LETTER FROM A TEA GARDEN

Published by TORC Publishing
Author's website
www.abioliver.co.uk

ISBN 978-1-84396-657-9
Also available in paperback
ISBN 978-1-84396-656-2
and as a Kindle ebook
ISBN 978-1-84396-658-6

Typesetting and pre-press production
eBook Versions
127 Old Gloucester Street
London WC1N 3AX
www.ebookversions.com

By the same author

A NEW MAP OF LOVE

Poignant, funny and ultimately uplifting – *Lancashire Post*

A New Map of Love is an acute and beguiling study of life, love and the endless flat-footed dance of men and women. – Sarah Dunant

Think Midsomer without the murders and you'll come close to this charming, old-fashioned story – *S Magazine*

Both funny and poignant – *Reader's Digest*

George Baxter is one of those rare characters in a novel that you feel you've known all your life. Full of hilarious set pieces and moments of tender reflection, *A New Map of Love* sneaks up on you, the last page is as lovely as the first. I loved it. -- Kit de Waal, author of *My Name is Leon*

For my family

LETTER FROM A TEA GARDEN

Abi Oliver

TORC PUBLISHING

1

October 1964

When the letter arrived, the truth is, I was a drunk, living out my pointless little life in this house. 'Mumsie's house,' I called it, though she had been dead for several years. It was in a deplorable state and, now I can be honest about it, so was I.

It was an Air Mail letter, pale blue, edged with red and blue chevrons and a hovering Air India aircraft on the stamp. At first, I assumed it was from my old friend Jessie Bell who still wrote from time to time. But it was not her loopy copperplate, which has hardly changed since we were eleven years old. Instead I saw a compressed, constipated-looking hand. *Lady Byngh, Greenburton House* ...

Persi – Marguerite Persimmon, my old nanny from India years – had been living back with us for eighteen months or so. (By us, I mean the doggies and me.) We were breakfasting off Mumsie's folding card table – this is the state we were in by then. Much of the house was unusable, including the dining table.

Once I'd read Roderick's letter the first time, I passed it to Persi. She peered at it over her specs, the chains she hung them on twiddling either side of her face. She laid it amid the crumb-strewn plates and a jar of Cooper's thick-cut and bowled that question at me.

'Well, do you think you could *do* India again?'

I looked away at the dogs, who had subsided now the toast was finished. The question hovered unpleasantly, like a wasp. I wanted to go and open the window and let it out. Even more I wanted a drink.

'So.' Persi was obviously going to keep on. 'Shall you go?'

'Don't be ridiculous. Of course not!!' It came out sounding pugnacious. It wasn't what I intended but it was how my voice often seemed to emerge these days. The letter lay dangerously close to a tea-sodden patch on the cloth and for some reason I reached over to move it out of harm's way. 'In any case, he's invited both of us.'

Persi removed the spoon from the marmalade, sucked on it as if it were a lollipop and laid it with deliberation on the sordid cloth. Her specs were dangling round her neck now and she looked like a rather clever heron.

'He's *your* nephew.' And then she winked at me and for a second I saw the Persi of long, long ago. In those days people could not keep their eyes off her. Even now she is striking, in her way. 'You're being wooed, El-e-a-nor-a.'

I was obviously feeling over-sensitive because this needled me like mad. Persi still has a Canadian accent, though not quite like that of any other Canadian you'd ever meet. It has intonations all of its own and drifts off into parodies of USA accents and a *pukka* English one when required. And she has played on my name in that teasing way, drawing out every syllable, ever since we met more than half a century ago, when she was eighteen and I five. But that day, her saying it in the way she used to when I was an infant – on top of the boy's letter, for goodness sake – felt like

4

someone plunging a garden fork into a pile of leaf mould and stirring it about. It was the leaf mould of my own past life and it was far from comfortable.

I had not set eyes on Roderick, my nephew, since he was an infant. The boy is my late brother Hugh's son. After thirty years of not a word, the previous summer, Roderick had invited me to his wedding, here in England. I wasn't going to trouble myself going all the way to Kent for *that* jamboree. After all, I didn't know the fellow, he'd never shown a jot of interest in the family and I never much cared for Jennifer, his mother.

Not wanting to let the side down, I had gone to some lengths to send him a decent present. Certain things are expected in these circumstances. And I felt sorry for the boy. You could say that Hughie let him down disgracefully. But he and this new bride of his, Virginia (née Perkins, or something rather run-of-the-mill sounding) didn't bestir themselves to come and visit here when they were in the country for the wedding. So that was that. They took off back to Assam, *au revoir,* tatty bye. I did wonder why in heaven's name he had gone back to work in tea when everyone else was leaving India like the proverbial rats, but there you are. They were gone, all possible disturbance over and done with.

Come Christmas, a packet of tea arrived, tip-top Orange Pekoe, with a card, *From Roderick and Ginny, with our love. XX!*

And now, this letter out of the blue. *I so regret that we have so little family ... So sorry for not managing to visit ... Ginny's mother was very ill by the time of the wedding and died soon after ... Would very much like to get to know you ...*

'Well,' I said, trying to ignore all this inner compost shifting. I found I needed to breathe in rather deeply. The girl's mother dying like that did rather change one's view of things. 'I suppose

5

he doesn't have anyone much except that mother of his.'

Persi pushed her chair back from the table, grasping it ill-advisedly with both hands to pull herself up. She already had a bandaged wrist from a tumble with a tray.

'Persi, for God's sake, the legs'll give way!' I grasped the teapot in view of approaching calamity.

'If we were to eat at a proper table for once,' she grumbled, stacking the plates. I've never fully understood why, everywhere she goes, Persi feels compelled to turn herself into someone's servant. She moved away to the back kitchen with her flat-footed, slapping tread. At seventy-seven she was spry but over-ambitious.

I thought I heard the words 'pig-sty' drift from the kitchen. What the heck had got into Persi? She seemed in a particularly spiky mood herself.

When she reappeared for the toast rack, so tarnished as to appear like pewter, and marmalade, I reached for a ciggy to avoid looking at her and said, 'He's going to want to know about his father, isn't he?'

Persi's bandaged hand stilled on the Cooper's lid, her face solemn. 'I imagine so,' she said.

Pulling on my Wellingtons in the porch, I realized my hands were shaking. My two dogs roiled about my legs, barking. Mumsie's old Lab, Honey, is a quiet old soul. But the Cairns, Bertie the grizzled one, Jack a toffee colour, kept leaping up and catching their nails in my skirt as if a walk was a barely dreamed of novelty.

'Do get *down*,' I bawled, shoving their tangled leads into the pocket of my old tweed coat. Over my mess of hair, I crammed a floppy brown turban with a streak of dried white paint along it. 'Yes, walkies! Go on, you blasted creatures.'

I stepped out into an October morning so bathed in slanting sunshine that it might have softened even my gristly old heart, had it been in an available state. I was far too busy scrabbling in my pocket for a Benson & Hedges, cursing the wretched matches. Finally, sucking in the harsh balm of it, I steeled myself to look at the house.

I had only taken it over within the past five years. Before Mother inherited it, her brother lived there, our Uncle Hat. Even though I now owned it, it never really felt as if it was mine, this splendid house. And what presented itself before me that morning was a symmetrical but unmistakably decrepit Georgian beauty, something wrong everywhere I looked: tiles missing, window paint cracked, moss everywhere. The flowerbeds were a tangle of weeds and leggy rose bushes and the evergreens bordering the long drive had grown so immense and menacing that even our whistling postman, who was used to it, arrived looking fraught.

It was a relief to be outside, that morning, away from Persi's probing. She had taken to watching me like a hawk to see if I was drinking. Since she arrived to live with me, I had definitely cut down. I had her to thank, though at this moment I felt anything but grateful because *by God* I wanted a drink and she felt like my gaoler.

From the back of the house I could run the dogs straight up on to the downs. Bertie and Jack shot off ahead like furry barrels of enthusiasm. Honey and I lolloped along together. My hips were giving me their usual gip. I've always been large busted and hipped – supposedly feminine, good for childbirth, ha ha – none of which, by then, felt in the least like a blessing. Worse was the gouty nagging in the joint of my right foot making me wince at every step, but which *must not* be mentioned to Persi.

I did look up enough to notice that the trees were alight with rust. There were hedges of shining red berries and the field to my right had been ploughed into chalky furrows, scored across with shadow in the sunlight. My soul was not entirely dead, just muffled in eternal winter.

The path leads across hummocky grass to the stepped flanks of Greenburton Hill, an ancient fortification – Iron Age? Saxon? I can never remember facts of this kind. It looks out over Greenbury, a village of spring lines and streams, down there to my right. The main road is a dark, cartographic line in the distance, running through Greenbury and up the hill over the chalk downs.

'Lovely.' Smoke wafted out of my mouth. Even in trying to pay tribute to nature I sounded crusty, as if I were barking orders. I had started to feel similarly dismayed when confronted by a looking glass: my face had taken on the look of a very fed up St Bernard. A grog-blossomy one, at that.

'Oh *God*,' I muttered. 'Oh God, oh God.'

I held my hands up in front of me, palms down. Nasty, beefy great things, dreadful yellow stains on the right-hand index finger. And shaking. I just couldn't stop it.

They're strong, capable-looking fingers – as if you play the piano for hours every day ...

Those old, ridiculous words surfaced in my mind like a cork bobbing up through water. Ridiculous then as now: flattering as they were, I never learned to play a note. *No*, I thought. Things were stirring and I most definitely did not want to greet them. *No, no*. The urge for a drink, for my oldest and most reliable friend Johnny Walker ...

No. Sun. Yardarm, etc. New rules – must be kept. You've kicked it before. You can do it again.

8

Memory ambushes one. It was that damned letter intruding. Family: something I had long been resigned to having none of. I suppose, when the wedding invitation came, I had hoped … Nothing came of that. But then, that packet of tea – and now the boy suddenly announcing that *he* wanted family.

I stopped to look out towards the distant, twin mounds of Wittenham Clumps. Instead, I saw Hughie and me, on this very hillside, he fourteen, I twelve, together in this alien land. It was one Easter, when the house still belonged to Uncle Hat and it was our latest billet for the school holidays. In those days the house was brown and mannish inside: coffee-coloured walls, leather chairs.

Uncle Hat was not quite like other people. You'd find a hedgehog in the kitchen or once, a goose with two goslings. And there were dogs and cats and – mostly outside – goats and a Shetland pony and among them all, our dear uncle, forever bumbling about. I don't know exactly what was wrong with Uncle Hat. He couldn't seem to be a chap the way regular chaps were supposed to be in those days. They had had to take him out of school. Whatever the case, he was a gentle soul and he was always kind to us.

One afternoon, Hughie and I came and sat on the side of this hill. It was the first time I saw that my brother was growing into a man. His voice was breaking and was a bit unreliable, which embarrassed him. It was chilly, but he was wearing shorts, rather too large. Hugh was not ept with clothes – something always seemed to be awry. He had olive skin and, sitting close, I saw the hairs on his legs like a water-weed flow, which disappeared into his grey socks. He was a solid boy. In fact we were similar in many ways, nothing delicate about us, and we both had the same dark, wiry hair. It was the only time since we were very small that I ever saw him cry.

By the end of the holidays, wrenched apart once again, I went back to school longing for him. We had been so close and we didn't really have anyone else except Persi. I remember thinking, if only one could marry one's own brother! It would solve all those dreadful husband problems, which loomed before us girls like the great wall of China.

Another memory steps out from behind this one: Hughie with the cook's son, Akbar, at Panchcotta. Our house and its lovely garden with beautiful trees was fenced off from the main tea estate. Pa was the assistant manager, just as my nephew Roderick apparently is now. A monsoon downpour is just fading away and there they are, two stark-naked four-year-olds, using a gigantic puddle as their paddling pool, running through it, shrieking. I, a sturdy toddler, am standing watching, always feeling as if I have too many clothes on and forever trailing after those little boy gods. The rain is gently falling, the air bloated with moisture, a grey haze to the light. But the sun is beginning to claw out round the edges of the clouds, lighting the splashing droplets. Hughie's and Akbar's little bodies are each gleaming shades of brown, and they are both giggling in torrents of their own.

Standing there, on the downs, I could feel that smooth mud under my toes, the way my soaked clothes clung like a second skin and all the laughter bubbling up inside me. Our sweet time of Eden, Hughie and me – and Akbar and little Shonu and all the pets, untouched in our garden paradise, before its wall was stormed by our future.

India. *Do you think you could* do *India again?*

Two figures were moving along the path towards me. Hardly

10

anyone ever walked along this way. Jarred, I watched them come closer, side by side. One wore an anorak of an unpleasant red, the other a dark blue one. No dog that I could make out.

'Bertie! Jack! Leave!' But I raised my voice to no avail. The dogs of course rushed enthusiastically towards the young people, who seemed nervous.

'They won't hurt you!' My attempt at being informative from a distance emerged as a parade-ground roar.

They were mere children, a thin, pale boy and a girl whose ginger curls clashed unpleasantly with the red anorak, holding hands, blushingly in love. The very sight of them made me feel weary to my depths.

'Morning!' I greeted them briskly. 'They mean no harm.'

'Mornin'.' They spoke in chorus, sarcastic, not looking into my face. I heard them giggling once they had gone past.

I closed my eyes. In the darkness appeared a bottle of Johnny Walker, my personal vision of the heavenly city. It must be nearly midday, I thought, surely?

Opening them again, I fumbled for another cigarette and lit up, hauling smoke into my lungs. How must I have looked to those two deplorable children? I took in the state of my coat: the grubby patches and ash burns and hem of brown tweed poking out at the bottom. I saw myself through their eyes, a scruffy old duck in a queer hat with paint smeared on it. I had nice slender ankles once, not bad legs altogether in fact. But just then they were sunk into black Wellingtons – men's ones, at that.

Stubbing out my fag viciously on a field post, I stomped on after the dogs, cursing the pain in my foot. And what's more, I thought, to hell with Roderick and his wife and his blasted assistant's bungalow! Damn his letter. Why couldn't the wretched

11

pup just leave me alone? And why write in that flannelling way, as if he actually cared a fig about getting to know me? What did he *want*?

'How much have you had already?'

Persi's latest interrogation made me savagely irritable. Battling to control myself, I managed to get the bottle back on to the drinks tray without dropping it.

What the hell had got into her? Normally there were looks, a certain amount of muttering over the state of the house, but during this period when we had been living together again, Persi had avoided any sort of confrontation. And I had pulled back on the booze, hadn't I? New rules, a certain amount of order. But we had never met anything head on, had skirted over surfaces like a pair of water boatmen. And what was wrong with that, pray? Where did poking about in things ever get you?

'Persi, I do wish you wouldn't creep about like that.'

The reason I had not heard her was that she was in her stockinged feet. The sight of them disarmed me. Maddening as she was, there was always something that could soften me towards Persi. She still had surprisingly slender feet and well-shaped toes, but then she had always been one for sensible shoes. When she wore shoes, these days you could always hear her slap-slapping along.

Just for a second, an image returned to me of the soles of Persi's flat nursing shoes as she knelt in the ward of that heat-seared infirmary in Calcutta, elbows on the bed, waiting, praying with every fibre of her …

Persi, in her pale blue frock, was hugging herself with her spindly arms. Instead of that bland mask she was so good at, her face looked unusually stern.

'It's my first,' I said, though I know the way I spoke implied, *I don't see what it has to do with you.* But that memory, the hospital bed, had blunted my tone.

'Oh no it isn't.'

'Second then.' I felt just like a child again, being ticked off. I took my brimming tumbler and sat at the card table as nonchalantly as possible. The space available for normal living had shrunk right down even in Mumsie's time: whole rooms filled with heaven knows what, then abandoned. The dining table was unusable, still stacked with her things. Mumsie was not well towards the end. But even now, I had yet to find the strength or stomach for the crazed clutter of it all. Doors remained closed, spaces to be reclaimed, like in Bluebeard's castle.

The dogs lay scattered, dozing, about the floor. I patted my pockets. 'Now, where have my ciggies got to?'

Persi was still looming over me. It was as if, with her standing there, like a wall, something tilted in those seconds.

'The first was barely a nip.' I could hear the sulk in my voice. Truth was, it was my third Scotch. In the space of half an hour. Before lunch. Why could I not just own up? Didn't I want life to be something other than being chained to the bottle?

But then Persi, in the odd way she often did, went into retreat.

'It's barely a quarter to,' she grumbled. Turning her back on me, she pushed her feet into her waiting shoes, black, elegant, despite having low heels. 'No JW before midday.'

'Well, I damn well need it today.' I picked up my drink, trying to steady my hands. The weight of the crystal glass, the pungent fumes and burning taste were my friends – my only friends apart from Persi. They brought down upon me a pall of warm, blurred forgetting.

Persi renewed her assault that evening.

Johnny Walker time again. My pegs. We didn't call them pegs in India for nothing. They were the drinking hooks on which I hung my day. It was sundowner time, dusk already at the windows, sweet whiffs of leaf smoke seeping in on the evening air and the warm gravy smells of Persi's beef casserole bubbling in the kitchen, sending the dogs into a lazy state of yearning. Knives and forks were already laid on a clean cloth which covered the mouldy holes in the table's green felt top.

Miss Marguerite Louise Persimmon, brought up in some Puritan pocket of Canada, was a lifetime teetotaller, a state of being which I have always considered baffling to the point of idiocy. She sat sipping tonic water, which would at least have had some point to it if we were still warding off malaria.

'Eleanora,' she announced in her creaky voice. 'You are going downhill. Worse than ever. And this house of yours –'

'Mumsie's house.' I could hear my tone turning facetious. 'Not mine. Though I grant you, you'd never have moved in if she was still alive, would you?' Persimmon, for all her Christian virtue, had had very few good words ever to say about my mother.

She stared at me. 'I've kept my counsel all the while and I've been watching it happen. But now, what with this nephew of yours, Rodney ...'

'Roderick. Though I can't see what –'

'Since you moved in here you've deteriorated and you know it,' Persi said with the ruthless honesty of a once professional nursing sister getting back into gear. She still slept with her red Queen Alexandra's cape on her bed – and Enid's as well – on the

14

coldest nights. Reverting to a professional role, her accent became more formal and English.

I felt the words fumble their way to me through the buffer of booze. I regarded them with lofty detachment.

'Look at this house.' Persi was getting into her stride now. 'You can't go blaming those lousy burglars for all this. There's hardly a room left fit to live in, what with all your mother's darn hoarding and the dogs and clutter.' She waved a spindly arm. 'The way you're going along, we'll be living in the coalhouse soon.'

She was bolt upright in the chair. I sat back. It was like being at the mercy of a vengeful dentist.

'Look at you – your clothes, your hands! You live like a tramp. You're a boozer – and smoking like a chimney stack! One day you're going to burn the whole darned house down!'

'I don't smoke upstairs,' I protested. But befuddled as I was, I could see for sure that something was going on. This was not normal. In fact, it was unprecedented. Sometimes it had even felt as if Persi was afraid of me. Or at least deferential. I had always put it down to her coming to live with me, for no payment or anything of that sort. It only began to dawn on me then, with a pang of sympathy for the old girl, that I was not the only one to be rattled by Roderick's letter.

'You need to *take yourself in hand.*' She underlined each word, shrill now and more Canadian. 'Or you'll be gone before I am.'

'No I damn well won't,' I said, nastily. Scotch nasty. 'Is that all you're worried about? Having someone to look after you?'

Persi leaned across, sudden as a cobra, and snatched the glass of Scotch from my hand. She set it down out of reach.

'When have you ever looked after me, *Nora*?'

This went through me like a cold, sobering shower. Nora. My

mother's name for me when in disparaging mood, which she was in often enough. An unflattering name; a servant name. And the worst of it was that, within this attack, I could hear the unbroken skein of Persi's love for me, her devotion, her own long griefs.

I stayed slouched in my chair, lost to a befuddled nastiness of emotions, longing, but not daring, to get up and go after my glass. I stared down at my walking shoes, the bunion bulge on the left joint.

There was a silence. Persi sat back, relaxing her spine as if exhausted. She plucked at her long skirt as she crossed one leg over the other and took a slow sip of tonic water.

'What's brought this on, Persi?' I forced myself to be gentle. Even I, half-cut and callous as I was, could make out that not all the distress in the room was mine. And I knew that distress of old. 'Do you think *you* could do India again?'

Persi stared past me for some seconds, towards the window and the darkening garden. The dim light softened her face and she looked young and old at once, this woman whom I had known almost all my life. Dear, dear old Persi. I could just make out a tiny, compulsive twitching at the left side of her lips. Her throat moved and she looked down. Surely not tears? I thought, praying, dear God, no. I was suddenly filled with an old, soft longing to be able to give comfort, but being simply unable. It was a skill I had somehow lost when barely in possession of it.

Finally, Persi pulled herself up straighter again, drawing the blue edges of her cardigan close about her. And met my eye.

'I daresay,' she replied, with a wave of her bony hand, with the stiff marrow of a woman who has nursed the wounded, not just in India but in France and Egypt. 'Why not? The boy wants us to come and we have the funds. And frankly, Eleanora – it might help shake you out of yourself.'

'But we can't!' I was filled with sudden back-pedaling panic. 'We can't just go off like that. What about the dogs?'

She stared back at me. 'Oh, don't be so ridiculous.'

2

Jorhat, Assam, February 1965

We landed at Dum-Dum airport in the middle of the night. Already, as I moved stiffly outside and stood clinging to the rail of the steps down from the aircraft, there it was. I took a deep breath, the smell wrapping itself about me in the darkness.

There was nothing gradual about this arrival, none of those first hints on the sea breeze as a ship eased its way into Bombay, or across the Bay of Bengal, navigating the Sundarbans and upriver to Calcutta. Instead, now and all at once, that smell, full force, like nothing else; the warm, capacious, complex stink of the land, as of the pelt of a vast animal.

As I stood there within the dome of dim airport lights, I had that old sense of all that was out there beyond, of the enormity of life going on. Calcutta lay in the distance and all about us, this great land – loving and cruel; magnificent, appalling.

'Oh my,' Persi said, turning at the top of the steps. 'Can you smell that?'

'I could hardly not.' I was snappy, emotions aching in me too powerful to begin on. Just that smell, already beginning to unearth whole parts of myself, buried deep.

'Some things don't change,' she added.

To my surprise, as we limped together across the tarmac, Persi slipped her arm through mine.

'Best foot forward,' she said, sounding so ridiculously *pukka* British that I burst out laughing.

'Oh, Persi,' I said, full of fondness. 'When did I ever manage that?'

We waited in the airport, an elegant, dimly lit place with pot plants arranged round the walls. We had come back to this place where day is night and night day, any sense of the clock so different from England. Bodies lay like mummies at the edges of the arrivals hall, while other people sat wearily on the chairs, shawls wrapped about them. A woman crouched, flicking dust about the floor with a grass brush. After a time, a grizzled man in a shirt and *dhoti* approached with a huge kettle and stack of tiny clay cups.

'*Chai?*' Squatting on hairpin-thin legs, he poured a cup for each of us. Persi produced a few *paise* she must have kept for years. What I really wanted was a damn good drink, but tea was better than nothing. I cupped the rough little pot in my hands and smelled the sweet, milky steam.

'Why did we ever leave here, Persi?' I said. Smells, tastes: all of me felt like a numb limb coming back to life.

Persimmon sat straight-backed as usual, feet side by side in her black lace-ups as if at a prayer meeting. If she was tired it did not show. If anything, she seemed already younger, energized by being there.

'It would have been undignified not to,' she said at last. She turned to me for a second, with one of those piercing, grey-eyed looks of hers. 'No good clinging on when you're not welcome – if we ever were. Things have to end.'

'Jessie Bell stayed on – in Mussoorie.'

'Huh,' Persi said. I think she always thought Jessie was, in general, a bit daft. 'Well, she was born here.'

'So was I.'

'Yes. Well.'

I wasn't sure what that meant. For a moment I was seized by longing for Jessie Bell's family's little house in the sprawling hill town of Mussoorie, a yellow bungalow clinging to the mountainside, the pea-green room where we used to sleep, the sloping garden bright with roses, love-in-a-mist, hollyhocks …

'That's where Hughie and I should have gone,' I said.

Persi frowned over her little *chai* cup. 'Mussoorie?'

'Hughie could have gone to St George's College. There was no need for him to go to England – for either of us. I don't think Pa would have sent us away.'

'Your mother wanted you to be English – as well as wanting shot of you, of course,' Persi said with her occasional merciless truthfulness.

'Not Hugh. Me, yes.'

We looked at each other and laughed. There seemed nothing else to be done at four in the morning in an Indian airport, with the past moving in to greet us.

Everything was white, blinding, when we climbed down from our second, smaller aircraft in the morning. The flat, scrubby land was flooded with sunlight, the windows of the ramshackle buildings and fishlike body of the plane giving off such piercing brightness that I walked across with my eyes almost closed. After being up all night without a drink in sight, I was feeling dreadful.

I had seen nothing much from the plane, but I traced it in my mind. From Calcutta we flew east, tracing the outstretched arm of the Brahmaputra until she bent at an angle, flowing south to meet the mighty Ganga as she became the Padma, the two joining hands to form the wide, lazy Meghna River, splaying out through the delta islands of the Sundarbans to the sea. I ached to see them, these embracing rivers of my heart, but below was only a pale haze. At this moment, we could have been anywhere.

Persi and I trailed along behind the other handful of passengers. Even though it was the cold season it was warmer than I remembered. My armpits prickled unpleasantly, my body felt creaky and my head was throbbing. Despite the new hairdo, I felt old and frumpy and done-up. All I could think about was being in a cool room with a bed and a bottle of JW to keep me company. It had been an emotional night and I wasn't ready – not in the least.

'Auntie! Er … Lady Byngh!'

I squinted at the low airport building, a very basic place now we were out in the sticks. Everyone except us had vanished inside and someone was holding the door open.

'Aha!' Persi sounded aggravatingly cheerful. Despite being thirteen years my senior, she was bearing up a lot better. 'The reception committee.'

'Oh God.' I fumbled uselessly in my pockets. 'I need a cigarette.'

But it was too late for that; we were almost there.

'At least he's here,' Persi said. 'I don't know what you're complaining about.'

'I'm not complaining,' I said. Complainingly.

And there was Roderick. He was not what I expected, which was absurd, because he didn't look in any substantial way different

21

from when he was three years old. In fact, he seemed surprisingly familiar. He still had a round, pink face and a tendency toward plumpness – as much as is ever possible in India – shaggy brown hair and pale eyes which still had that defenceless expression of his. He was the image of his mother, though Jen was always a good deal sprucer and a great deal less disarming than this rumpled figure in front of us.

'Aunt Eleanora, at last! How nice to see you again.' He had all the public school moves, of course, good manners, gave a quaint little bow before turning to greet Persi with a handshake. 'And this must be Miss Persimmon!'

Persi tilted her head, held out a hand and said gravely, 'Good to meet you, Roderick.' I was relieved she didn't put on that hokey-jokey character from across the pond, the way she sometimes did in social situations.

'Hello, Roderick,' I said, wondering for a moment whether he expected to be kissed. As I'd left it a bit late for this, I stuck my hand out as well and he offered me some plump fingers.

'Well, well,' I said, as we went to retrieve the suitcases. I was doing my best to sound jovial, though I'm not sure it came off. 'You're Hughie's boy. You don't look in the least like him.'

'So they tell me,' Roderick said. There were two remaining cases side by side and he picked them up with no apparent effort. 'Shall we get out of here? Car's outside. You must be keen to relax. I've got some water in the car. It's getting rather warm.'

I couldn't help having a good look as him as we followed and I realized that what I had said was untrue. He had Jennifer's colouring but his middling height, the grey flannels worn too long in the leg, shirt coming untucked, his hair dishevelled and showing a little balding patch, all in all a lack of talent in dealing with clothes – he was Hughie all over. And in the midst of this shambolic appearance and pouchy face, a straight, distinguished nose that has passed down through generations of Storr men with no interruption. I found myself wanting to blurt out, 'Your nose – I do like your nose!' Mercifully I managed to keep this deranged offering to myself.

In fact as I walked along, wanting to tell him to be careful with my bag but not daring in case it led to questions, a feeling started to come over me that I had noticed before at times in my life. In situations to which I do not feel equal – which have been numerous – it's as if a sort of inner tide goes sucking out inside me, leaving me with a sense of detachment from everything, where I have neither animation nor care about what happens. This was rather how it was as we first stepped out into Assam.

Roderick waved away offers to carry the bags and numerous hopeful rickshaw drivers and led us to a black Ambassador, its bulbous form glinting in the sunlight.

'I managed to borrow it,' he said. 'I didn't think you'd be comfortable in the jeep.' He settled Persi in the front and, to my relief, I was to go in the back. The tide of my adequacy ebbed further. I needed a drink, desperately. I sat back and closed my eyes for a second, thinking about my suitcase, my cardigan-wrapped bottles snug inside, the thought of unscrewing the cap, the burning, friendly liquor … *Oh God, oh God.*

'A chance for a snooze if you like, Aunt,' Roderick said before he closed my door at the back.

'Thank you, dear.' I looked up at him and managed what I hoped was the smile of a benign auntie, despite my throbbing head. But I would not be sleeping. Oh, no.

Heaven only knows how, but as he shut my door, Roderick

managed to jam his own finger in it. I heard a yelp of pain, the door opened hurriedly and closed again and the boy disappeared for a few moments, apparently bent over in agony.

'What's going on?' Persi asked, twisting round.

'He caught his finger. Remind you of anyone?'

'He shut his own finger in the door?' She was frowning. 'How the heck?' Roderick appeared then at the driver's door. 'Are you all right, dear?'

'Yes,' he said in a constricted voice, starting up the car. He had wrapped a handkerchief round the finger. 'Quite all right.' He offered us water from a tin flask, then swiveled in the seat, his face suddenly bashful. 'I can't wait for you to meet Ginny. She's a great girl. And we've some news to tell you.' He let off the handbrake. '*Chelo*, let's go.'

I sank into the back seat. The stately old saloon car with its slippery seats, low to the window: already that felt like home. I forgot about the drink I was craving. I looked and looked, catching drifting snatches of Roderick's chat.

'I started off at Cinnamara,' he was saying.

'Ah, HQ,' Persi observed. Cinnamara is the biggest garden in the Jorhat Tea Company's region.

'But now Ginny and I are at Rungabari, of course we still see a lot of the old faces in town, at the Club.'

Persi's head was in front of me, her thick, old-snow-coloured hair coiled into slides and pins. I ran my hand over my own head, still startled by the feel of it. Before we came, Persi had insisted we get tidied up – well, most importantly, that I did. 'You look like some crazed beast.' So we popped off to the hairdresser's. Persi had a trim and in a mad moment I had mine all cut off, into a sort of Eton crop. It seemed the only solution. In fact, because it's so wiry it arranged itself into little waves across my head and looked surprisingly chic. Even the old St Bernard face looked a fraction more cheerful. It was still a shock looking in the glass though and every time I did, I thought, silly old fool.

'You look ten years younger,' Persi announced when she saw it. 'You'll have the chaps flocking.'

'Oh ha-flaming-ha,' I said. 'That's all I need.'

Outside the window, the yellowish road unwound in front of us. And bit by bit, I allowed what I saw to reach me: a pale winter sun lighting tired, scrubby trees, wayside stalls of biscuit jars, packets, matchboxes; dashes of colour, pink or parrot green of a sari, shining emerald on a cockerel's neck as it dashed away from the wheels, the glint on the bell of a cycle ridden by a man, head wound round with a cloth, his feet, in *chappals*, curved down over the pedals. Flashes of light off water in the drainage channels along the road made me narrow my eyes. People, children, *pi* dogs. I allowed my lids to droop for a moment.

Soon I was looking out at acres of tea bushes, pruned flat-topped for winter, the spindly shade trees dotted across them, bringing scale and variety to a horizon of bushes. The gardens were quiet as it was not the plucking season, but a few workers could be seen scattered amid the bushes. Two women close to the road righted themselves and *salaamed* us as we passed.

I had resolved to keep any emotion tucked well away, but the sight of it, the smell, the light ... Home. Where I was born. The deepest part of me – oh, yes, home.

We bumped over a level crossing, the railway tracks curving away between banks of tea bushes and, soon after, turned in through gates beside which was a green and white sign:

RUNGABARI TEA ESTATE – *Jorhat Tea Company.* Another yellow road to bump along. Roderick glanced back over his shoulder.

'There's the *burra* bungalow.'

It was a grand *chung* bungalow – two-storied, thatched – with immaculate gardens, a huge banyan tree spreading shade.

'The factory's straight along here, about a mile. And here's our *chota* bungalow!'

We turned in at the gate of the assistant's bungalow, a much more modest, single-storey affair, and so similar to my childhood home, the tin roof and white walls, the verandah running halfway around it, that I felt as if someone had taken my heart in their hands and was squeezing it. I closed my eyes for a moment.

As the car braked, a dog rushed out barking shrilly and there were sudden movements: a knot of people emerging on to the verandah.

'Ah,' Roderick said, 'Ginny's arranged a welcoming committee.'

My first, far-off glimpse of the new Mrs Storr-Mayfield (neé Perkins) gave me the impression of a mouse-haired twig in a mint-green frock and I doubted that she could have organized anything of the sort. The household had most likely arranged itself around her in the ways it was long accustomed to doing without any bossing from the new *memsahib*. She stood on the verandah steps in front of the group of servants. Though standing on a lower step, she was still their height, pale like a stalk grown in the dark. I found myself antagonistic, prepared to meet one of those tight-lipped, snooty English misses that India seemed to recruit – or to create, I've never been sure which.

The dog was a short-legged, brown and white creature of indeterminate breed – mostly Jack Russell, I guessed – and he was a welcome diversion.

'Hello, old chap!' I greeted him heartily, once released from the car. This would be so easy if it were only dogs we had to deal with. He jumped about, licking me, before tearing off again.

As I straightened up, I saw the young wifey advancing upon us from the bungalow steps in neat little heels. She had a sickly look, certainly the wrong complexion for this climate. Reassuringly, she was not a classic beauty, or even especially pretty, but nor was she as insubstantial as I had assumed. As she approached, I saw a strong-boned face, dark eyes, with rather thick brows and a wide mouth. Rather odd looking, in fact, yet I found my eyes drawn to her face with a kind of fascination.

Let's get this over with, I thought. Then at long bally last I can get a drink.

'Lady Byngh – and Miss Persimmon – welcome to Rungabari!' She had a deeper voice than I expected; deep but not harsh in any way. Though slender of build, close up she looked quite wiry, as if she might easily heft a hay bale. She spoke very formally, adding, 'Of course, you both know all about these places better than I do. No, Nip – down!'

The dog had come rushing back and she made as if to grab him.

'It's all right,' I said, patting him. 'There's a good chap.'

'Oh, good.' She gave a faint smile. 'I'm so glad you like animals.'

She came close and offered her sallow cheek to be kissed. We brushed against each other with supreme awkwardness. She then did the same to Persi, who looked taken aback but gamely did her best with this unfamiliar carry-on.

'I do hope your journey was not too tedious?'

It was the usual social chit-chat, stilted, functional. But she had a steady look, caught your eyes and held them, in a way that was disconcertingly direct. It was a strange combination. Goodness me – inwardly a groan was rising: *Take me to my room! Let me just get the cap off that bottle!* – we were going to have to spend three weeks in the company of Roderick, who seemed pretty daft, and this odd girl.

'We're so glad you have come.' Her face altered and she cast her husband a glance of the sort of adoration one felt might have rubbed off after a few months of marriage. 'Aren't we, Pod?'

Pod? Good God, I thought. And then, *Be nice, Eleanora. Just for once try to get something right.*

'We were so sorry not to visit you in England,' Ginny said. 'But Mummy ... I'll explain.' She stopped, looking stricken for a moment, as if interrupted by some inner vibration, and put her hand over her mouth.

'Are you all right, darling? 'Roderick drew his hand from his pocket as if to comfort her, then gazed aghast at the blood-soaked hanky wrapped round his finger as if he had forgotten all about it and shoved it swiftly back in again, wincing.

'Yes, of course,' she said, recovering gamely. 'Now, this is our little household.'

The servants were standing in a semicircle behind her, smiling with a mixture of duty and naked curiosity.

'This is Bholu, our *chowkidar*. If you need anything, let him know and he'll pass the message on – I'm sure you know the drill. You can get him to come by calling out ... er ...'

'*Koi-hai?*' I suggested.

'That's it!' Roderick said, beaming. 'I see you haven't forgotten!'

A number of others were introduced – the bearer, Nirad; Iqbal the cook, Raham the *mali*, who looked after the garden.

Persi and I stood, listening, *salaaming* and perspiring. I felt very crotchety, worn out and quite desperate for a drink. I could see our hostess was not the cut-glass type I had expected, that for all the social chat she looked out of her depth. All the same, I felt certain other emotions towards Virginia Storr-Mayfield, the daft little puss. I have to admit, they were not noble emotions – they were those needling, unpleasant, *what-do-you-know-about-life?* feelings, to which I was rather prone in those days. Life, I find, is an endless challenge to one's generosity.

And when she and Roderick stood there, side by side, hands touching, I thought I had never seen two people look more like lost children. It came to me with a shock, that each of them was quite some years older than my mother and father were when they embarked on this life, with far less possibility of escape.

'What are you up to, Eleanora?'

Persi's voice reached me, muffled, from the bathroom attached to our room.

'Nothing!' I called back. 'Unpacking.'

I had not fully considered what it would mean, having to share a room with Persi. Not just my hands but my whole body were shaking by now. We had been forced to sit for a brief time on the verandah with a tray of tea, looking out at the garden. It wasn't unpleasant – anything but – and if someone had just produced a glass of Scotch …

The lawn was edged with shrubs and there were beds of roses

close to the house, each surrounded by a ring of white-painted stones. At last Roderick said he must go back to work for a time, and he showed us to our room. This bungalow, like the one where we lived at Panchcotta, is a one-storey affair built on a *chung*, or platform, raising it above the ground to keep it above water during the rains. It was a relief not to have to climb stairs.

The room felt very familiar: whitewashed walls, two dark wood-framed beds with mozzy nets separated by a little table with a water jug, glasses and a small pottery vase containing a yellow rose. There were the usual teak chest of drawers and a couple of rattan chairs. The floor was smoothed boards with a small rug between the beds. All was pervaded by a faint smell of Lysol. It was only when I looked at the wall above the bed that the familiarity became unnerving. There was a painting of a sea estuary, the sails of little boats flecked across the ruffled water and a harbour in the distance. The knot in the wood at the left bottom edge of the frame and every detail of the painting were known to me the way I know my own body. I didn't say anything then.

'So, have a nice little rest and we'll see you later,' Roderick said, teetering in the doorway. He had a boyish way of lifting on to the balls of his feet while he was talking to you that added an air of wanting to get away.

As soon as Persi popped into the bathroom, I dived into my case.

'I heard clinking.' Her voice emitted from the bathroom with an oracular echo.

There was no time to fiddle about looking for the silver toothmug. I was wobbling like a badly set junket by then, but I managed to screw the top off the bottle and get a few good swigs down me before stashing it back in the case. After pulling a few clothes out on to the bed, I returned the case to the floor, carefully laying it flat. I'd have to go easy. Only four bottles. Had to make them last.

With the JW warmth stealing through my innards, I breathed in deep and went to the window, reaching out to touch the glass. It felt cool and slightly dusty. In our day here, the windows of houses like these were covered with a deep blue muslin which filtered the light. There were shutters still, the same as I remember, which could be bolted over the windows to help keep out rain and insects. I was looking out from one side of the house where there was nothing much in view except the cookhouse, a little building some yards away with a corrugated iron roof. Beyond were bushes. A child was playing on the grass, in an enormous pair of shorts and naked from the waist up. I narrowed my eyes for a second. Akbar? No, of course. Not Akbar.

As I stood there, I expected for a moment to hear the soft sound of music from along the verandah. Mother would sometimes put on her phonograph. Nocturnes and waltzes would drift to me as I lay on my bed across the room from Hugh, the piano notes flowing like the waters of paradise through my early years. *I'm back here. My God, I'm here.*

'Did you bring hooch with you?'

'For goodness' sake!' I turned, horribly jarred by the interruption. Persi stood in the doorway, hand on bony hip.

'Just a nip,' I said nonchalantly.

'Huh.' She advanced on her open suitcase and took out her Bible, laying it on the night table as if in retaliation.

'Well, they might be teetotal like you,' I said. 'I can't survive all this without a drop.'

'You're your own worst enemy – always have been.'

31

This seemed rather sweeping, as statements go, not to mention wounding. And the worst of it was she sounded sad. She leaned over the bed, arms braced to lift her suitcase to the floor. In the middle of this she seemed to lose all strength and slumped forwards.

'Here – that's too heavy to lift like that.' I went and took one end and we lowered it together and slid it to the floor and against the wall.

'Thanks,' Persi said in a dry voice, sitting on the bed to slide her shoes off.

'Have a lie down,' I told her. 'It's been a hell of a day.'

'Just for a few minutes, perhaps.' She sounded ashamed, as if giving in to something. But she still sat, rubbing one stockinged foot against the other, pulling pins and combs out of her hair, which slowly uncoiled at the back.

'So,' I said, sitting down on my own bed. 'I think Mumsie would have called Virginia "the sort a man might eat for breakfast".' Mother had various disparaging terms for other women: jolly lumpkin, fat swallop, shrinking violet.

Persi, making herself comfortable on the bed like a nesting river bird, gave me one of her looks. 'And why would you want to go quoting her, exactly?'

I looked away, ashamed, though not wanting to admit it. Sometimes Persi's Christian resolve to be unerringly positive about everyone until given reason not to be wore me down. But I knew she was right – and not just about Virginia, about giving the child a chance. Sometimes I feel as if my entire upbringing was a schooling in how to live in opposition to your better instincts.

'Just for a few moments,' Persi said muzzily.

When I looked at her a moment later, she was already asleep, flat on her back. Her face, smoother in that position, lost its severity. I watched her fondly for a moment, remembering the very first time I ever saw her, in the flat in Marine Drive, wearing that giant pair of gumboots. Since then, how many touching points there had there been in our lives, at the very best and worst of times ... For I second, then, I was back, standing beside her, the sky and slow waters of the great river at our feet aglow with evening, her arm about my shaking shoulders, watching the very fibre of my heart flow away downstream.

I got up abruptly, glancing at her as I crept over to the case and managed a couple more swigs. Careful, old girl, I thought, replacing the bottle. You've got to behave yourself. It might be your last chance. For what, was something I didn't want to go into.

I took my jacket off and lay down, still in my skirt. The last thing I heard was the whistle of a train and its long, fading rumble, not far away at the edge of the garden.

'So, Auntie – a drink?'

Roderick's blessed words came to me across the living room, into which we had emerged after a long nap. I felt refreshed and ready for things. Especially things like a glass of Scotch.

The place had the layout I remembered – the living room extending through the house from front to back. Most of it was a sitting room with leather armchairs, side tables, on one of which was a modern looking gramophone, the cane magazine rack, plant holders in china and brass, the rug on the floor – all so familiar. At the back, furthest from the doors to the verandah, was a small dining table and chairs. I had half forgotten, but now I was back here, so little seemed to have changed. There were electric lamps now, their dim light battered by moths as much as the old oil lamps ever were. But the rest, the walls with their panels joined by brown wooden battens, the canvas ceiling, the hovering of the servants and feeling of being never truly alone anywhere, the sense of the immense land outside, blanketed in darkness. All this was exactly as I remembered.

When these longed for words were uttered, I was sitting looking out through the doors to the verandah while Persi, in her grey frock, roved about, peering at things. She had already been equipped with her glass of tonic water.

'Ah,' I said casually, as if such a thought would never normally occur to me. 'How nice. What've you got?' He began a list of Scotch, gin-fizz, sherry …

'Scotch,' I interrupted swiftly. 'Marvellous.' He was a Johnny Walker boy, thank the heavens! This made me warm to him immediately.

'Coming up. Ice?' He was at a side table arranged with decanters and glasses. Persi was bending over the low bookcase. She pulled out a volume and squinted at it.

'Just one,' I said, possibly with too much cheer. My rations in the suitcase were obviously going to stretch further than I had feared. I can admit now how much time I spent in those days calculating just when my first drink would be permissible – and the next and the one after – full of fury if anything got in the way of it. With a feeling of sudden joy I lit up a cigarette and sat back in the chair.

'This yours, Roderick?' Persi said, in a languid tone, holding out a book with a faded dust jacket.

'What's that, Miss Persimmon?' He was pouring.

'*The Terracotta Temples of West Bengal*,' she read. Persi liked highbrow stuff like that. I was pretty surprised there was any such thing in this house. I would have expected a few Anglo-Indian cookbooks, light romances, an Agatha Christie or two. But I did spot a few volumes of poetry as well. He obviously had an unusual blend of tastes.

'Oh, yes.' Roderick placed a satisfyingly full glass on the table by my chair. 'Carterton and Dutt. Yes, I picked it up in Calcutta. I have seen one or two of the temples – Vishnupur and so on. They're astonishing. I've told Ginny we must go and have a tour sometime.'

Persi thumbed through for a moment, peering through her specs, then slid it back on to the shelf. I was about to comment on the painting in our bedroom, which had hung in the room Hughie and I shared as children, when Virginia made an entrance. She had changed into a straight little snip of a dress in pink flowered cotton – quite the fashion at home though one could see more of her legs than perhaps was strictly required. Her hair was loose and lightly curled up at the ends. There was a touch of pink on her lips, blue at the eyes, mascara. The roses in her cheeks, I guessed, were from the rouge brush.

'Drink, darling?' Roderick waved a hand over the table.

'Oh, no thank you. I'll just stick to water.'

God, I thought. Another one. Quite soon, she invited us to come to the table.

'Chicken again, I'm afraid.' She rolled her eyes, pulling her chair in. There was still something chill and closed about her, but she was trying to be social and play the hostess. 'We'll all look like chickens soon. I hope you're all right with curry? They do that better than anything else.'

'Oh, I think we'll be all right with curry.' Persi smiled. 'We've eaten plenty of it in our time.'

'Oh, yes.' Another faint smile. She reached out to pour us a glass of water and managed to knock over the little vase with a single rose bud in it. 'Oh, dear. I'm so sorry!'

Virginia seemed about to rush off somewhere, but Roderick put a hand on her arm as Nirad appeared with a cloth.

'Oh,' she said again, this time sounding irritated. 'Yes, of course.'

Poor girl, I thought, she really is rather nervous. After all, it was Roderick who has invited us two old trout to visit, no doubt out of some sense of duty, and she was to be stuck with us.

The food was delicious. The taste, the sight of the servants' hands bringing the dishes, their low murmur in the background – Nirad and a young lad, both Hindi speakers, I gathered – the gentle tilt of the head each gave when addressed ... How can I explain? It wasn't about being waited on, not that, it was just the way people were. As if I had been touched deeply in myself with a familiarity, a sense of home for which I had been waiting many years.

I should come back, I thought, as I took a mouthful of rice, stained yellow with turmeric. These two are here now, after all. And my old friend Jessie Bell up in her Mussoorie cottage, who had vowed that India was her native land and she would never leave.

'Has it all changed a lot here, Lady Byngh?' Ginny leaned over towards me. I realized I had said very little and was grateful to Persi who had been managing some pleasantries about the garden and Roderick's work and so on. We had both smartened up a bit and Persi, with her hair fastened up and a light cream shawl over the frock, looked gracious and kindly. Which I suspect is more than I did.

I looked across at the girl. Despite her putting on a good show, there was something not right about her. Even with the rouge, she looked pasty again, her face moist with perspiration, though it was not a warm night and Persi and I were wearing shawls.

'Not all that,' I said, 'from what I've seen.' I smiled at her and tried to sound as jovial as possible. After all, I did want the girl to like me, didn't I? 'Cars and so on have changed, of course. Pa used to go about in an old Tin-Lizzy, they were called. A Ford T, I think it was. That's when he wasn't on a horse. The roads were hopeless in the rains – a sea of mud. You'd get marooned for ages at a time. But this house' – I looked around me – 'is not all that different from what I remember. Except the bathroom. In our day it was a tin bath and a *punkah* – not these electric fans! So, how are you finding India, my dear?'

'I'm getting used to it – gradually.' The girl sounded vague and I could see that suddenly she was hardly managing to talk. She had her head down, her eyes darting back and forth as if looking for an escape route, and she was breathing quickly, as if in a dreadful panic.

'Are you all right, dearie?' Persi asked.

'Excuse me. I'm so sorry.' She got up and with no ceremony pushed her chair out of the way so that it fell over on one side and dashed from the room.

'Oh, dear,' Roderick said, righting the chair.

'Gippy tum?' I asked pleasantly.

'I ... er, something like that,' he said, sitting down again. 'I'm sure she'll be back in a moment. Sorry, Aunt Eleanora.'

'That's quite all right,' I said. 'We all have our moments, out

37

here.'

'Another drop of whisky?'

I feigned hesitation. 'Perhaps I will.'

'Tell me,' he said, refilling my glass, generously, I noticed with approval. He seemed to leap in, awkwardly, as if not knowing how to broach the subject. 'You and my father – you must have shared a room, as children?'

There was emotion wrapped up somewhere in his tone, but tightly, not spilling out.

'Yes,' I said. 'The house was just like this – only two bedrooms. *Ayah* slept in with us as well. Nancy, her name was. Hughie and I were great playmates – although really his best ever companion was Akbar, the cook's son. They were round about the same age. I used to play with Shonu, the *mali*'s daughter.' Much to Mother's chagrin, though she could hardly stop us.

Roderick's round face was turned to me, filled with a hunger that was plain to see. What a child he seemed, this man of what, thirty? A hurt child. It was there in the round grey eyes, the look of someone desperate for crumbs. Don't ask, boy, I thought. Don't ask too much. Stay on the surface, it's safer.

'Do you remember this, Miss Persimmon?' He turned to her, politely, to bring her into the conversation.

'No,' Persi said, sipping her blasted tonic water. 'That was before my time.'

'I'll tell you one thing about your father,' I said. But Virginia reappeared then, looking more cheerful.

'All right, darling?' Roderick said, half rising.

'Do sit. Yes, I'm quite all right.' She sank on to her chair and continued. 'Look – we need to say, darling. I can't go on like this.'

'I did say we had some news,' Roderick said bashfully.

'The thing is, I'm having a sprog – we are, that is.' She blushed and burst into giggles. 'And I feel absolutely ghastly. I've been chucking up every morning and half the day as well. When we went to the Club last weekend I ended up heaving into one of the flowerpots!'

I couldn't help a snort of laughter at the thought of this delicious scene. I also couldn't help warming to her slightly. So of course – she was preggers. That was what you did when you got married, wasn't it? I somehow hadn't reckoned on this being part of the picture and it came as a shock.

'I had no idea it was all going to be so foul!'

'Darling,' Roderick said reproachfully. Evidently, he had rather more romantic ideas about the portage of children.

'Sorry.' But she was still giggling, probably relieved to get it off her chest and for a moment she and I were both chuckling. I went through the social motions, congratulating them, but I certainly had mixed feelings about this news. Oh Lord, were we now going to have nothing but baby talk for the entire visit?

'Congratulations to the both of you,' said Persi, who was always capable of kind diplomacy. 'I'm sure you've made your families very happy.'

'Yes, jolly good,' I said, raising my glass. 'Well done all round!' I realized this made it sound as if they had won a horse race, but what does one say on these occasions?

Once we had made this happy toast, Roderick said, 'Come along now, Aunt Eleanora. Tell me more about your memories – and my father's?'

'Ah, let's see.' And here I must admit, I felt a certain devilment. It was the announcement that did it, of course. Sometimes you can't help it, in older age, when your life has not delivered all it might. You envy the young, the serenely married, the ones who manage to have all they need, frankly and legitimately. It seemed she had everything that had been denied me – even my beloved India. Even if it was not clear to me that she really wanted it.

'I had entirely forgotten about this.' It was true; a memory appeared, whole, in my mind as if a door had been blown wide.

Roderick, face expectant, leaned back as the servants took the plates away and replaced the first course with a fruit salad. Then he twisted in his seat to face me, holding his glass like a child waiting for a bedtime story. Virginia leaned her elbows on the table. Two moths danced round the lamp.

'Well, one afternoon – I would have been three I suppose, so Hughie was four going on five – we were all having our rest after lunch. It was very hot, that sort of hot which presses you down on to the bed and you want to lie all stretched out, so nothing is touching anything else. The *punkah* was going, I remember. Sometimes we used to hang a bit of wet sacking across the door to cool things down. Neither Hughie nor I were actually asleep. We'd been playing about a bit. *Ayah* had been trying to quieten us both down. We didn't seem to be affected by the heat quite like the adults. I suppose it was being born here.'

I could feel myself making claims. My birthplace. My place.

'We heard a noise coming from our parents' room – next door, like here. It was Mother: not a scream exactly, but she cried out. A few moments went by and then Pa came into our room.' I laughed at the memory, remembering the sight of the dark hairs running down Pa's chest and belly. 'All he had on was his shorts. He said, "Come on, you two, come and see this," and led us into their bedroom.'

I could see they were both rapt by this point and I was rather

40

enjoying myself.

'We couldn't see anything to begin with. Ma and Pa had been lying there having their nap, with the doors all ajar to let in a breeze, such as there was. Anyway, a bee flew into the room. Soon another came, then another and another and in just a few moments, while they lay there still as planks, an entire swarm had flown into the room.'

'Oh!' Ginny said. Her eyes were wide, blue smudgy shadows beneath them. 'How horrible! I couldn't bear it. Whatever did they do?'

'There wasn't much they could do, except lie there. Father told us they stayed absolutely still, hardly breathing, while the swarm droned about over their heads. But quite soon the bees disappeared, except that they could still hear them. There was a peculiar, echoey sound – almost like someone snoring.'

'Heavens,' Roderick said. 'I've seen plenty of swarms outside – but I never knew they might come indoors.'

'Pa realized the bees had flown into the wardrobe. When he crept over and had a look inside, they had fastened themselves on to an empty coat hanger. He let us peep in, and there they were, all hanging down like a sort of black slick.'

I looked at Roderick – at him and not at Ginny.

'This was where Hughie came into it. Pa said there was nothing for it but for him to try and pick up the hanger himself and carry it into the garden so that he could hang them from the branch of a tree. He lifted them ve-ery slowly and carefully out of the cupboard, saying to them, "There you go, little chaps," or something. He liked animals and other creatures, Pa did.'

'My, my,' Persi said, sounding amused. 'I've never heard this one before.'

41

'The bees all stayed where they were, hanging down like some odd sort of garment, as Pa started to inch his way across the room. And Hughie said, "I want to carry them." Mother of course was saying no, not to be so ridiculous, and of course the problem, as Pa pointed out to him, was that he was nothing like tall enough. So, still holding the bees, he managed to lift Hughie up with the other arm, and once he was high off the ground, Pa very carefully let him take the hanger off him and hold it. I remember Hughie's face. He had the hook with both hands, holding it right away from him as far as he could. He was concentrating so hard, I thought his eyes would pop out. They took them outside, very slowly, and hung them from the branch of a papaya tree. The bees didn't fly away immediately, they just stayed there, all in a funnel. But by that evening they were gone.'

'How extraordinary,' Ginny said. 'My goodness, you think of snakes and scorpions and things, but ... We must always close the door, darling!'

Roderick had a half-smile on his face and I could see he was affected in some way by the story. A crumb from the past had come his way. I took a sip of my drink.

'That's a very good story,' he said. 'Is it true?'

'Of course.' I drained my glass. I was getting a bit tight. 'Why would it not be true? Then there was the time when the Kraits fell down on to their bed ...'

'Kraits?' Ginny asked, those eyes stretched even wider.

'Snakes,' I explained. 'Venomous.'

'Stop that, Eleanora,' Persi said quietly.

'It's just,' Roderick went on, looking rather wretched, 'I'm never sure, when people tell me about my ... my dad.'

'Dad' instead of 'my father' was sweet. It wounded me,

because it brought Hughie close again.

'Why did you come back here into tea?' I asked him. 'After all, we were a spent force here, long ago.'

'Well …' He gave me a painful smile, running his finger down the side of his glass. 'Truth is, I'm pretty wretched at everything else – except writing the odd poem. And I suppose I just wanted to know.'

'Know what?' Persi asked.

Ginny sat quietly, watching us all, but I noticed that suddenly her eyes seemed full of a blazing passion of some sort. There was a lot to this young woman, I saw, feeling suddenly curious about her.

'I don't know.' He shrugged. 'The family business, I suppose. What it was – is – like.'

'So,' Ginny said suddenly, as if something had occurred to her. She leaned forward, elbows on the table, her arms shapely and ivory white. Her tone was formal, cautious. 'Your father, Lady Byngh …'

'Oh, don't call me that, please,' I said tetchily. 'That's all a lot of nonsense. Eleanora will do well.'

'All right.' She gave me one of those looks, direct, surprised. 'Eleanora, then. He would have been Hugh's father – my father-in-law's father? What was his name?'

I felt all prickles suddenly. Naturally, the girl wanted to know who was who in this family she had married into. My Pa, my lovely father. Yet I tensed, feeling my breath become shallow, as if I were a fierce dog, guarding the private, overgrown territory of my own heart.

'My father and Hughie's?' I tried to sound breezy. 'He was called David Storr-Mayfield. Storr only, until he married Mother.

She was a Mayfield and the Mayfields thought they were a big noise.' This did not seem quite the moment to start explaining about the family business. 'She wouldn't give up the name.'

Ginny frowned, trying to piece things together. 'So, Pod, did you know your grandfather – David Storr-Mayfield?'

'No,' Roderick said. He had a bewildered look, as if this thought had scarcely ever occurred to him. 'I mean, I knew he had been in tea, but I never actually met him.'

'You wouldn't have met my pa,' I said breezily. 'You see, he took his own life one sunny morning, the poor, silly darling. I was only four myself at the time.'

'Persi?'

We were lying in our narrow little beds. She had said not a word to me since we came away from the others. I could hear her shifting about and I knew she was awake.

'What d'you make of them?'

There was a silence before she said, 'They're good people.'

This wasn't a lot of help. As I say, I put this frustrating lack of analysis down to Christianity.

'Why did you come out with it like that? It wasn't necessary – or kind.'

'Don't know.' I was ashamed. I didn't know. Sometimes, though, I get so weary of pretence. 'He wants to know more about Hugh, doesn't he?'

'So tell him. You've got memories – he wants to hear. But you didn't have to begin like that.'

'Well, that's one more thing he knows now,' I said brutally. 'And there's all the things *I* don't know.'

'If you don't know, you can't tell him, can you? He just wants a little piece of his father, that's all – he had little enough.'

After that there was silence. But I couldn't sleep for a long time after I could hear Persi's polite little snores. Lying there in the dark, hearing the whining bark of a jackal somewhere far across the garden, I thought, I'm not the only one with memories. I should have asked if she was all right. Not that she would be likely to say, though. But now we were away from that wretched house – Mumsie's house – things felt different, as if we were able to see each other with gentler eyes.

I lay on my back, wide awake, smelling the insecticide. The *chowkidar* went padding along the verandah and back. Soon after, a train passed, rumbling slowly, letting out its lonely, fading whistle to the night.

That night, for the first time in more years than I could recall, I dreamed about both of them. I woke as dawn approached, with that old, unbearable feeling I hoped I had left far behind. I could no longer lie with that and I creaked my way out of bed, taking the blanket, to sit on the verandah.

There was no sign of the *chowkidar*, but the little dog came pattering along. 'Hello, Nip old chap,' I whispered. 'Have you come to keep me company?' I stroked his head for a while, hoping my own kennelled doggies were all right.

A moment later I heard someone stirring in the other bedroom. I stiffened, dreading one of them coming out and my having to be social at this time in the morning. There was a pause followed, unmistakably, by the sound of Mrs Storr-Mayfield chucking up in the bathroom. Eventually she subsided again.

Soft voices came from the cookhouse to my right, and I could smell wood smoke. Otherwise, all was quiet. I sat amid the morning birdsong, looking out as pearl light touched the trees and wiry, dew-silver grass, recalling other gardens, other dawns.

3

Panchcotta Tea Estate, Assam, 1904

It was my fourth birthday. I lay half-covered by a sheet, looking up through the white haze of my mozzy net. It was the hot season, the waiting dawn already steeped in heat, but not yet with the force with which it would slam down later in the day. Mother complained constantly about the heat, but to me, a child of India, it was normal.

I could just see the top of Hughie's black, fuzzy hair as he slept on his cot, his back to me. Nancy, our *ayah,* lay on hers against the far wall, a neat S-shape in her blue sari. I could hear the *mali* splashing water out beyond the verandah, humming to himself as he gave the flowers a drink.

I was excited, but I could not at first remember why. My waking thought was not 'It's my birthday!' but to smile at Ganesh, who was sitting on the mattress by my pillow. Pa had given him to me, a little statue of the elephant god made of turquoise resin, cross legged, one hand raised in greeting. He had wide, jaunty ears and a big belly as if he had swallowed a pumpkin whole, that was what Pa said.

'Tubby.' I poked him. He made me feel happy.

'What d'you want to go and give her that for?' Mother asked.

'Horrible pagan thing.'

'What's horrible about it?' Pa said. 'It's an elephant. I think he looks very jolly.'

I sat up, wishing Hughie would wake.

'*Mali!*' Mother's voice came from outside, shrill. 'Take it away – that's it, away – go!'

Mother would not learn 'those dreadful languages'. She insisted on addressing the servants in English until they caught on to what she meant.

The splashing moved further away to be replaced by other sounds: the jingling of a little bell, voices and laughter, and there were feet climbing the verandah steps. Our door burst open. *Ayah* leapt up with a shriek and Hughie woke, sitting up in fright.

Standing in the doorway was Pa, in his riding clothes, his black hair dishevelled and face all smiles. Looking just as amiable was the brown pony beside him, whose halter he was holding, which had a tinkly bell attached to it. *Ayah* made a noise of not entirely pleased surprise at finding a pony almost in bed with her and scuttled to crouch on the other end of her mattress. But she smiled then, showing her big square teeth, pulling the end of her sari half across her face.

'Happy birthday, Nellinora!'

Pa brought the pony right up to my bed and folded back the net. A soft, grey nose snuffed enquiringly at my arm. It felt lovely and I giggled. It had bright, cheeky eyes and I could smell the warm pony smell.

'He's for you, darling. Happy birthday.' Pa leaned down and kissed me.

'Oh!' I stood up and wrapped my arms round the pony's neck, nuzzling his wiry mane. He jerked his head and the bell tinkled. I sank down on the bed again, gazing at him. What a present – a whole world of horse! Hughie already had a black pony called Tinker. Now it was my turn.

'What will you call him?' Pa asked.

'Jingles,' I said, at once.

'Jingles it is then.'

'Ganesh likes him.' I lifted the statue to the pony's questing nostrils.

'I daresay.' Pa laughed.

'Do put that dreadful thing down.' Mother had swept into the room and stooped to peck my cheek. She smelled of soap and cologne, so different from Nancy, whose smell was of hair oil and fennel. 'Happy birthday, Eleanora.'

I heard a giggle from the door then and saw that Akbar had crept in and was looking round the doorframe, hand pressed over his mouth. Peeping round him was my friend Shonu, the *mali's* girl, a year younger than I was, with her huge eyes and mop of unruly hair. Hughie jumped out of bed and ran out with the two of them.

'Hugh!' Mother called. 'You come back here!' But he was gone. I could hear them giggling outside.

So I was left with *ayah* and my love affair with a pony, and with Mother and Pa, whose own love affair was far more star-crossed than I had the years to realize.

This tea garden world, to me a place of wonder, was the only one I knew in those five years – the same years in which my scholarly, unthrusting father failed to attain any sort of promotion, a theme on which Mother held forth frequently.

'You ought to be moving up to manager by now, not bringing

up your family in this little hovel.'

Mother had come from Money. She found it provoking, having to face the fact that this was not a position they could buy their way out of. Pa was too busy interesting himself in other things to be regarded as garden manager material.

So, we stayed on in our one storey. No *burra* bungalow for us, like the manager's next door, which was a two-storey thatched building of what seemed palatial magnificence. We had hardly ever been there because the children of the current manager and his wife were much older than Hughie and me and had disappeared to somewhere called 'Home'. Although Mother and Pa went round sometimes, it seems as if the large, mustachioed manager and Pa had very little in common and his wife, Mother said, was 'a jumped-up guttersnipe'.

One afternoon, when I crept out from my afternoon nap to the sound of Chopin, I found Mother pacing the room in her long skirts, her hands clenched to her chest, weeping and muttering savagely. It frightened me and I ran away.

The life of a planter's wife is lonely, but Mother made it more so. She loathed India and everything about it, even the other Europeans.

That birthday morning, instead of riding off to work at the tea factory at first light, Pa took me for a ride, bareback on Jingles. He wore only a halter and I held a neck strap with my plump, tanned fingers, my legs stretched across his sleek back, bubbling over with happiness. I had Pa to myself, the lovely smell of warm horse and his movements under me and, all around, the sounds of the wakening morning.

The *mali* limped over to the gate – he had a tubercular hip –

grinning as he opened it for us to go out on to the track through the estate. Pa led me along the yellow road as the sun rose into a parched sky. The sea of green tea bushes stretched away on every side, divided into neat parcels by sandy tracks and drainage ditches and dotted with shade trees to protect the delicate tea shoots from the merciless sun. Scattered about the fields were the bright saris of women plucking the leaves into their baskets, before the worst of the heat. Two of them who were close to the road called *'Namashkar!'* touching their foreheads and smiling.

I rode, my eyes shaded by my *topi*, smelling Jingles' sweat. My tall, solid Pa turned and smiled from under his own *topi*, his dark-eyed face crinkling.

'How is he, Nellinora? A good little chap, eh?'

I nodded, already in love with Jingles. And Pa greeted the people we met. He seemed to know everyone and every language. He had a passion for it and in his spare time he was compiling a dictionary.

'If there was a way everyone working here could understand each other it would all be so much better.' Already there was Assamese, Bengali and Hindi and some of the other workers were brought in from other parts of the country.

I never understood why Mother got so furious about this dictionary – not until I was much older and realized that in the five long years that planters had to work for the company without being allowed to marry, in their need and loneliness they often turned to native women. Mother never seemed quite sure what had gone on, but she would say furiously, 'Ah, I suppose *your sleeping dictionary* taught you that.' I had no idea at the time what she meant.

'It seems obvious to me,' she would say, looking up from her sewing, or a magazine she had had sent from Calcutta, now long out of date, 'that the only sensible thing to do in this country, with all these ridiculous languages, would be to teach them all English. It would make the place a damn sight more civilized.'

Pa would smile patiently, but he had given up trying to talk to her about it. Even kitchen Hindustani was beneath Mother, however much Pa pleaded with her to learn. She would not bend to anyone else's terms.

Sometimes, perhaps because he needed to talk to someone (Mother and the estate manager not being the right someones), Pa showed his complicated project to Hughie and me. It was a roll of sheets of paper, each divided into four columns, the left-hand column headed ENGLISH; the others, the words spelled out in English letters, headed ASSAMESE, BENGALI, HINDUSTANI.

'I'm trying to keep it alphabetical,' he explained once, frowning. 'But you see, I can only manage it for English speakers to refer to. If I have a word like, let's see, Soil, it can only remain alphabetical in one language because Soil, or Snake, or Sun don't necessarily begin with an 's' in any other language and the alphabets are not the same – d'you see? So I can only make this make sense to an English person at the moment.'

'But that's all right, isn't it?' Hughie said, trying to be helpful because he could see, as I could, that our father was suffering in some way. I thought it was all because of the alphabet being different in all the other languages. I didn't know how to make it better.

Pa smiled wearily. 'Well, it's a start.' He rolled up the papers and tied a cotton thread round them. 'I sometimes wonder whether, if everyone in the world spoke the same language, it would be a better place.'

He wrote poems about such things. His heart ached for the wounds of the world. As it turned out, he didn't even speak the same language as our mother, let alone everyone else in the world.

That morning, of my fourth birthday, he led me along the main road through the estate until we could just see the iron roof of the tea-processing factory through the trees. He stopped, lifting his hat to wipe the sweat from his brow.

'Now,' he said, 'some horses know how to find their way home. But Jingles is a rather new chap round here, isn't he, so I can't just point him in the right direction and say "Off you go" to you both. We'd better go back and fetch old Minto so that I can get to work.'

'When he's bigger he'll know the way,' I said. 'Like Minto.' Pa's big chestnut horse with the white blaze could have trotted about the estate with his eyes shut.

'This little one is not going to get any bigger, Nellinora,' Pa said. 'You'll outgrow him before long. But he might get a bit wiser, eh, little chap?' He stroked Jingles' neck. 'Come on, birthday girl – *hazri* time. Let's beat the sun and get home.'

As Pa led Jingles back into our compound, I saw a splash of colour close to the verandah steps. It was the orange of a sari, and a tiny little woman was standing there, arguing shrilly with the *mali*.

On seeing Pa, the woman sank to her knees and touched his feet. Pa didn't like it and gently told her to get up. She was bony like a grasshopper, with a red marriage mark on her forehead, thin hair scraped back and rings all round her ears and in her nose. She kept beating her chest with her hand and talking fast in a whining voice.

Pa dismissed the *mali*, who limped away, muttering. He said something to the woman, but he seemed defeated, shrugging at her. Her whine grew even higher and more unhappy. I wanted Pa to make things right, but he didn't seem to be able to. In the end, he told her to go and she yanked the end of her sari tight over her head and slunk away down the path.

Mother appeared on the verandah in her morning dress, pale yellow with tiny pink flowers. Her golden-brown hair was elegantly pinned back. I knew Mother was a beauty because everyone said so and, though they did not exactly say so, that I was not.

'What was all that?' she said. 'Did I see one of those junglies? She's got a nerve, coming in here.'

'Oh, Alicia,' Pa said, turning to fiddle with Jingles' halter, though there was no need.

'I don't know why they don't know what's good for them,' Mother said, straightening her cuffs. There were a lot of conversations about the 'labour problem'. It was hard ever to find enough people to work the tea gardens. Most of the Assamese were quite happy working their own land, thank you very much, so why come and work for us? Other workers were tricked into coming many miles to Assam from other parts of India and then found they could not leave. She stared at Pa. 'What did she want?'

'The usual. Come on, Nellinora.' His voice changed. 'Off you hop. Bring your leg over.' As I slid down stiffly from Jingles, Pa looked across at Mother. 'She wants to go home. They were all told they'd go home.'

'Huh,' Mother retorted, turning away. 'We'd all like *that*, wouldn't we? Come along, Eleanora – breakfast.'

I followed her skirts. Father stood watching us, holding

Jingles. I could feel that he was still there and I turned. His eyes were full of unhappiness and this was not what I was expecting, not on my birthday, selfish little thing that I was. The orange lady had been anguished too and the sadness of each of them seeped into me, darkening the day. Pa was too sensitive to the world. I've found that survival depends on how much of the world's misery – or even your own, come to that – you allow right inside you. I had a sensitive father – but I was also schooled by Mother.

There were a few Europeans we met who seemed to think that people are just people, of the same value as they are. The Scottish missionaries, the Revd and Mrs McTeer, were like that. They worked in Jorhat Town and Mrs McTeer always seemed to have a group of singing children round her. Pa got along well with her. But there were those like my mother who imagined one had to make divisions. Her pink English skin and place of birth (though what's so particularly special about Berkshire I'll never know) making her of absolute, superior value. She was a 'Christian' who was bored by church, a person in the so-called religion of love who seemed to have not the first idea how to go about it.

There would not be another birthday like that, with Jingles, the dogs and all the other pets – Snowy and Lop my rabbits, Raju the rusty-haired macaque monkey who used to steal my doll and dash off into the trees – no tea and cake in the garden.

Next summer, Hughie was due to go 'Home' to school and Mother was to go with him on furlough. With this looming, in the February of 1905, in the cold season when the garden was quiet, Pa suggested we have an Indian holiday. In all his time there he had barely seen anything except for Assam and Calcutta.

We embarked on a long, rattling train journey, waking to find ourselves in the south, a place of temples and seaside and greener, lusher altogether.

This is how I remember it.

We are in a retiring room at a small-town station called Mettupalayam. The station offers a few retiring rooms, very plain and white. Mother and Pa are in two hard beds pushed side by side in the middle and Hughie and I on folding cots at the side. There are bars on the windows and one of the shutters is half open, letting in the first morning light and the smell of coal smoke.

I'm lying on my cot with a muzzy, hollow feeling, having been sick in the night. Mother got up to see to me. There has been a great deal of noise in the night: the station racket, shouting when a train pulled in, its chugging sounds as the train got up steam again, doors banging, a dog barking and *chai-wallahs* calling on the dark platform. Had I not been sick, I might have slept through all this and then I should never have heard the other sounds. It felt like a bad dream because they were voices I could not seem to recognize. Was that Mother, that snake-like hissing and whispering? And that other voice was surely Pa, soft at first, but then it broke open:

'I can't stand it, Alicia. Have you any idea what you're doing to me?'

Terrible sobbing, choking noises seemed to go on and on – and that other snake voice, furious, 'Stop that – in heaven's name, David. It's so pathetic!'

Lying here now, in the morning light, I hear an early train's hissing and its mustering steam, whoomp, whoomp, outside. Smoke drifts in through the window. A *kak* appears, perched on the shutter, grey-suited with a black hat, not like English crows, which are like clumps of flying charcoal. Its claws rattle and it peers down at me, *kaaa, kaaa … Kak. Don't call it that – speak English. It's a crow.* But it's called *kak* – it says 'kak' … There are children's voices, someone sloshing water.

I turn over, away from the half-open window, the shutter and crow, the pale sky … And this is where my memory somehow goes wrong, because then, on this last morning of my life – this known life – I lie there under the Indian railway sheet and I hear a shot. It can't be, that shot, however much I have persisted in remembering it in contradiction to the facts. It is the sound my memory supplies to accompany the hiss of the train, the smoke, the crow.

When we wake properly, Hugh, Mother and I, Pa is gone. For one of his little walks, Mother tells us. The morning is all confusion; the Station Master's Office – an Indian station master, small, with gentle hands – the blind man outside, bony as a hat stand, leaning stiffly into the wall, his eyes milk white …

It does not take long to discover what has happened because a huddle of villagers come from outside the town, who have found him – exactly how, or where, no one ever tells me. My Pa walked out into the remains of the night and laid himself down in front of the first morning train as it got up speed, thundering south towards Coimbatore.

Mother had the dogs shot, that I do know. Are those the shots that my mind has soldered on to the other memory? Did I even hear them? I've now no way of knowing.

We had to leave Panchcotta. I remember a church, brown inside, 'Abide With Me', a hymn I've never been able to sing since. After that, all I can remember is Persi.

Bombay. She was wearing a stiff blue dress and a pair of Wellington boots. The boots were the first thing I saw because I was sitting on the floor, a thick rug beneath me. The house belonged to my new stepfather. Mother, it appeared, had been on her way out in any case. On her 'rest cure' in Calcutta, she had met a P & O man, over for a visit from the Bombay office. His name was Peter Kelner. Very quickly, they got married. What Mother had been planning originally, I have no idea: the dread divorce, or a life of pretence if she had left Pa? But she was a widow, so that was that. I only pieced all this together much later and hated her for it.

One thing I do recall is her parting from Nancy. I hovered in a doorway, perhaps somewhere in Calcutta, perhaps in a hotel. Mother and *ayah* were sitting side by side on a bed, their backs to me. Each had an arm round the other. Nancy's red and gold bangles pressed against Mother's pearl-grey blouse; Mother's arm draped diagonally like a grey sash down Nancy's back. Both were sobbing. Mother, especially, was weeping in a way I only witnessed on one other occasion. Nancy was not coming with us to Bombay. Mother had taken her on in Calcutta and she came to Assam with us, but she was a Bengali and Bombay was too far for her. She had returned home and planned to find work back in Calcutta. I still can't quite believe what I saw. Mother had such a superior way with the servants. Come to think of it, I can't recall what Nancy's real name was – it was Mother who called her that.

Persi told me later that Nancy had seen Mother through the birth of her first child, a boy called David, who died of a fever after a month. That was another reason why she hated India so much: she blamed the country for killing her son. Once she had had Hugh, she vowed she would not have any more. And then I went and made my presence felt. But with Nancy, who was so sturdy and reassuring, there was a womanly bond I never saw Mother make with anyone else, even though up until then you would never have known it – oh no, the *memsahib* was not supposed to fraternize with the servants.

She was never a happy woman, my mother. At twenty-three she had felt left on the shelf. Her younger sister Frances had not only married, but managed to bag some sort of lord and was living on a grand Suffolk estate. Their younger brother, our Uncle Hat (because he wore a battered straw panama seemingly night and day in all seasons) was not quite all there in some way – though he was a sweetie, and always so good to Hughie and me.

So when Mother, at some village party, met a chap – Pa was reasonably handsome – home from India on furlough, no doubt desperate for a woman, she leapt at it. God alone knows what she thought. It's not as if he hid from her the fact that he was a tea planter. But she wanted marriage, quick as a flash, and it must have sounded swanky. Off to India, you know, all silks and palaces, maharajahs and riding elephants wherever you go, all that storybook guff – was that what she imagined? Sometimes she said to Pa, 'If I'd wanted to marry a farmer I could have stayed in Berkshire.' After all, it was very isolated, very lonely for the wives. Hardly anyone for acres around, miles to the Club to see people who mostly bored her, no glamour, which she liked. Mostly no one to talk to but us – a husband who was England born but one of those Englishmen who loved India as part of his own soul. And Hughie and I were little Anglo-Indians for whom the country was simply home. Ironically, the only true friend Mother ever had, for all her crashing snobbery and prejudice, was Nancy.

There was an *ayah* in Bombay but she could never replace Nancy and did not last long. Perhaps we were little monsters. We were two very unhappy children, who wanted our Pa, our animals, our home, not to be stuck in some stranger's house on the side of the Malabar Hill in Bombay. I can remember very little about it until Persi arrived. I can't even recall Hugh being there or anything we did. It was later, in England, when I made my deliberate decision never to feel anything. But the habit had already long begun.

Mother, who was having to contend with a busy, previously single man who had no idea about children, especially dreadfully unhappy ones, decided we needed an English nanny to get us ready for as early a dispatch 'Home' as possible. Persi was what arrived – neither English, nor in fact a nanny.

Persi was an escapee, a motherless child, a piece of flotsam. But she made an impression. There was the voice, Canadian, slightly cracked in tone even then, the fact that she was a head taller than Mother and therefore passed off as older than the only just eighteen years she really was; the long, languid body dressed in severe shades and that head of thick, sensuous hair, wavy chestnut with auburn lights in it. And the Wellies. She arrived during the rains, not from Canada but from a few streets away. Persi had originally fled across the Atlantic to work in England, then answered an advertisement which brought her to India to look after a small boy called Ralph. Poor little Ralph was dead before she even completed the crossing. So she came to us.

I'm ashamed that I can't remember more: what she said that day, or her long, strange, interesting face as it looked when we first set eyes on her. What I do know is that from then on, one way or another in so far as she was able, Persi was always there.

The other occasion when Mother wept was when she parted from Hugh and me only a few months later. It was because she was parting with Hughie, not me – of that I'm quite sure. But Persi was with us and for me, by then, she was home. She stood between us, straight as a wash prop, holding our hands as we squinted into the glare from the deck of the P & O's *Himalaya*. The ship hummed and vibrated and Mother, all on her own in the crowd on the Bombay dock, shrank smaller and smaller, waving her hanky.

'That's right, wave bye-bye,' Persi said. We raised our hands obediently. Hughie was sobbing. Mother may have been crying again, but she was too far away to see. And then we could not make her out among the other hatted mothers and wavers teetering at the edge of India as we took our leave of its hot breath on the breeze.

Persi's skirt was a green tartan and I remember my face brushing against the pleats, how rough it felt as we lost sight of Mother.

'All right now, piglets,' she said in her kind, but commanding way. 'Let's go and see if we can find something nice to eat, shall we?'

The voyage was rough and Hugh was mostly confined to his bunk, spewing yellow stuff into a bowl. Persi and I were perfectly all right. The young men on board loved Persi. They were drawn to her as if she gave off a magic aroma – though in truth that scent could only have been a mild disdain. She had left Canada and her widowed, religious fanatic of a father to escape a marriage. He must have seen even then that she was not a man's woman because, young as she was, he had rushed into an 'either marry or here's some money to get out of my hair' sort of position.

Persi was pleasant enough to all these young men – on the surface. And she was *herself*, incorruptibly and cheerfully. But she was never, ever biddable and even that seemed to be what drew them to her, as well as that face, the extraordinary hair. She would have the occasional dance in the ship's ballroom, in her only slightly glamorous, sage-green frock. But she cared not a jot what any of them thought – about her or about anything else.

Rain, the copper shine of wet leaves, a black door under a cobwebby porch somewhere deep in the countryside, a heavy knocker. School. And we, a tall, copper-haired woman and scruffy, brown child, waiting outside.

Before she leaves again, Persi squats on the scuffed parquet floor looking into my eyes with her intent grey ones as if trying to bleed strength into me.

'I won't be far away. I'll come when I can and I'll write you every week.'

She kisses me goodbye and, at the last minute, pulls me briefly, tightly, into her arms, even though there is some other person there, exuding impatience.

This is England. Everything is cold and grey: the sky, the stones, the days. The only colour is Persi's blue coat and the lights in her hair and suddenly she is gone.

A black iron bedstead, a deep dip in the middle of the thin mattress which I try to wrap my arms around, for want of a flesh and blood person. A long attic room full of children like me, between four and six years old. One who is three, her thighs red-raw in the mornings from urine. I wake, already crying. I think

I shed all the tears I had for a lifetime during those first weeks.

Smells: the cheapest of soap, ammonia from morning sheets slicing into our nostrils, boiled cabbage, boiled onions, potatoes, swede, anything you can boil the guts out of with never a hint of spice. The sickening stink of rubbery grey stew.

There are high ceilings, iron-framed windows, their panes spattered with rain, but blurred and half-hearted rain, not like at home. One afternoon, the air sickly with leaf rot, I pick up an apple from the grass, half green, half tan and spongy to touch, barnacled with mould. I have never seen a green apple before.

And letters, each week, with Persi's neat, looped handwriting. No longer in my mother's employ, but still, there she is, always in touch, telling me sweet, cheering things. One week, about a dog she saw in a London park and that she has a landlady called Mrs Tickell; another, that she has started training to be a nurse at a hospital called St Bartholomew's and that my brother is all right, is settling in and she hopes I am too. Mother writes once a month, about weather and Bombay parties, about people I don't know. That's all I recall about my first school.

This second school was in Buckinghamshire and that's where I met Jessie Bell.

Some girls brought their own animals to school if they lived in England. Otherwise the school was a holding pen for the children of Empire. I don't think Robert Bell, Jessie's father, ever realized quite how amateurish the place was. He was a learned, in some ways innocent man and had thought about keeping Jessie in India. But he was a botanist or agriculturalist or some such, and often on the move. And the Bells had heard that Langley Down was a happy school (which in some ways it was, if you like ponies and giggling in hedges).

Jessie, who had mousy curls and rosy skin, never came up against the problems I faced.

'Are you Indian?' (The right answer to this, of course, not being 'Yes.') 'Look at your hair – and you're brown as a berry. Eleanora's a *chi-chi*!' Hugh told me he had just the same.

'No!' I used to say furiously, because it was said so accusingly that it must be a shameful thing. And also, because it was the truth. But I was swarthy and dark-haired and never entirely got away from this accusation, especially as Jessie and I sometimes exchanged chat in Hindustani as a way of shutting them out.

As I grew, I became top-heavy with a large bust. While chaps I came across later were enthusiastic about this, other girls resented it like fury. Jessie never had any of this. She was an average sort of plump, with buck teeth and specs, and I remember her always laughing. I thought about inventing a father for myself since the next question issuing from the young snoots, 'What does *your* father do?' was unanswerable. I thought about saying my father was a prince or a maharajah. Since they persisted in thinking I was Indian anyway, I might as well do what seemed the ultimate in pulling rank. I never quite dared and mumbled that my father was dead.

But somehow, they found out about Mayfields.

'Ha ha, Eleanora's Pa works for Crappers!'

For a good while I was nicknamed 'the Crapper'. I used to hit girls who called me that, even come out with Bengali curses that Akbar had taught to Hugh and me. But that only made things worse. Sometimes rage swelled in me, so strong that I thought I might trample them on the floor – until I managed to freeze it over. I felt nothing, stopped reacting and they got no satisfaction out of me.

Just as boarding school teaches you to cry quite silently, so it also teaches you to kill your own anger, or any other inconvenient emotion. I can't say I learned a great deal of anything much more useful than that.

During the whole fourteen years of my banishment to England's cold exile, I went home only once, when I was twelve. I only lasted a couple of days in Bombay with Mother and my stepfather, Peter Kelner. Persi had long nicknamed him 'the Mynah' because of his capacity for keeping up an endless, vacuous social chatter. But he and Mother were strangers to me. I hated it there and decamped to Jessie, who went home every two or three years, and the snows of the hills.

Persi, whose hours were dictated by the hospital, would come when she could and take us out from school, about once a term. There'd be a tramp in a sodden park, a picnic and paddle in a river or a cake in a teashop – I never cared what except for being with her. During the holidays, while we were still small, Hughie and I mostly stayed on at our respective schools with the other colonials whose parents had not managed to make arrangements or had forgotten completely about them. But the next stage was Uncle Hat, in Berkshire – presumably when we were deemed old enough more or less to fend for ourselves.

That Easter when Hugh and I stayed with Uncle Hat and sat on the hillside at Greenbury, I would have been getting on for thirteen, he fourteen. It was the holiday after we had been home to India for that dismal Christmas. I'd gone to Jessie, but Hugh, also escaping the Bombay house, travelled to Assam. He had always wanted to go back, but straight afterwards I had not been able to get a word out of him about it.

Now it seems odd, how many things we didn't talk about, how much of our time together was spent *not* saying things. We were apart a good deal of the time and we hardly ever wrote each other letters. Yet there was still a deep bond between us.

It was only then, sitting on a hummock of grass in a stinging April wind, rows of fuzzy green wheat shoots stretching before us, that he told me about Akbar.

'I went back to Panchcotta,' he blurted. I looked round, startled. Hugh was facing straight ahead, England-pale now, the wind blowing his wiry curls about his forehead. 'I wanted to see it. I couldn't really believe it would still be there.'

I sat hugging my knees. His words made my stomach clench. We were both hunched with our collars up and I was shivering.

'Was *ayah* there?' I asked.

Hugh glanced at me with a frown. 'No, of course not. She came back to Cal with us – remember?'

'Oh, yes.' My mind had rearranged the past. Panchcotta, with Nancy always there. I felt as if I had been punched.

'I went to see Akbar – I thought he'd be there for ever.' I could hear the roughness of tears in his voice. 'That he would just grow up and be a cook like his father.'

He stopped for a moment. I didn't look at him.

'His pa was still there. When he saw who I was, he …' His voice broke then. Those sobs had been waiting there a good long time. 'I'd never seen … one of them … you know, cry – like that.'

It had happened three years earlier, when Akbar was eleven – so Hugh would have been as well. The rains arrived, and the lower lands all flooded. The tea garden was on slightly higher ground, but the paddies filled and the drainage ditches were overflowing. Akbar caught a fever. They looked after him, did everything they could. The garden manager had him taken to the hospital and his mother camped by his bed night and day.

'His brain swelled,' Hugh told me. He was really crying now, couldn't help it, poor old lamb. My own throat was aching like mad and I put my hand on his back. Why couldn't I weep, not even then? We were so hopeless with emotions, no flaming idea what to do – with our own or anyone else's.

'In two days, he was dead. They couldn't save him.'

Hugh looked me full in the face, his eyes red, cheeks wet. 'Remember what he was like?'

Of course I remembered: the thick fringe, his grin with those tombstone teeth, his eyes shining with mischief, the thin, whirring legs. Akbar the Great, we used to call him.

Hugh drew his hand roughly over his eyes. 'There would have been no point in telling Mother.'

Of course not. Mother would have said with disdain, 'Who?'

'Shonu?' I asked. Shonu with her curly mop and dancing eyes. 'Was she still there?'

'I s'pose so. I didn't see her.'

We sat looking at the heavy clouds over the downs. I knew that each of us, in our minds, was in Panchcotta, in the sun, among the animals and the bright flowers, running on the grass with Akbar.

We never spoke of it again.

Come 1914, there was war, which for me meant being marooned in England. Persi was gone – she joined the Queen Alexandra's nurses and was abroad. Mother, who never seemed to be stuck for money, paid for me to stay pedalling slowly along at school until I was eighteen. She was all for sending me off to some finishing school after that, with a view to me 'coming out'. Thank God, the war ended before that.

4

1965

The young Mrs Storr-Mayfield took to her bed during the first days of our visit. I couldn't help thinking that this dose of infirmity was well timed to avoid our company. Roderick kept apologizing, saying she could not seem to stop being sick. In a way it was a relief. In the circumstances, I must admit, I found it easier that she kept out of the way.

'Don't you worry,' I told him. 'Persi and I can find our way about. And we don't need to be rushing off on excursions.'

We ate a meal in the evenings with Roderick and I tried to find nice little things to tell him about Hughie, as did Persi. We took pity on him. And he was eager to hear. He was a good man, I realized. Not unpleasant company. But lost, somehow. And he was worried about his young wife. Persi hastened to assure him that sickness when with child could well be a sign that the pregnancy had taken well.

'Really?' Roderick said doubtfully. 'Well, the poor girl, that's all I can say. It's wretched.'

The second night, he said, 'By the way, there'll be Club night in a couple of days. You must both come along and meet everyone.'

The Jorhat Gymkhana Club was the social centre for all the tea gardens in the area around Jorhat Town. I had known it well once and, hearing its name, I felt a tightening inside me at the memory.

'Of course,' I said. 'That would be very nice.'

The rest of the time I spent looking about me, absorbing, longing mostly to be alone. Persi, who seemed to feel the same, didn't bother me. She was quite happy drifting about or sitting reading or dozing. I wandered the garden in the bright winter sun, with Nip following me about, running here and there. I relished the girth of the giant banyan at the edge of the garden, the ants building giant nests among its leaves. I took in the soft sounds of workers calling to each other, the sight of saris spread flat to dry on the grass, each a flag of colour, held by stones at the corners; by the sight of a cow standing in a low, watery spot the other side of the fence, stalked by its white egret companions.

In the cool, late afternoon I – or Persi and I – walked through the gardens. We followed the sandy paths between parcels of tea bushes, exchanged greetings with workers, with children carrying firewood home in bundles on their heads. I drew in the evening smells of the vegetation, of woodsmoke and cooking.

We didn't talk much. Each of us was lost in our own thoughts and memories, like two people standing at the edge of a well, looking down into depths of tenderness and loss which were beyond words to express.

In the mornings I would rise early and sit on one of the cane chairs on the verandah, wrapped in my shawl. Sitting out there, even by the fourth day, it still felt to me quite extraordinary that I could be here again.

Memories kept rising like clouds of birds. Some I wanted to look at, others I ordered in no uncertain terms to take themselves off into the murky dawn light. But that morning I could not help rising with them, beyond my shrouded view of the garden to the estate with its miles of trimmed tea bushes and shade trees, swooping beyond over the villages and the levées bordering the river. The waters of the Brahmaputra meander along skeins of channels in the cool, drier months, but in the summer monsoon the river swells, pouring from the gullies and white peaks of the Himalayas, growing many miles wide, flooding the land and, in my mind, forever carrying the greatest loves of my heart. And all around, the jungles of Nagaland and along the Burma border, which meant war, which meant Japs, which meant ...

Oh Hughie, Hughie, my big, soft, lost brother.

Go thoughts, fly – do, please. I am not adequate to my own emotions.

The garden was coming fully into being with the sunrise, grey lifting to green, warming the flowers to their full red and yellow. I was about to move inside when Nip, hearing something, got up and tootled along the verandah and I turned as Virginia said softly, 'Hello, little chap.'

Oh Lord, I thought, jarred. Now I was going to have to deal with this one.

She came closer, barefoot, very pale and wrung-out looking. She had her arms wrapped round herself in her white nightdress with a long brown cardi over the top. Her eyes were dark in her face, which looked suddenly younger and sweeter with no make-up. She forced a valiant smile.

'My goodness, Virginia,' I said. 'Should you be up? How are you feeling?'

71

'Good morning.' She stopped, still not sure what to call me, but stepped forward, seeming encouraged. 'I feel pretty shaky. But I've had my first morning chuck and I've just managed to eat a couple of glucose biscuits. It feels as if it's passed for the moment. 'I'm not sure I'm very good at being pregnant.'

'Do sit, dear.' I indicated the other chair and she perched on it, tensely upright, still hugging herself. I noticed that she had chubby toes, like a young child, and the sight of them made my throat tighten. 'You've not been having an easy time,' I managed to say.

She acknowledged this with a tilt of her head and I found myself appreciating her. Mercifully she seemed not the sort to make a big fuss.

'Roderick has gone out for a while. And there's tea coming – there should be enough for both of us.' Once again, she tilted her head. Things felt different from that first night. Since then, we had seen very little of her. Now, she seemed so young and different, not playing a part. I liked her directness. 'I know you said to call you Eleanora – but it's a long name. Might I call you Auntie?'

'D'you know ...' I found myself feeling almost bashful at the inner warmth this suggestion created in me. 'That would be very nice.'

Virginia looked at me in apparent surprise. 'All right, then. And please call me Ginny. No one uses Virginia unless they're cross with me.'

'Ah, well, that I'm not.' I laced my fingers in my lap and she began to relax back in the chair, cautiously, wincing. Hanks of hair slid over her shoulders. She was soft, like a child. I could not but think of the tiny being unfurling deep within her. But I firmly closed the door on this thought. There are those who have and those who do not. Such is life.

'My muscles are all sore.' She rubbed her ribcage.

'Not nice.' I hoped I sounded sympathetic.

'No.' She made a half-comical face. 'All in a good cause, I suppose.'

A faint ceramic clinking signalled the arrival of the tea brought by one of the young lads, barefoot. He put the tray down, smiled and departed.

'*Chota hazri*,' I said, nodding towards the tray, which held the tea things and a plate containing four more of the glucose biscuits and two bananas.

The girl stared at it. 'I just can't get used to people waiting on me. It was me who had to do the waiting at home.'

Nip sat between us, bright-eyed at the arrival of the biscuits. And I had one of those brief moments when you see yourself suddenly – here I am, sitting with this rather lovely young woman, talking, as if I am someone who can conduct herself like that. It felt miraculous.

'I was so sorry to hear about your mother,' I said. 'I gather you spent a lot of time looking after her?'

'Well, yes. I did whatever I could. By the end she was so very ill …'

She drew in a deep breath but there did not seem to be tears. She pulled the edges of her cardigan together, hugging herself.

'Is Miss Persimmon still asleep?'

'Yes. Dear Persi. She's very game, but she does get rather weary these days.'

Ginny gave me another of her direct looks and I saw in them an appealing capacity for human sympathy. 'I gather she's an extraordinary person – nursing all over the world and so on?'

'Yes. She is extraordinary. In a great many ways.'

The girl was sipping her sweet tea cautiously as if weighing the odds as to whether it would stay down. She nibbled on one of the biscuits. I took one and it tasted strangely delicious.

'I do like your hair,' she said, startling me. 'So brave. I don't think I'd have the courage to cut mine so short.'

'Ah, well.' I spoke breezily, though I felt ridiculously gratified. 'It was born out of necessity really – proper birds' nest before. Nothing to be done but cut it all off.'

'But it's lovely strong hair.'

Strong hair. Yes, that's been said to me before. Changing the subject, I said, 'Do you like it here?'

She paused. 'I think so. Some things about it, anyway. But what I don't like is … There's too much *suffering*. I suppose one gets used to it – but is it *right* to get used to such things? It's only been a few months, I suppose.'

I appreciated her attempting to be honest. In my day, so many things were 'marvellous' or 'simply ghastly' – a kind of reflex without much real thought or feeling.

'There's a *lot* to get used to,' she said, frowning slightly. 'And I miss my mother. But of course, even if I were at home, she's not … here any more.'

'You were close?' I supposed some people must be close to their mothers.

'Very.' She looked gratefully at me. 'Although by the time she died she was … She had already left us, the mother I remembered, anyway. But you see I worked for Daddy as well – he's a dentist and I was his assistant: nurse, receptionist all in one. The surgery's in the house. And with Mummy upstairs, we were all sort of together. There's only me, you see. She had me and then fell ill, just a year or two later. And … Well, I realize now, you spend your life on tiptoe, trying to help, trying not to upset anyone, worrying about Mummy and how she's feeling, and about poor Daddy, soldiering on. You ask me how I feel at any given moment and the truth is, I hardly know what I feel for myself.'

She looked up and I did see tears then, which she wiped away, though not with shame, just as if they were not something she wanted to dwell on.

'I was the life in the house, you see. I never really thought I should get away or marry.' After blowing her nose, she added. 'Actually, I *hated* being an only child. I mean, I know we're all alone, ultimately. But while we're alive, we're like stars in a constellation. Those other stars – the ones we're closely connected to, the people we love – they're everything. What I want now is lots of stars, lots of *children* – faces at every window!'

I couldn't help it, I was damnably moved by this, and as much by her confiding in me. Faces at the window, a man you love … *Oh, dear girl, you are more blessed than you could know.*

'You've come a long way,' I said. 'For Roderick.'

'He's a lovely man.' She looked at me as she said it, quite straightforwardly. There was nothing soppy about it.

'Yes,' I said. 'I er … I can see that.'

'The only trouble is …' She unfolded her legs and lowered them, leaning forward for a second to put the cup down, then carried on heatedly, as if everything needed to come tumbling out.

'When you're having a baby, no one will leave you alone. I can't tell you how glad I am that you and Miss Persimmon don't have any children! I wish I'd never told anyone. I'm sick to the back teeth of some of those women we meet at the Club – and Mrs Farley, the manager's wife. She's got three children. They just keep on and *on* about it – reminiscing and telling the most *horrible* stories. They think they're being kind but I can't imagine how they think it's of any help to me to hear all about their heartburn and stitches!'

'I would imagine,' I said, carefully, 'that no one else's stories are much help in that area. It's a bit like life in general; you have to go through it in your own way. Golly,' I added. 'What a sage old owl I sound – and how would I know?'

'But I agree, Auntie! That's what I think. That damn Mrs Greening keeping on and on about her piles …' She giggled then, hand over her mouth for a moment. 'I mean, I didn't even know what she meant by "piles" until … Oh dear, sorry. I think I might be going to be sick again.' She got hurriedly to her feet and darted off.

I watched her, smiling. But straightaway, seeing her young, expectant body moving away, her talking about all of it, awoke the old longings of my body. Memories started to prod at me, the hardest ones of all. Not yet, I thought, panicking, forcing them away. Please no – I'm not ready.

There was a sound which could only be Persi approaching, the slap, slap of her shoes. Nip woofed and dashed to greet her, his nails clicking along the verandah. Persi was draped in a brown blanket, her hair a thick white plait over one shoulder.

'Morning,' I said. 'There's still *char* in the pot.'

'Morning.' Persi sounded fresh as a daisy. She folded herself into the chair vacated by Ginny, rested her elbows on the arms, hands clasped. For a moment she turned her head and our eyes met, then she looked out again, across the garden towards all that lay beyond.

5

1919

There are years, decades even, in which I wonder what I did with myself. Not that I was expected to do anything much, except find myself a husband. Mother had lowered her sights on that, given what an awkward booby of a thing I was. My titled, handsome knight was now to be – well, anyone remotely eligible who, in her words, could 'abide' me.

In the spring of 1919, I lay in the bath in Peter Kelner's house in Bombay and I was in heaven. I was home, home, home! Even the sight of that room, the tin bath with its raised brick surround, the wooden thunderbox and the handbasin filled me with joy. Finally, after the years of war spent hanging about at school with Jessie, knitting balaclavas and socks while the fiancés of our poor and in some cases, increasingly deranged, teachers were picked off one by one – at last we had arrived back. Even Bombay felt like home, even Peter Kelner's bath!

I looked down at myself, my stomach curving gently out of the water, smooth and caramel-coloured as a sandbank, the wet tangleweed of hair between my thighs, my sizable breasts, lolling a little to each side, and my strong legs, feet pressed against the end of the bath. The ends of my hair floated close to me.

I had not looked at myself properly in I don't know how long. For a start it was too damnably cold in England most of the time for more than a brisk sponge down. And it just wasn't done. We all dressed and undressed like nuns, under the bedclothes or the tent of a nightdress. Our fortnightly baths were taken in our underwear. It felt a guilty and dangerous thing, taking in the sight of my unvisited body, this object that – I had picked up this view from somewhere – as a girl, was a wayward instrument. It possessed unmentionable traits – periods, babies – and had to be safeguarded fiercely.

Mother appeared through the door without knocking. I drew my knees up instinctively, feeling the blood rush to my face at the very thought of being *seen*. After all, I hardly knew this woman who had the advantage of me by being fully dressed, a primrose-yellow blouse tucked into a jade-green silk skirt reaching well down her calves, her hair elegantly arranged in a chignon. I suppose she had aged – of course she had, her skin more textured, white hairs threaded through the brown – but she did not seem much different.

'Ah, Eleanora.' She paused, a hand on the door before stepping in and closing it behind her, quietly, as if her being there was a secret.

I wanted to say, 'Please get out. Go away and leave me alone!' But she came over and let herself down into the cane chair, arranging her skirt carefully before looking up at me. A warm, almost shy smile came over her face, the alluring, enveloping smile of a beautiful woman. Seeing that look for the first time in a great many years I came close to breaking down. It utterly disarmed me. It was a look of love, I thought, *her* love, that I yearned for even though I barely knew it.

'It's very nice to have you home, dear,' she said, sitting straight and formal.

It was all I wanted to hear. I swallowed and gazed back at her, shy as a lover myself.

'It's nice to be back,' I said, my voice gravelly. Oh, the understatement! The joy I had felt as the blurred chaos of Bombay had come into view, the incense and dung-smoke-scented land of my heart. The sight of a papaya or the orange loveliness of the flowers on a golmohur tree sent me into inner spasms of joy.

But there had been shocks as well. When I opened my mouth, the Hindustani I thought mine for ever, fluent and thoughtless in my Eden years, had rusted into forgetting, so that I floundered. Shocks in seeing that Peter Kelner was almost bald (not that I cared), that I saw the squalor and suffering of 'my' country with new, adult eyes, that I was old and changed myself. Even so, it was amazingly good to be back.

'Well –' Mother, beginning to revert to the mother I remembered, was appraising my body. 'I see your skin has not got any paler.'

Awful, the feeling that gave me. English winters, wartime shortages and insipid stodge had left me the palest I had ever been in my life, but she still saw my olive colouring as something of a curse. Under her business-like stare I felt as if my body was melting into a shapeless lump, like very old custard.

'So, our job is to get you married off. Now the war is over there'll be some sort of proper season at last, I'm sure. We'll have a few days settling-in time and then I'll get you to as many parties as I can. You can dance, I presume?'

'Yes,' I said. That was something we had at least been taught, though dancing only with other girls, I was used to the men's role.

That would have to do.

Mother sat back and folded her arms, as if trying to identify the words for a hopeless case, then got to her feet.

'What you'll have to do,' she said, going to the door, 'is work your way up. Don't for pity's sake settle for the first box-*wallah* who asks you to dance. But at least if you've got some sort of partner you'll get more invitations and it'll give you a chance to look round. Of course' – she turned, having already opened the door – 'your clothes are atrocious. I'll get the *dirzi* in. He's very good at copying designs. We'll scrap your old rags and start again. Just don't go putting on any more weight.'

She left me lying in the tepid water, taking with her that moment's illusion that she was actually pleased to see me.

'Hughie, may I come in?'

It had taken me a few nerve-twisted moments, standing outside the door of Hugh's room, to find the courage to knock. Once the war ended, Hugh had stayed in England for a time – in hospital for some of it though he wouldn't talk about why. Eventually he sailed to India. From the moment he arrived in Bombay, looking terrible, I knew he would soon be gone again. Not that I blamed him.

It was a horrible time. All my nearest and dearest – in other words, Hugh and Persi – had been away for such an age, and when they came back, all of us were changed in ways that we could hardly understand ourselves, let alone communicate to each other. Jessie Bell's brother Duncan had died at Ypres in 1917.

Persi had worked as a Queen Alexandra's military nurse in hospitals in France and then in Alexandria. I had very little idea of what she had seen, nor of how much she must have been suffering. She had lived and worked closely with Enid, another QAIMNS nurse, for more than two years. Not long after the war ended, Enid announced she was getting married. Persi never once spoke to me about this period but, knowing as I do now Persi's capacity for complete devotion, it must have been bad. Enid was her first real love, I think. Persi was back in India now, working in a civilian hospital in Calcutta, right at the other side of the country.

And then there was Hughie, my once sweet, sensitive brother.

He had been here for a month, while I was still being trotted round the 'season' amid the dregs of the male emotional wrecks. I was beginning to feel like one myself. I was so excited when Hughie arrived back. My brother, at last! And then the shock of him, his silence, the clipped sarcastic responses. I tried to ask him about Mesopotamia, about what it was like – after all, how was I supposed to know? He gave me a hard look.

'There are a great many flies,' was all he said. He had an angry, superior wall around him. I almost gave up trying to approach him, but that day I must have felt so lonely that I went to try again, knocking on the door of his little room at the end of the corridor.

I heard him mumble something. The brass door handle felt cool in my hand as I turned it, leaning on the wood of the door, a knot of desperation in me. *Hughie, come back, please don't leave me behind.*

The room was narrow, white and monkish. Mother had asked the maid to put a vase of lilies on his side table. They were vivid orange cannas, which seemed lurid and out of place in this austere room. Their thick scent was mixed with the smell of shaving cream. His window looked out on to the garden at the back, and in the patch of sky I could see thuggish clouds gathering.

Hugh was sitting up on the bed, a pillow upended against the bedhead. He was dreadfully thin and all his clothes hung on him. With his new, cropped hair and jutting cheekbones, he reminded me, sadly, of some sort of poultry.

As usual he had a book in his hand, like a shield, lowering it, with its faded blue jacket, just enough to look at me over the top of it. The expression in his eyes was neither welcoming nor unwelcoming, as if he barely knew who I was.

The last time I had seen him, before they sent him away, was the Christmas of 1916, at Uncle Hat's house. We played chess together on Christmas Eve, and then drove to the midnight service in the village on a crisply cold night, stars glittering through the darkness of the lanes. We had been close then; perhaps the closest ever. He had told us about his training, joked that it was just like a continuation of school. One night, walking in the dusk over Greenburton Hill, he hinted at how afraid he was of what was to come. I realize that Uncle Hat was the only other male on earth to whom he could have confessed such a thing. We stood in the dying light, looking down the hillside where smoke rose from fires in the village cottages and our uncle provided a podgy, comforting figure beside us.

'Poor Hughie,' he said. 'Wish I could do it for you, old boy.'

'Don't you worry, Uncle Hat,' Hugh said fondly, nudging shoulders with him. 'I'll be all right. They won't be expecting you to go, will they?' Anyone could see Uncle Hat wouldn't last half a day in the army.

But that was the Hughie I had carried with me through the remainder of the war, praying that he would be all right, worried sick, especially after Duncan Bell was killed. And this was the brother that now, in the terrible loneliness of my Bombay life, I yearned to talk to.

I didn't dare let go of the door to begin with. There was something about the way he was looking at me, standing there in my silly flowery frock and my sandals on those polished floorboards, that made me feel utterly foolish, as if I was a waste of existence. That was one thing about the war, you see; it made many of the women seem foolish fripperies in comparison to the men. As if our lives were pointless, gossamer things with no substance. What had I done for the past five years except tread water at school in England and knit a few balaclavas?

We regarded each other for a few seconds before I broke my gaze and looked down, unable to stand it. I could feel my cheeks burning, tears not far away.

'Sorry,' I said.

'What for?' He sounded genuinely confused.

For being such a stupid waste of time, I wanted to say. But I did dare to look up.

He put the book down and pushed himself up further on the pillow. There were a few seconds in which I heard a bicycle bell and Geeta, one of the maids, calling to someone outside.

'You coming in then, sis?'

This was so much better that the lump in my throat ached even more. I closed the door and sat, as he invited with a sweep of the arm, on the side of the bed. He had laid the book face down. We never did talk about the war. It was as if, then, it scarcely mattered what anyone had experienced, set against the mere fact of their survival. If you were alive and still had all your limbs and a vestigial sort of sanity, you were deemed to be all right. Hugh had been horribly ill, we knew – malaria, sand fever, dysentery and some other infections. By now, apart from his skeletal frame, he *appeared* more or less all right.

There was a silence. I tried looking directly at him.

'Grim here, isn't it?' he said.

'India?'

'Not India. *Here.*'

Mother was as adoring of him as ever, at least in the way she always referred to '*darling* Hughie', but in fact had no real idea what to say to him. And Hugh had always loathed Peter Kelner, 'the Mynah', a vacuous, clubbable, golfing sort of chap with sandy hair and a perky moustache.

'Yes.' I tried to joke: 'At least she's not trying to marry you off though.'

'Don't you believe it,' Hugh said, grimacing. 'She's started talking about some girl called Lady Gertrude Fearsome-Fortitude or some such.'

I burst into relieved giggles. 'There isn't anyone called that!'

'Something like that.'

I couldn't think who mother might have had in mind, but knowing her social climbing tendencies, this did not sound surprising.

'Do you want to get married?' I asked.

Hughie stroked his chin in a humorous way. 'Well, let me think ...' A split second later he added, 'No!'

We both laughed. My spirits soared. This was so much better. He had been so sardonic and closed when we were in company. I had a glimpse of my old brother, only now as someone sharpened and witty.

'Do you, Nellinora?'

'I suppose I'll have to.' I plucked miserably at the white bedcover. 'What else am I going to do?' I looked helplessly at him. 'What shall *you* do?'

He sat up straighter, as if with an injection of life.

'I shall go back to England. I'm going to Cambridge.'

'Why?' I said stupidly, barely even grasping that he meant the university.

'I'll study the Natural Science tripos,' he said. It was the first real animation I had seen in him since he came back. He turned over the book and I saw that the pages were covered with faint print, interspersed with symbols and equations. 'Science is the future!' He was aglow, but I saw with a prickle of discomfort that there was a certain look of mania in his eyes. 'Science is what will save mankind! Empiricism! Truth!'

'But what do you mean, truth?' I said, puzzled. It was hard to live in India and ever believe only one thing to be true.

'Truth arrived at by evidence, by experiment!' He launched into a monologue about all the different ways in which science was developing and would alter life as we knew it and how he did not yet know whether he wanted to branch off into medicine or into physics and astronomy. He seemed feverishly excited. I found myself shrinking back into my usual loneliness, after the brief glimpse I had had of real contact with him.

'Well,' I said, getting to my feet. 'I'd best let you get on then.'

I wasn't envious – the prospect of real study and cleverness had never been offered to me at all. But I felt bereft, as if a door had slammed shut. He could leave – move away into a new life that I could never know or understand.

Within a few weeks we saw him off at the quay in Bombay on a ship to England, that small, cold land for which I had little affection. By the time I saw him again, I too was a different person.

And did I want to get married? It was what one did, the way one made a success of life as a female. It was the vast, overhanging cliff whose summit, rope or no rope, we were expected to conquer, and thus attain the right to look down on the spinster and the childless wife, the widows and the making do's – those who had had to surrender a marriage of satisfactory status for what they could get.

Yes, I wanted marriage. But what I really wanted was moonlight and roses and all the things in the songs. They were what I thought was meant by love, because I really hadn't the first idea.

The war saved me, in a way. God knows who I might have ended up with at a dreadfully young age. Mother bemoaned the slaughter of our men – of course anyone would. It was a catastrophe of inhuman folly. But what she meant was that before the war there was an abundance of spare chaps all eager to gobble up girls of almost any description. By the end of the war, we outnumbered them by far. Because the man situation in England was even worse, the Fishing Fleet took off, shoals more girls taking their chance on steamers to the East to enter the 'catch your man' game in a different place.

Mother pushed me round the Bombay circuit. There were evenings spent in large houses with gaudily dressed women – including me, my pièce de résistance being in peacock-green satin – and servants in white jackets with drinks trays. And of course, the precious males, all of varying degrees of peculiar.

Cattle market hardly does it justice. It was more like a zoo of rare and strange species: the drunks, obsessives and recluses, the ones visibly shaking.

I had a few gowns I wore in turn. As well as the peacock green there was a baby pink tulle, a peach silk. I'm not sure why I felt such an impostor in them; more like a battleship out on manoeuvres than a girl seeking her mate. Especially in relation to the Indians. The small-boned grace of so many of them made me feel like a ham-joint.

One such evening, during the hot months of 1920, I was standing just inside the verandah doors of one of those elegant Bombay houses, trying to catch anything in the way of a breeze, already squiffy from some fizz drink or other, on the very edge of things, as ever.

'Hello! You look as if you could do with some company!'

A neat little chap stood before me, about thirty, I suppose, with clipped, black receding hair – and clean shaven. Moustaches were disappearing at that time, perhaps too much of a reminder in the style of Kitchener. He held his hand out as if dispensing a favour.

'Cyril Parfitt. Major Parfitt to give you the full handle!'

We both laughed rather pointlessly at this.

'Eleanora Storr-Mayfield.'

'Oh, I say. You must be part of the set here? I'm only down on leave, from the Ambala Cantonment.' He was dressed in civvies, but you could tell he was military: the hair, the brisk, upright bearing. 'Can I top you up?'

He clicked his fingers at one of the waiters and as I set about my rather strong drink, we carried out a bit of small talk in the faint breeze through the open doors. Beyond, stretched the wide lawn, flares softly lighting the path through the shrubbery.

Cyril had very intent eyes, brown and shiny, and a way of staring into your face as if he was deeply interested in you, or that's what I thought, silly little thing. As I sipped, he told me a little about Ambala but mostly kept firing questions at me: my family, my school, how long had I been back, ah, my brother had been out East, had he? He made a show of chuckling at my replies and made sure my glass was topped up again. After a time – I was quite squiffy by then – he suggested, as they all inevitably did, that we take a turn round the garden.

'Do come and see Mrs Carew's rose beds. There are none to match them.'

He guided me by the waist: men did so manoeuvre one about in those days, as if one were a horse or a rowing boat. As we stepped out on to the verandah, one of the servants, a young, serious lad who bowed a great deal, met my eye. I've always wondered what he was thinking. Had he seen Cyril on patrol before?

With Cyril's hand still on my back, I accompanied him across the grass. It was dark by now, the air soft and smelling of grass and cigarette smoke and jasmine but I was wearing heels and kept turning my ankles in the spongy grass. I paused and took off my shoes.

'All right?' Cyril said, leaning down solicitously as I unhooked them with a finger.

'The heels do sink into the grass rather.'

'Do take off your stockings as well, if you like,' Cyril said. 'No one can see.'

I thought this a very odd remark, as well as obviously untrue since there were other couples scattered about the garden. 'It's quite all right,' I said, with *memsahib* stiffness. I could feel the cool carpet of grass through my stockings.

'Have you seen the bower?' he said, right on cue. 'It's just round here, do look.'

I found myself steered into the bower, which was of course lovely, with glimpses of moonlight between sprays of small pink roses cascading down over an iron frame. Once inside, their scent was all about me. And so – immediately and without ceremony – was Cyril. Talk about hands, knees and bumps-a-daisy, the man was like an octopus with a train to catch. There were wooden benches around the inside and I found myself on one of those, my spine pressed uncomfortably against the stone of the wall and Cyril's tongue sliding about in my mouth. I had never thought moonlight and roses would mean something as frightful as this.

When I managed to say, 'What on *earth* do you think you're doing?' in as indignant a voice as I could manage, he yanked me even closer against him and ... Let's just say he had been banged up in the army camp at Ambala for a lengthy stretch without a woman in sight, or not a European one anyway, or so he told me.

'Well, that's not my fault, is it?' I said.

'You're a game-looking girl.' He really was awful and his breath stank of Scotch and onions. His hands were up under my skirt as if he thought I was just going to ... 'Come on, play along. Don't be a tight little bitch!'

'Take your hands off me!' I gave him a good old shove, but he came at me and slapped my face with the back of his hand. It hurt like hell and I thought, right, I'm going to scream now – who cares who hears? I let out a sound and he clamped his hand over my mouth. Somehow, I sprang round and stuck my finger hard into his eye and as he was cursing, I dashed out of there, although I left my shoes behind and had to sneak back and fetch them. I ran into him later in the house and he muttered some sort of apology, but I wasn't having it. He was one of the worst I met, but of course a lot of the best men had been lost to the trenches. It began to feel frightening, as well as demoralizing.

I had had more than enough of being paired off with pimply engineers, of standing out for dance after dance because there were too many girls. Bombay itself was all right, the city, Chowpatty Beach for days out. But soon after the Cyril incident, which left me feeling soiled and shamed, I had had enough. I had what felt like an irresistible invitation from Jessie Bell. Her father was studying strains of tea in Assam, she accompanying him as his assistant. For a few months, they were to be working in Jorhat. Would I like to come and stay?

Would I!

And that's how my life changed, in just a few weeks.

II

6

Presidency Hospital,
L.C Road,
Calcutta.
June 5th 1920

Dear Eleanora,

Well dearie, your letter fortuitous. Thank the Lord for Jessie and that father of hers, busting you out of there (Mynah and all).

Timing could not be bettered. I have a little surprise for you. Presidency a marvellous hospital and a calm billet after the war, but I'm after something deeper. Off to try vocation with sisters over on the delta in Barisal. Have been able to delay a few days so will meet train at Howrah, June 20th as suggested.

Yours with affection as ever,

Marguerite (Persi)

I caught sight of her from the train even before we had slid to a halt in the shadowy cavern of Calcutta's Howrah railway terminus. Persi, already taller than most people around, was dressed all in white. You could scarcely have missed her, even among the crowds on the platform, the railway coolies weaving through with bundles on their heads through everyone waiting

95

for the train to pull in.

The moment the locomotive braked fully all hell was let loose. Though in general I enjoyed travels by rail, it was the end of the hot season. I was very keen to escape this sizzling compartment in which I had been stuck for two days, in the company of a young girl with Shorthand and Typing – 'Gosh, is it always this hot?' – heading to some office in Calcutta and a sad older lady who had come to help her widowed daughter and three grandchildren to return to Warwickshire. Though I sympathized, I had heard quite enough about the life of 'poor Cynthia' by the time we reached Bengal.

Even once I had wrestled my bag out of the door, waving away help, Persi remained standing in exactly the same place, like a rock in a stream. Actually, she gave me a bit of a shock. She was still very thin and was wearing a long white frock, her splendid hair tied back in a plait, which hung forward over her shoulder. Golly, I thought, she looks like a nun already. I was none too sure about all this religious carry-on and what it was all about.

But I felt a huge rush of happiness and affection at seeing her. I had got away, and here was dear old Persi! I was wearing a crumpled frock, was drenched in sweat and must have stunk like a polecat, but I flung my arms round her and felt her embrace me, gently, in reply.

'Hello, Persi.' I grinned up at her.

I had only seen her once since the war, when she had stayed with us for a couple of days in passing, on her way to Calcutta. She had been positively gaunt then, worn to the bone, and I wanted to spoil her and make her rest. I had scant success with that, but she was cheerful enough.

'Hello, Eleanora.'

Persi was never one for great displays of emotion. She was one for getting on with it, staunch with deeds, not words. But when she looked down at me that morning, amid the racket, the smells of coal smoke, rotting things and *bidis*, I could see all the fondness and concern she felt for me in her eyes. Were there even tears? I wanted to hug her again but knew she wouldn't be having that.

She waved away the hovering coolies and the two of us each took a handle of my little bag and made our way out among the few Europeans and the crowds of saris and *dhotis*, the *chai-wallahs* and vendors with circular bamboo trays of peanuts and sweets on their heads. At the front of the station, we found a brougham with a horse that looked a little less moth-eaten than the rest.

'I suppose Mumsie wanted you booked into the Great Eastern?' Persi said as the horse set off at a trot, off, the bell on its bridle jingling.

'You could have come too,' I said.

Persi gave me one of her looks. 'I've got a room for you at the hospital. Rather simple, but we can come and go as we please.'

I watched eagerly through the little window as we crossed the pontoon bridge, seeing the river spreading beyond, busy with coloured sails and the city closing in around us. I drank in the sight of my city. The monsoon was soon due to break and heat bludgeoned down upon the streets. Though we were under cover the little carriage was hot and stuffy. Yet, I still felt invigorated. Bombay, and Peter Kelner's house, had never been home to me, and Mother's relentless marriage campaign had sapped me. But now I was starting to feel my spirits return. We stopped abruptly, the carriage-*wallah* cursing at something ahead. I looked round at the busy streets and up at the buildings, realizing now how much it was like London – but so much nicer.

'Dear old Cal,' I said.

'Mm,' was all Persi said. She looked out dreamily, as if seeing visions far beyond my ken. Goodness, I thought, she really has become religious. She had always been Christian, of course, as opposed to Church of England like most of us. It must be the war, I realized. It seemed to have made people far more religious or far less. But I felt I wanted to bring her back to me. I nudged her and made a face.

'It was very naughty of you to write "the Mynah" in your letter. Mother might have read it!'

'She wouldn't know what that was, surely?' Persi said. 'Anyway, I can't imagine she would have been interested.'

I loved her for conspiring with me, the way that despite her rigidness in some things, she was always, in the end, on my side.

After the baking turmoil of the city and the baksheeshing children surrounding us when we set down in Lower Circular Road, the nurse's quarters felt like a cool refuge. The windows along the corridors had their blinds pulled almost closed and nurses in white moved along them with almost silent tread.

We climbed echoing stairs and Persi opened the door to my austere little room, containing nothing but a black iron bedframe and thin mattress, a small white chest of drawers and a rickety table and chair. Looking into this monastic-looking cell was when it hit me. I threw my case on the bed and went plummeting down after it so that the springs cranked.

'Oh, Persi! You're not really going to be a nun, are you?' It sounded such a desolate thing. 'You're not going to leave me?'

All those feelings rose in me again, the echo of footsteps

moving away from me, of backs turned, leaving me in strange places.

Persi was standing looking down at me. She tilted her head.

'Leaving you? When have I ever left you, really and truly?'

She softened then, as she sometimes did, smiled and sat beside mutinous little me, taking my hand. Both of us were slippery with sweat, but that hand in mine felt like the most loving caress I knew.

'It won't make so very much difference, will it?' she said. She was always so strange looking, with her long face and eccentric ways, but always captivating. 'After all, you already live the other side of the country, and if you go and find some beau who will sweep you away …'

'Oh, that's never going to happen.' I was very low after being pawed about and humiliated all this time. 'No one's ever going to want *me*.'

Persi's grey eyes looked into mine with steady kindness.

'Eleanora.' She spoke so seriously that I felt her words enter me as she said them. 'You are and have always been a loveable girl. You mustn't ever doubt it, no matter what –' She cut herself off and with her other hand reached up and laid her palm on my hot cheek for a moment. My throat tightened again and I couldn't look right back at her. I felt so lost and insecure and unloved after all that carry-on in Bombay that I just wanted to howl, but I barely knew how these days.

'It only takes one, after all,' Persi said, withdrawing both hands and rubbing them together. I raised my eyes to see her smile. It was as if something in her had deepened over the years. Or perhaps I mean smoothed. Some of her spikiness had been filed away. 'And the rest don't matter, do they? Come on, dearie, let's go and get a cup of *char*, shall we?'

Persi had already completed her work at the hospital. She took those days with me as holiday, allowing herself treats she would not normally have indulged in or had time for. She had her hospital pay and I suppose she was not really going to need that where she was going. I so often forgot that Persi came from money, that in fact she was rather a classy kind of lady, when she allowed herself to be. And that week she let herself enjoy.

We wandered the city in the cooler parts of the day; across Chowringhee in the morning to the lung of the *maidan*, the great park at the heart of the city, green in winter but the grass now parched and flattened by innumerable games of cricket. We went to the Victoria Memorial, to Eden Gardens and the Botanical Gardens. We walked beside the Hooghly at sunset, the air thick with smoke, watching the boats being allowed to pass along at sunset, once the pontoon bridge was opened. On Sunday we went to the morning eucharist at St George's Cathedral.

Above all, we ate. We haunted the smart environs of Park Street, ordered numberless *nimbopanis* – lime sodas – in the heat, went to the Grand and to Firpoys on Chowringhee to order the best spiced dishes we could find and we tucked into European cakes in the fancy cake shops.

'I'm beginning to feel myself expanding,' I said, as we sat beside the shaded window in a café one afternoon, with ragtime piano music tinkling away in the background. In the street passed European females in washed-out colours, while the Indian ladies paraded in red and azure, emerald and turmeric, fabrics so vivid that the sight of them gave one a jolt of pleasure.

'You won't expand,' Persi said, licking cream from the side

of her mouth. 'This is *food*. Not like all that abominable English suet.' She took another mouthful of her cream horn and chewed with a relish that made me wonder for a moment at her suitability to be a nun. She had left the white dress behind that day and was dressed in a vivid green one, patterned with sprays of red hibiscus. I had seen heads turn in Park Street. Did she think this was the last time she would be able to make the most of these things, eat cream, flaunt her femininity – no, perhaps not flaunt, but allow at least? Not for the first time, I felt quite a frump beside her.

'Got room for another one?' I grinned, polishing off my own cream slice.

Persi sat back as if pondering. A gaggle of Indian children in school uniforms were at the counter with their well-to-do parents, squealing over the cakes.

'You know,' she said, 'I really think I might. When the rush has died down.'

Once we were settled with a pot of tea this time and more cake – a cream slice for Persi and for me, a new experience called a 'chocolate bomb' – she said, 'So how's Hughie?'

So far, we had kept our chit-chat light and humorous that week, but now I felt myself tense up.

'In Cambridge, Emmanuel College. You know Hughie – he's never been any good at writing letters. All he ever talks about is molecules anyway.' I tried to make a light of the hurt I felt at Hugh's abandoning me so completely.

Persi was looking at me with an odd expression. A waiter with a tea tray distracted her for a moment and she lowered her gaze, but I had seen something in her eyes.

'Have you heard from him?' I asked, casually.

Persi could never lie. 'Once or twice.' She took a mouthful, as if to enforce a full stop upon the conversation.

I was full of sudden rage, a sour swell of feelings. In that moment I hated Persi and I hated my life and everyone in it. Why was it that Hugh could be bothered to write to Persi, but not to his own sister? Or mother for that matter, though that I could more easily understand. Persi had shown both of us far more care than mother ever did. But why would he write to Persi and not to me? Was the bond between Hughie and Persi stronger even than the one she had with me? I felt so angry and left out that I realized I was scarcely breathing.

'Well – how is he?' I stabbed the shell of my chocolate bomb with my fork.

'Hard to tell.' Persi must have heard the barb in my tone because she sounded almost apologetic and was trying to give me an honest answer. 'As you say, obsessed with science.'

I was trying to calm myself, to control the rush of jealousy I felt. My emotions frightened me. I was not used to them and to find such a feeling directed towards Persi of all people ... Of course, when she came to see me when I was at school, I knew she had been to see Hughie as well. It's just that I thought of Persi as being *mine*.

'You mean he sends you equations?' Still, there was bitter sarcasm.

'He doesn't say much at all,' Persi said gently.

That was what it was; she was gentler nowadays. My nasty feelings seeped away. What on earth did any of it matter? Persi was *ours* – she was good to both of us.

'Why are you doing it?' I asked her, in a small voice. 'Becoming a ... Going to Barisal?'

She considered this, elbows resting on the table, hands

together under her chin, the fork dangling from her fingers.

'The Mother House is there, but they have a smaller place here in Cal. I met one of the sisters, Sister Ruth. I mean not just met; *talked* with properly. I just knew that … Well …' She lowered the fork and cut a neat slice of cake. 'That I had to wear a veil.'

On the face of it, this sounded a pretty odd reason to me. 'But you wear one in any case,' I argued. 'You're a nurse.'

Persi gave me another of her looks.

'You're not going to go over to Rome, are you?' This was a frightening thought. In those days I found the thought of all nuns pretty terrifying, never mind Roman Catholic ones.

'No, the order is Anglican. C of E if you like.'

I still felt she was hedging.

'But *why*, Persi?'

'Well.' She laid her fork down and sat straighter. 'You know, Lelly, I'm thirty-four years old. I want to *do* something while I've still got time, something that matters – to me, at least. Give service. And at my stage in life, I feel that if I'm going to be married, I'd really be best off marrying God.'

On our last night in Calcutta there was a sunset of the sort you only see in India. We were walking by the wide old river and the sun went down like a blood orange. Even in this tumultuous city, an almost reverent stillness settled in the air as the light faded, gold, pink, the reflections chopped into the water's surface.

There was a deep, tremulous feel to that evening as Persi and I ambled along together, the way one feels when something is about to end and when one knows it is ending, as if each remaining moment is delicately enshrined. Boats plied the water, some laden with jute, with bright, rectangular sails. People passed us on the path, voices lowered, in that same mood, as if the very air was sacred. Persi's white frock softened to peach and my tanned arms were so dark I might have passed for a native – but then I am a native.

'You will keep in touch, won't you, Persi?' I still felt I was losing her.

'Don't be silly. It really makes no difference. I'm joining a religious order, not going to the moon. And in any case, I'll be a novice for at least two years. I'll be here some of the time. You can't just join like that. They might chuck me out long before then.'

'No they won't!' I laughed. But I found myself hoping they would and ticked myself off. She had something she wanted – I should try to be glad for her. It was not as if her life had been much freer as a nurse.

She slipped her arm through mine and I smiled in the dusk. We stopped to look across the Hooghly. Its old river smell was tinged with sewage and the breeze carried incense and smoke from the fires that flickered orange and gold on the opposite bank: in other words, the smells of home. And she, beside me, was the nearest thing I had ever known to home. I was full of love for her and gave her thin arm a squeeze.

'Godspeed, Persi,' I said.

We parted the next day at Sealdah, the Eastern Railways Station. My train for Guwahati in Assam was due to leave before hers, so she had time to help me into a Ladies' compartment. But I just could not bear to let her climb down and leave me there, so I went out to the platform again with her.

Amid the hubbub of preparations for departure, we hugged each other. This was a rare thing and made me feel as if she was going off to a place where none of the rest of us would be able to follow.

'Good luck then, Persi,' I said with what seemed like fatuous cheer, as if the religious life was a horse race.

'Give my love to Jessie, won't you?' She smiled, but her voice was thicker than usual, I knew I wasn't imagining it. 'And Eleanora – come and visit us, won't you?' I felt she needed to go, to contain her emotion. She touched my shoulder, turning away. '*Namaskar*. God bless.'

She stooped to pick up her little hold-all and as she walked away, a very singular sort of bean-pole among the crowds of saris and vendors and coolies, it occurred to me that that little brown case most likely held everything she possessed in the world.

I have never been good at unlatching myself from people and I could not bear to turn away until I had my last glimpse of her, that slender movement of white before she disappeared amid the crowd.

7

'Ellie – Eleanora!'

Jessie Bell met me off the steamer with a motorbike and sidecar. I spotted her energetic figure, one arm raised among all the sudden crowds and hubbub of disembarkation after the slow journey upriver. I waved back and we weaved towards each other.

'You're here!' Her pink, bespectacled face beamed out from under a solar *topi*, tied firmly under the chin. She flung her arms round me and I felt such a wave of joy at seeing her, at being wanted by someone, that I almost felt like blubbing. We had not seen each other since the war ended and we had finally escaped that school. In the meantime, Jessie had grown up and become if anything, quainter, but also more womanly – even though a woman whose plump thighs were wrapped in khaki slacks, a white shirt that strained across her bosom and a pair of scuffed chukka boots.

After the time I'd had of it in Bombay with all that season and party strain, seeing Jessie was a tonic. The thing about Jessie was that she really never gave a damn what anyone thought.

'Here –' She handed me a pair of goggles, leather things which had to be tied at the back. 'You'll need these, believe me.' She fixed her own on and soon she was strapping my case to the back of the bike and settling me into the sidecar. I laughed as she hopped over the saddle. Imagine what my mother would say!

'Good Lord, Jessie,' I said. 'Look at you!'

Jessie grinned down at me. 'One has to get about. Pa got it for me. Right – hold on to your hat.'

We roared away from the river, along the pale sandy roads of home. Looking back, it was one of the happiest moments of my life. A grin spread across my face as the wind blew my hair to rags and brought smells of *bidi* smoke and incense to my nostrils. We were in Assam, all the Bombay ghastliness blowing away like the dust we were raising along the road behind us.

Jessie's family were to be billeted for a few months at Cinnamara, the head garden of the Jorhat Tea Company, while Jessie's father did research at Toklai, the Tea Research Centre. Jessie, who showed no sign of participating in any 'season' or being taken round any other sort of cattle market, was helping him.

'We may, however, be able to grant Jessie a wee holiday, now we are graced with a visit from Miss Storr-Mayfield,' Robert Bell said, twinkling at me over the dinner table that night.

The family had been given the use of a planter's bungalow. And though none of us mentioned it directly, I think they were glad to have another person sitting in the fourth chair at the table, which would once have been occupied by poor Duncan, who had not returned from Ypres.

Jessie's father, dark-haired, bearded, drily humorous, made me feel part of the family. As did Mrs Bell, a kindly, quietly eccentric soul, who seemed more *distraite* than I ever remembered her being. I suppose it was grief. That first night she sat at the table in a powder-blue dress not buttoned up quite right, her faded brown hair in a straggly bun, saying things like, 'Would you care for another wee spoonful, Eleanora?' Although she was English, Ellen Bell had taken on some of her husband's Scots phrasing.

It was never clear to me whether Jessie had in some strange way taken on the role of her brother. We never spoke of it. But Mrs Bell seemed to have no particular plan for Jessie or obsessions about her marriageability; it was like having shackles taken off, being there, in this sparsely furnished, sincere place, and away from my mother.

Jessie and I spent free and unsupervised days in the moist heat of Cinnamara. The weather was due to break any day and the air was thick, seeming to press at one's temples. We lazed around or wandered about the gardens, all of which filled me with pleasure and nostalgia. We sat for hours in the verandah's shade, sipping tea or *nimbopanis* and talking, talking. I told her some of my grim experiences with Men I Had Danced With. Jessie seemed to have no interest whatever in men, nor sense of pressure that she should. She laughed like mad at my stories and I laughed too, until both our faces were wet with tears.

'Oh, Ellie, how perfectly ghastly!' she said, her homely face collapsing into giggles again after some further mortifying detail. 'Well, you'll be quite safe here. There really aren't many spare men about.'

But she was not quite right about that.

Club night. The Jorhat Gymkhana Club is not one of the ones scattered about deep in the countryside, but on the edge of Jorhat Town. It was a tradition that the planters and others gathered on a fixed night of the week. There would be entertainments and games and it was a chance for people scattered across the area in remote gardens to have a get together. I had been there many times when I was very small, with Father and Mother, with Hughie.

We drove there in Robert Bell's car, Jessie and I in the back, the windows open to let in the hot, languid air. Jessie was fanning herself with her boater. The back of my skirt felt sodden after sitting on that slippery seat on this sweltering evening. As the sun set, the light was tinged with pink. Other cars were turning into the Club grounds, a few rode in on horseback and a tonga or two came clip-clopping in, carrying those who lived nearer at hand. As this club was in the town, a wider mix of people came to join in, not just planters.

'I believe there's a show on tonight,' Robert Bell said to us over his shoulder as we turned into the drive and the expanse of green playing fields surrounding the Club.

As the Club building came into view with its tin roof and long, covered balcony extending all along the upper floor at the front, I found myself flooded with memories and a sense of strangeness at how things stay the same when we ourselves change, or at least, we believe we do. And for a few moments I connected with the me of Before – the Eden me.

Downstairs was the bar, a children's room, dance floor and billiards room. All of it was in a style similar to the houses: white walls inside, criss-crossed with wood battens and all rather homely.

Robert and Ellen Bell knew a lot of people there and they left Jessie and me and took themselves off into the energetically chattering huddles. Many of them were planters who lived out of town, along with their wives in their smartest cotton frocks, the families greeting each other, so animated, so relieved to be in a crowd of their own people again after the long days on far-flung plantations. Jessie and I went upstairs – there was a bar upstairs as well when the place got crowded – to the long balcony. And how familiar to me was each tread of those stairs as I climbed up there!

'Gin fizz?' Jessie asked me.. I was just getting settled into one of the cane chairs and my reply was drowned out by a burst of laughter from a nearby table followed by cheers and clapping. Jessie and I looked at each other, smiling.

'What d'you say?' Jessie cupped a hand round her ear.

'Please!' I shouted. 'Plenty of fizz!'

'Right-o. Back in a tick!'

I sat looking out over the balcony at the green space spreading beyond, big enough for horse races, golf, all sorts. In the soft light of dusk, I could see a few children running about, the glow of their pale clothing as they followed the movements of a red ball. Hugh and I had run out here, the grass dry like a mat in the heat, or spongy after the rains. I could feel how it was to be those children, the caressing air about their cheeks …

There was some amateur theatrical going on in the long room next door, where there was a stage, from which kept coming the thump of feet, a trumpet blast, then outbreaks of applause. More laughter came from the table to my left, the overdone cackling of people who are already rather tight and determined to have a good time. Glasses clinked; smoke drifted from their cigarettes.

I glanced at them, feeling exposed, as you can when sitting at a table clearly on your own. My green frock, silky and too tight, was riding up my thighs. I shifted, tugging it down, and folded my hands primly in my lap. My hair, then, had grown down to my shoulders and I had fastened it in a loose knot at the back to keep it off my neck. It made me feel a bit of a Plain Jane – but then I felt that already.

I was starting to wish Jessie would hurry up. Knowing her, she had been waylaid and was chattering to someone. For something to do I opened my little bag, beaded with mother of pearl, in search of ciggies.

'Are you in need of a light?'

I had barely been aware that someone was sitting on my right, just behind me. A hand appeared, a brass-coloured lighter and a flame jumped into life.

'Thank you.' I turned to see a large, bear-like man, his white shirtsleeve seeming to glow in the muted light as his arm stretched towards me. I made out a full brown beard and thick hair, strands of which fell forward as he leaned over, and he raked it back with his hand.

'Pleasure,' he said, as I tilted towards him to light up. He snapped the lighter shut, leaning away from me while he returned it to his pocket, straightened up and gave me a smile. It was a shy smile and for a physically well-built, broad-shouldered man, he seemed to shrink into himself, as if to occupy less room. In those seconds during which we observed each other, I took in more: the white shirt covering a large scale, muscular body, a long, big-boned face and an immense, rather wonky nose. His eyes seemed blue, or grey in the gloom.

'Not seen you before, have I?' His voice, though deep, was soft.

'No –' I was saying, just as Jessie appeared, swooping down on us with glasses clinking with ice.

'Bill! How lovely to see you!' She leaned down before he could get to his feet and light, acquaintance kisses were exchanged. 'This is my old chum, Eleanora. We were at school together, "at Home".' She made an ironical face, settling her wide hips wrapped in a floral cotton frock, in the chair. 'Ellie, this is one of our neighbours – sort of, when it's fifteen miles or more! Bill Ashton. Not on your own, are you, Bill? Oh, of course – Betty and the boys are off on the lollipop run, aren't they?'

Jessie began to look as if she had regretted her remark about 'Home' and schools – or at least the tone in which she had delivered them, since Mrs Ashton was clearly in the process of delivering 'the boys' to one of those self-same institutions.

At that moment another man appeared from somewhere – thin, black hair is all I remember, nothing remarkable. Afterwards we could not recall his name, so Jessie said, 'Let's call him Reg,' which made us both laugh. We all decided to sit at the same table and after a bit of shuffling about, I ended up sitting between Jessie and Bill Ashton, who was to my right, by the balustrade, looking out over the grounds.

'Yes,' he explained to me as Jessie chatted to Reg or whatever his name was. 'My wife wanted to be there herself to settle Jimmy, our second son, in. He's only five, you see. Dougie, our first, went over with a chaperone and – well, it didn't suit the little chap too well, going off like that.'

'Does it really suit anybody?' I said. I had had a few good glugs of my gin fizz by then and was ceasing to care too much what I said. But in fact, by some strange instinct, I felt I could say anything to Bill, even then.

He looked startled. 'Well ... I mean, I suppose ...'

'Did you go?' I blundered on. 'Like that?' What I was really asking, I suppose, was, are you one of us? Were you born here, or there, in this supposed 'Home'?

'Yes.' He eased back in his chair, seeming to relax a fraction. 'I was born in Jamshedpur – Father was a steel man. I was seven when I went.' He gave a little laugh. 'Jolly good, though. Makes a chap of you.'

'Does it?' I thought of Hughie. You could safely say, I suppose, that Hughie was 'a chap'. 'I went when I was five, with my elder brother – he was almost seven. Mother wanted us out of her hair after Father … died.' I felt drunk and brutally in need.

Bill Ashton looked utterly taken aback again. Now, I thought wearily, knocking back more fizz, is the moment when he gets up, says he needs another drink or there's a chap he really must see – anything to get away from me.

It's true there was a bit of a silence between us then. The lamps had not yet come on and across the tables the faces were shadowy in the dusk. There was much boozy laughter. Children played, giggling, up and down the wooden stairs. Jessie was chuckling at something 'let's call him Reg' had said and I wondered if she was interested in him. We never talked much about such things. Not, as it turned out.

'I have wondered at times,' Bill said. He was still there, to my rather foggy surprise. 'Well, you know.'

He looked across as me as if he genuinely wanted me to say something. As if, in the gloom, his eyes were saying, Is this really right, the way we do things? The one true British way, which leaves anyone who falls out of step feel they are at fault, that there is something wrong with them? Is this really the right way to be? Although Bill seemed the usual public-school type, necessarily jolly and guarded, the sort I met everywhere, even then his surface seemed very thin, crackled like the glaze on a vase, with something real and in need close underneath.

I knew that my own life wore across it the dark break that was Pa's death and that since then nothing had ever felt truly right.

Suddenly everything seemed to come into collision inside me. Some instinct about Bill. And the fact that I was here, back in the dear old Club where everything had once felt good and true, that on that carpet of grass below the balcony I had once run about with Hughie and the other children, free and unbroken.

I looked into Bill Ashton's enquiring eyes and had a terrible urge to fling myself into his arms, to take comfort, leaning up against that large, cliff-like presence. To my utter horror, I burst into tears.

'Oh, my dear,' he said. After a moment he leaned in and took my hand, which caused his hair to fall forward again and made me cry even more. It was quite appallingly embarrassing, but I just could not stop.

'Ellie, whatever is it?' Jessie turned to me and everyone was full of consternation. I could feel people staring at me from the other tables.

'It's all right.' After a few moments I managed to put a cork in it, pulled my hanky out of my little bag and fixed a smile to my face. 'I'm quite all right!' I was being hopelessly jolly now, even managing a laugh. 'It's just me being sentimental. I haven't been to the old Jorhat Club in many years – all very silly.' I wiped my eyes and said to Jessie, 'Nothing to worry about,' and turned to Bill again. 'Do tell me about your little boys?'

'Sorry about turning on the taps like that,' I whispered to Jessie as we drove back to the Cinnamara garden.

'Don't give it a thought,' Jessie said kindly. She was also pretty tight and quite relaxed. She yawned. 'So – you met the Gentle Giant, at least.'

'Oh, you were talking to Bill Ashton, were you?' Ellen Bell

114

said, sleepily. 'Nice man. And two dear little boys.'

So dear, I thought bitterly, that it must be obligatory for them to live on the other side of the world. But I kept my trap shut. What on earth had come over me?

The car's headlights moved jumpily along the pale road, edged with scrubby green. Every so often a face swam out of the darkness; native faces, men walking at the edge of the road; the sudden white of two bullocks pulling a cart for which we had to veer quickly to one side. Jessie slumped her head against my shoulder, snoring slightly, and her mother also drifted off to sleep. I looked out over the dark landscape, smelling the night, the feeling it gave you of the immensity of the land about you.

And I kept seeing Bill Ashton's face turned towards me, as if imploring, 'Tell me.' It was an extraordinary thing; I couldn't seem to stop thinking of him right from that first meeting, as if we had recognized something in each other and each of us desired something from the other. Not desire of the pawing, calculating sort I had had to put up with in Bombay. But a need of a quite different sort, which both moved me and made me tell myself I was being utterly ridiculous. Quite apart from the fact that he was married with two children, Bill Ashton must be touching thirty-five and I had only just turned twenty. And yet.

I saw him a week later, in Jorhat Town.

The Toklai Tea Research Institute was not far from the Club and Jessie, who was now working with her father again, took me along in the sidecar of her bike. The monsoon had arrived by then. The air was buffeting wet and plumes of water sprayed from the wheels.

'Sure you'll be all right?' she said, as I climbed out, windswept and damp, at the entrance to Toklai. I could just make out the long, pale building beyond the gate. 'I'll be finished by one.'

'Of course!' I was looking forward to having a wander round on my own. 'Got my brolly!' I waved it at her. 'I'll wind up at the Club. You can come and find me.'

With the humid morning heat beginning to build, I pulled my hat well down over my eyes and set off slowly along Club Road. Very soon, my cheeks were puce and I was drenched in perspiration.

'*Memsahib?*' A hopeful rickshaw-*wallah* hovered alongside me. He pointed to the sky. 'Raining, raining.'

I searched my rusty brain for the language that used to come to me automatically. All I could do was gesture with my hand.

'Walking,' I said, politely.

The young man tilted his head back and forth, as if at the eternal folly of European women, and wheeled round to pedal languidly back the other way.

I smiled to myself, trying to keep my face lowered under the shade of my hat brim, and to walk in the driest parts of the road. Damn it, it was hot and sticky! But so utterly good to be here. I was alone, for the first time. As I looked into the well-tended gardens of European bungalows, passing a few people here and there, the occasional bicycle or bullock cart overtaking me, I allowed the place truly to flood into me. Memories came one after another of Hughie and myself, of once walking this road with Pa to visit someone ... My heart buckled with it but it still felt marvellous, this flow of recall, feeling it, smelling the wet earth, the scent from beds of roses.

As I got closer into Jorhat Town, the road grew busier. Bicycles and rickshaws, bullock carts and flat carts piled with various loads: hay, engine parts, logs. The shops on the main road spilled produce to the street – potatoes, hay, rice, from which the shop-owners were pulling sections of tarpaulin now it had stopped raining. There were tyres, tools, pieces of machinery. Scrawny horses stood between the shafts of carts, cows stood in a contemplative manner half in and half out of shops; goats, hens and black pigs picked scraps from the shallows of the gutters. All the smells – the open sewers, running in a channel along the street, swelled by the rain, the sodden refuse stamped into the ground, dung cakes drying on walls for fuel, each with the shape of a hand imprinted on them and always, everywhere, the acrid whiff of smoke: all this had made up the pungent brew of my childhood.

As I passed a roadside shack selling bangles and other knick-knacks, I saw a young woman standing looking at the display. Her hair lay in a thick plait down her back. With one hand she was holding up one side of her pink sari to keep it out of the wet, while a curly-haired girl of only two years or so was pulling at the other, whining up at her. The woman turned to look down at the child and straight away I knew her.

'Shonu!' It just popped straight out of my mouth.

She looked across at me, her face stern from scolding the infant, and for a moment I thought I'd made a silly mistake. But I pushed the brim of my hat up and her face shifted into a wide-mouthed smile with square, gappy teeth, hardly changed from when she was a little girl. She almost ran towards me, tugging the startled child by the hand.

'Miss Elly!'

Releasing the girl's hand, she pressed her palms together, *namaskar*, bowing her head, and I did the same. We looked at each other then. She was so familiar, those bright, laughing eyes, a tiny scar under her left eye where she once fell over and cut her face on a sharp edge of stone; the shape of her, at once graceful and cuddly, as she had always been.

We laughed with joy at the sight of each other and only then I found myself speaking easily, fluently. Shonu and I were little girls again, chit-chatting as we had at Panchcotta in a Bengali–Hindustani mix-up. Yes, she was married, she told me, and still living there, on the garden. It was very rare for her to be in the town. This was their little girl, Anusha, and yes, she was all right. Husband all right, family growing – an older son at home. Anusha gazed at me. She was finer boned than her mother, and solemn.

'Miss Elly, you are looking very nice and plump!' Shonu giggled. 'You have husband now?'

No, I had to admit.

Shonu's brow crinkled and I received a good ticking off. Very soon I must marry! I laughed it off saying I was looking hard for a husband.

'You must not be leaving it too late.' Shonu wagged a finger at me. 'Or no one will marry you!'

I asked after Akbar's family and some of the others and we parted. With her graceful head movements, she said, 'Come to Panchcotta, meet my family.' At the last moment, after a hesitation, she moved towards me and we embraced each other. It brought tears to my eyes. I felt happier than I could remember, as if connected to my real life again.

The heat was becoming so intense I decided I would soon need a sit down. I turned back, feeling a welling sensation inside me, as if I was quite literally full of something champagne fine. I had got about halfway back along Club Road, clouds beginning to mount up in the sky again and the ominous atmosphere before a storm pressing down, when I heard the trotting hooves of a horse and a cart approaching behind me. As it reached me, the driver slowed the horse with a 'Whoa!'

'Hello. Can I give you a lift anywhere?'

Turning, with a jolt of pleasure, I saw Bill Ashton perched on the cart's narrow driver's seat. This made me happier than it probably should have done. It was so nice to recognize someone and be greeted like this.

'I'm only going to the Club,' I said. 'But I wouldn't mind, thank you.'

'It's going to come down again in a minute,' he said, reaching out his hand. 'Come on – hop up!'

By the time we were inside the Club, there was almost a twilight feel to the day. We carried our drinks up to sit on the shady balcony: a beer for Bill, *nimbopani* for me. Bill sat back, his body splayed wide, as one does instinctively in the heat. But it also felt as if that big, generous body and his personality were somehow open to me. The fans turned, languidly. Each of us pulled out a hanky to wipe faces and necks. I dabbed the creases of my arms.

Bill offered me a cigarette, lighting up for both of us, just as a growl of thunder began outside. I wondered for a second what each of us was doing here, drinking together, two people who were almost strangers.

'I wouldn't have expected to see you here in town,' I said. 'Aren't the gardens on the go full tilt at the moment?'

Summer is the main plucking season. From the early morning the gardens are dotted with workers plucking the baskets of leaves to be weighed into the garden factories for the processes of drying and fermenting, rolling and heating, the machines turning day and night.

'It certainly is. Second flush. Non-stop.'

Bill held his cigarette up and took a drag on it, then rested his elbow on the arm of the cane chair. I liked the shape of him, broad shouldered, bulky in his shirtsleeves. From the moment we met, there was something inevitable about Bill, as if I had somehow known him before, the sort of feeling that makes you believe you have had another life and are simply reacquainting yourself with someone you already knew – and cared for. He looked tired, a certain heaviness in the skin below his eyes.

'Only, we've had a breakdown. I'm waiting for a repair from the machine shop along the road.' He smiled. 'Time for a drink at least. You know all about it then?'

'I was born at Panchcotta.' I thought I had told him this, but I'd been so tight that night I hardly knew what I had said.

'How nice.' Another drag on the cigarette. He was shy, I could see. Every so often he passed a hand – big hands, with wide nails – over his bearded chin, as if considering things. But he did not seem in a rush to drink up his beer quickly and leave.

'Yes, it was. In fact –' I was about to tell him about meeting Shonu. I stalled, feeling silly. But he looked at me, looked deeply.

'In fact?'

I laughed, turning even pinker than the heat had made me already.

'It was a very funny thing. This morning, I ran into someone – a little friend I had in the garden at Panchcotta. She was the *mali's* daughter.'

As I spoke, water poured from the sky: a great swishing sound as if all our surroundings were being swept by a huge broom. It felt cosy under cover here in the Club, with rain drumming on the roof. I had to speak more loudly and we each leaned in closer to be able to hear each other, so that our faces were unnaturally close together. It was strangely intimate and I did not look at him most of the time while I was telling him about Shonu, and then about Hughie and Akbar, only glancing up now and then to meet his eyes. I said that seeing Shonu had made me feel *right,* sort of joined up again, and happy. I must have bubbled on at him, but the thing was I felt I could, and that he was listening and not mocking and that he understood.

'It felt as if I had met my long-lost sister,' I said. 'I never had a sister. I should have liked one.'

Bill hesitated. 'Yes,' he said. 'Me too.' He sat back for a moment to blow smoke away from my face, then leaned in again. 'I had a friend, in Jamshedpur. Mohan.' A warm smile spread over his face. 'I don't know now what his family did, now I think about it. But we used to play cricket together. We got along famously. But of course …' He reached for the tinny ashtray on the table to stub out the cigarette. 'After I went to school in England, I never saw him again.'

We were both silent. Our eyes met for a moment. After that things felt awkward. The rain started to let up and we had no reason to sit so close to each other. We sat back, exchanged a few more pleasantries about the gardens and about Jessie's family. I remember we laughed about the Bells – fondly. He did not once mention his wife.

'Well,' he said, eventually downing the last dregs of his beer. The light was coming back outside, the shine of water on everything. 'Best wade my way back and see if they've fixed the part. You're waiting for Jessie, you say? Be all right?'

'Of course.' I stood up. 'But I'll have a wander round the grounds while I'm here, even if I have to paddle, for old time's sake.'

It was already happening, I can see that, thinking of it now. At the time, when we weaved past the tables to the stairs, and afterwards, side by side along the shaded colonnade, I thought that the rightness I felt – alert, despite the damp, numbing heat; electric, alive – was because I was here at the Club, that it was to do with my past and my memories.

I stood beside him when we got to the cart, the horse gleaming wet. He did not leap straight up into the seat, but reached up to wipe it as dry as he could with his hanky, then stood, as if reluctant to go. It was only for a few seconds, but enough for us both to feel it, to look up at each other with a kind of enquiry and look away again. I felt a lift of something inside me, very physical, a surge of knowing something that my mind had not yet caught up with.

'Well.' He patted the horse's neck and it jerked its head up, startled. 'Better be off.'

'Yes, of course!' I said, probably in a horribly jolly tone.

He looked at me again then, really looked, as I was a strange object of which he was trying to make sense. Our eyes met for what seemed a long time. Somewhere there, it had begun. Both of us said later that each of us felt it even when we first met, that we *knew* each other. It's a very rare few people in your life who arrive in bold capital letters, right from the start. Then, I just knew that I liked him more than any other man I had ever met.

He climbed up, reins in hand, the wood of the cart creaking, and settled on the seat. That sense of being bereft began in me even then, the grief at someone parting from me that I have always had to repress.

'Cheerio, then,' he said, clicking to the horse to move along. 'See you around.'

See you around.

I smiled, and waved, in a polite way. He set off at a trot. The wheels whirled drops into the air.

I did see him around once or twice more during that stay. The gardens were busy, but he came to the Club and amid all the other socializing, we said hello. That, at the time, was all.

8

Jorhat, Assam, Christmas 1920

'I'm so sorry, Ellie,' Jessie said to me miserably, that Christmas night. She sank down on the edge of her bed, the other side of the room from mine, and put her head in her hands. 'It's been such a grim day.'

It was true that despite Ellen Bell's most valiant efforts, our day of church and a roast chicken dinner and games after it had been so shot through with poignancy that it had felt almost unendurable for all of us. Duncan's absence was a rent through the family so deep that it seemed impossible that it would ever heal. I only hoped that my being there helped them find the strength to lift themselves, just a little, out of all the heartbroken remembering of former times.

I sat beside Jessie, putting my arm around her plump body as she sobbed. Tears dropped on to the skirt of her Christmas frock, green raw silk, with red berries embroidered on the skirt.

'Don't be silly. Your poor parents – and poor you. You must all miss him so terribly.'

I felt foolish then, at my occasional sour feelings towards Hugh. He was alive – how fortunate I was compared with Jessie and her family!

Jessie put one hand over mine in my lap and squeezed it. I was wearing a crimson velvet dress, soft and reassuring to the touch, like an animal.

'I'm so glad you're here,' she said.

My goodness, I was glad too! At the end of August I had felt I must not impose on the Bells for too long and I went back to Bombay. By this time, my mother had more or less given up on me so there was less of my being carted about to all the parties. But mother seemed to be at the sauce bottle rather regularly these days and it made her more vicious. I was her useless spinster daughter, about to become of age and still lumping about the house and 'eating meals' at the Mynah's expense! She made no protest when I said I was returning to spend Christmas with the Bells in Assam.

'Believe me,' I gave Jessie a squeeze. 'It's a lot better here.'

Jessie wiped her eyes, put her specs back on. We looked at each other with a wry desperation and burst out laughing.

I had not arrived in Jorhat until just before Christmas and it was not until it was over that I heard that Betty Ashton, Bill's wife, was still away and that the two boys had not been in India for Christmas either. It was Jessie's mother who mentioned it, prefaced with, 'Poor man.'

'I know she's not sold on India,' Jessie said, pouring water into a glass vase – she and Mrs Bell were arranging flowers while I sat nearby. 'But what a way to go on, at Christmas as well! You can't help wondering about that marriage!'

'Now, now.' Mrs Bell, dressed in a shapeless, grey dress, was snipping the thorns from a rose stalk. 'You can never judge these things from the outside, dear.'

'Well,' Jessie retorted, 'I'd say you either co-exist in the same house or you don't, and she seems hardly ever to be there.'

When I met him again at the Club, soon after that, I already knew this about his home situation. But truly nothing had really crossed my mind by then about Bill and me. He was married and a good deal older, so I had shut it away. One's mind did not stray there. But socially I liked him and I was pleased to see him when we found ourselves once again in company at the Jorhat Gymkhana Club.

I was surprised by how pleased he seemed to see me. As it was a cool evening, Jessie and I went into the bar downstairs and Bill and another chap were sitting at a table to one side. The other man, somebody-or-other, was introduced as being from Cinnamara as well. We settled at the same table, Jessie chatting for a bit. Then she drifted off to talk to other friends and soon so did the other chap, leaving Bill and me.

Being alone together like that – of course we were not alone, the room was crowded, but it felt that way – I became suddenly aware of him again. This man in a thick green sweater who, despite his size, well over six foot, seemed to shrink, as if trying not to draw attention to himself. I wondered if he had been beaten harshly as a child – so many boys were – and it was sometimes a sign. And again, he seemed struck with shyness.

'I gather your family are in England?' I said. 'What a shame. I'd so love to meet your little boys.'

'Yes.' He shifted in his chair, patting his pocket for cigarettes. 'You know, doing the family rounds before going back for the new term. The little one is not very settled and Betty is very keen that they don't miss out on family.'

This seemed reasonable enough and Bill was doing his best

to appear cheerful. He smiled and took a mouthful of beer. But I could feel it, the mantle of sadness that lay over him, seeing other families here together. There were a few children about, some too young for school, others home for the holiday.

'How was your Christmas?' I was making small talk before realizing what a tactless question this was.

'I was taken in by the Fieldings,' he said with a wry expression. 'They're rather good at waifs and strays.'

'I know the feeling.' I laughed. 'I was rescued by the Bells – again. My mother makes me feel like a large, heavy piece of furniture she keeps having to move about and she's not allowed to give away!'

Bill stared at me for a moment. He was in the middle of lighting a cigarette. Startled, he took it, unlit, from his mouth and laughed, head back, such a full-hearted sound that I could only join in.

'Oh dear, how awful!' He held out the ciggy packet to me and we lit up. 'You poor girl. I'd forgotten how direct you are!'

'Blunt, you mean? Mother says she despairs.'

'Isn't that what mothers do, despair?' he said unguardedly.

I tried to make light of it. 'Yours too, you mean?'

Bill shrugged. 'You know the old rhyme:

"I've failed for the navy and army,

The Church and the law, so you see,

The only profession left me –

My last hope – an assistant in tea."'

'It can't be that bad, surely?'

'Not far off.' He grimaced. 'My mother set great store by writing. Thought I'd stay in England and do something very *pukka,* if not writing a great work, at least the law or something.

As it turned out, I'm a disaster with a pen in my hand. It all comes out wrong.'

'But it suits you here?'

He smiled then. 'It does.' I could see that he loved it – the place, the work. He stubbed out his cigarette. 'It's rather warm in here. Fancy a breather up top?'

We climbed up to the abandoned upstairs bar. The air was winter cool and I pulled my cardigan round me. We went to lean against the balustrade, smelling the cool grass, the eternal smoke from dung fires. It felt as if the Club was a ship, lights on in the hold below, from where floated whiffs of cigarette smoke and the rise and fall of boozy laughter and music. Its glow illuminated a margin of the grass and beyond that was darkness, as if of an unknown sea, the stars and a slim half-hoop of moon. It was just enough to pick out the planes of our faces.

Only then did it occur to me that I should not be here with him like this. We were alone, our arms sometimes grazing each other's as we talked, comparing the usually unspoken truth of difficult mothers. Bill had been sent to school in England at the age of six.

'She really didn't know what to do with children. Even my sister went when she was eight.'

'I was five,' I said. 'And my brother not yet seven.'

I told him, all of it: about our father, something I never usually disclosed to anyone. It felt right with Bill – truth, trust. I told him about Persi, about her going off to be a nun, and he asked if I missed her.

'Oh yes, in a way, I do.' But I knew as I said it that even if Persi were here now, I could not be honest with her about this, about the feelings flowering between Bill and me. 'She's always been there somewhere, in the background. She's really rather wonderful in her odd sort of way.'

Bill gave a small laugh. 'She sounds it. A lucky find.'

Even as we talked, so easily, there was that feeling, *We are here, but this cannot be happening, all this that I feel, because he is married and we are such different ages and it just cannot be …*

'I always hoped to do better with my own.' He looked down at the path as if to see if there was anyone there.

'I expect you do,' I said.

He gave a bitter laugh. 'I suppose I can't do much harm if I almost never see them. That might be the best you can say.'

He sounded unhappy and I didn't know what to offer in return.

'Sorry.' He turned to me, face deep in shadow now. 'I'm being a proper old misery. I find I can talk to you, Nella.'

'*Nella?*' I burst out laughing. His naming me felt so intimate.

'You look like a Nella. Don't you like it?'

'I … Yes, I do!'

There was one of those pulses of time, a second in which you know you might fall the whole way and there is that passing chance to draw back, not to let it happen. But I was in his arms and he was fleshy and passionate and I was moved by him, wanted him. It was utterly different from all the Cyrils. Kissing Bill was passion and comfort all at once. He put his big hand on the back of my head, holding me, so gentle while his lips searched mine. That hand, cradling me, that tipped me over to him like nothing else.

And so it started and neither of us could or would stop. I kept falling, gladly and full of joy.

*   *   *

I was not in fact a virgin by then. I let one of the Cyrils (in fact I think his name was Peter) deflower me one evening in the Mynah's house when they were out. I thought I'd get it over with and I didn't mind too much. He was a strange chap though. He was thin and muscular and evidently felt the need to give me a running commentary on everything he was doing as if he was running a training camp: 'Right, coming in now!' Even the adorning of himself in one of those ghastly, smelly rubber things: 'Nearly got him covered!' I found the whole episode sore and hilarious in a sad way and he never came near me again but at least I knew what was what. Give or take.

With Bill it was entirely different.

I couldn't go to him on the garden at Cinnamara. There were servants and workers everywhere.

'I've got a boat,' he told me. 'At Nimati Ghat.'

This was a snatched conversation when we were leaving the Club on New Year's Eve, amid the boozy, celebratory goodbyes around us. He leaned close and my whole body came up in goosepimples, feeling it was reaching out to him. He spoke very quietly, as if he could hardly believe what he was saying.

'How about tomorrow? Can you get away?'

'Yes,' I said. Come hell or high water, I'd be there.

There was no choice but to confide in Jessie. She was my best friend and I didn't want to tell lies. The shock in her eyes told me just how innocent she was about men. No, she said indignantly, of course she wouldn't tell her parents. I was going out to visit someone …

'But Ellie, what on earth are you *doing*? He's *married*.'

'I can't help it, Jessie,' I said. 'And it's no marriage, as you said.

I'll be careful, I promise.'

I didn't care – about anything except being with him. Here was this wonderful man and I was just stark staring bonkers about him. I needed, I wanted. I loved, so that I couldn't sleep for thinking of him.

The river, our mighty Brahmaputra, was winter-low, a broad, grey green between its sandy banks. We pushed off in Bill's long, punt-like boat from the *ghat*, passing the shacks and smallholdings of people living along the bank.

The sun gently lit the water. Bill paddled us downstream until we were away from any village life and could stop at a good picnic spot. We climbed out, pulling the boat up high on the sloping bank and carried our things – quilt, basket of food – to a patch amid the tall grass and shrubbery. We each looked round, instinctively, for snakes.

'Seems all right,' Bill said, spreading the thick quilt on the ground. I put the picnic bag down on one corner and bent to take off my sandals. As I looked up, Bill was kneeling, watching me.

'Oh, Nella.' He spread his arms and I walked into them. Bill put his arms around my waist and rested his head against me. I was moved, looking down at his thick, brown hair, seeing the lay of it, the way it crowned just to the left. I stroked my hand over it and heard him say, 'My God, Nella.'

I let myself sink gradually to my knees, our bodies lightly touching until we were looking into each other's faces and I could see the sad, shamed hunger in his eyes. Bill took in a sharp breath. This time it was I who put my hand to the back of his head, my other arm wrapped round him, pulling him even closer, and I reached my lips up to meet his.

After a time, Bill drew back a fraction, his eyes anxious. 'Have you ever –?'

'You mean – *been* with anyone?' I found myself blushing, wondering which answer he would prefer. 'Yes. Just once.'

He seemed to relax then, a fraction. 'So, I'm not … deflowering you. But I must … We must …' He had brought protection, those terrible rubber things, and turned away shyly to put it on.

'I hope to God no one's about,' he said, turning back to me, blushing. We were already mostly naked. 'You never know in India.'

If anyone was, after that we did not notice or care. Making love with Bill, his big, generous body covering mine, the quiet, intense enjoyment and relief of a man who wants, needs, was all I knew. And lying there together afterwards, the sun on us, holding each other, was the greatest bliss I had ever known.

'There's a place I know – up-country a way,' he said, after we had lain for a time, sometimes talking, sometimes just quiet. 'Very basic – you have to take pretty much everything with you. We might manage just a few days. Bhutan would be even better, but it's really too far.'

'Yes,' I said, without even thinking about it.

Here was this wonderful man, unlike anyone I had ever met, in my arms. We could love and laugh together, we knew the same long rootedness in this country, the same kinds of sorrow. And as we climbed back into the boat that day and paddled along the wide immensity of the river, I knew in a deep, certain way, that he was my man.

9

'I don't really know if Ginny likes it here,' Roderick said. 'Has she said anything to you?'

He and I were sitting up late, in the dim light, our chairs arranged to look out over the verandah. It was too cool actually to sit outside. Ginny had gone off to bed saying she felt queasy again and Persi said she was going to read in our room for a while. Possibly she was being tactful, leaving us to talk.

I was happy enough to linger and try to get to know my nephew better, this prospect being enhanced greatly by the fact that he was generous with the Scotch and I always knew I could count on a refill. Even as he asked the question, he was filling my glass. He sounded worried.

'She hasn't, no,' I said. Not in so many words, anyway, I thought. In the few days since our early morning conversation, the girl had been more reserved with me again, but I still felt oddly protective of her. Young girls always have to do so much *fitting in*. 'I'm sure she'll settle in perfectly well, but I expect she's feeling jaded about everything at the moment. You know, when the tum's a bit gippy. She'll feel better soon.'

I kept surprising myself. The voice I had heard recently in

England – my voice, that sharp, resentful bark – seemed to have softened. I found kinder, more reasonable words coming out of my mouth. A curious thing.

Roderick sat quiet for a moment, hands clasped over his little pot-belly. I could see even in the poor light that he had got his shirt buttons done up wrongly and his collar was askew. He was so like Hughie in that regard and it touched me.

'It's all happened rather fast,' he said. 'I wasn't expecting …'

'What, to be a father? It really doesn't take long to conceive a child, you know!' I said this rather too heartily and then regretted it.

'I know, but …' He shrugged. I thought, He's scared, poor lamb.

'The thing is, Aunt, I scarcely feel I know what a father is and I'm soon going to be one.' He looked at me as if gauging whether to ask the question. 'Will you tell me – about your father?'

'*Mine?*' This was not the question I had been expecting. There would be more questions about Hughie at some point and I really must try to answer them.

'He *was* my grandfather.'

'Yes. Of course he was. Well, he was rather marvellous. I was always closer to him.' I heard the warmth in my voice and I did the best to tell this young man about Pa, about his kindness to people, his love of India, his long project with the dictionary. And I explained just how ill-assorted was the marriage made by my parents. I told him – why not? – that Mumsie had had a long affair with the Mynah before Pa found out.

'The trouble was, he was so defenceless – he was completely devoted to her.' The echo of those distraught cries came to me then, in the retiring room at Metapullayam, on the last night

134

when I had a father, the last night of his own life. An ache moved across my chest. 'Poor old chap. My mother, Alicia, was not … she never showed him any understanding. She was not a happy person and I think India made it worse. She hardly knew how to be content, I don't think.'

Roderick seemed to be drinking this in.

'I wish I'd known him,' he said.

'You would have liked him. He would have liked you.'

He gave a little gasp, as if what I had said had actually had a physical impact. He sat forward, head down, resting in his hands. To my consternation, I realized, when I heard him making breathy, gulping sounds, that the pup was on the verge of weeping.

'Come on, old chap,' I said, heartily. 'Buck up.' And was then furious with myself for sounding like a callous gymnastics teacher.

'I'm sorry.' He sat up, taking in a shuddering breath. 'I've just felt very – alone in the world. Because of Pa, I suppose. Going like that. I know it was the war and everything, but Mother always said he had deserted us, war or no war.'

Typical Jennifer, I thought. Of course, that was the basic truth, but she could have spared the boy that.

So, I told him more about Hughie as a boy – about Panchcotta and Akbar, about school.

'I'm not sure how he got on at school,' I said. 'He'd never say a word. And then we were all stuck because of the war. I saw more of him after that, for a time, in Bombay. He had been out East and I suppose he wasn't in too good a way then, really – none of them were. But he went back to England and to Cambridge and I know he wrote to Persi now and again. The rest of us – well, he just cut us off. And then …'

I stopped. Perhaps this was one of those things he did not need to know. But he was waiting.

'I was back here in India when all this happened – Persi was as well. I gather Hughie had some sort of breakdown, towards the end of Cambridge. He never finished his studies, I don't think. He was –'

'What?' Roderick leaned forward and I saw his round face loom towards me. 'It's all right. Tell me.'

'I believe …' I kept my voice light. It wasn't the sort of thing anyone talked about. 'He had to go and be looked after for a bit, in a sort of hospital somewhere.'

'A mental asylum?' His voice was soft, fearful.

I nodded. 'Poor lamb. For about eighteen months, I believe. But you see, so many men were in a state at that time. The war took it out of them.'

Roderick sat back, silent. Eventually he said, 'Poor Pa.' He sounded emotional again. So like his father, so like mine, I thought. Gentle souls. Gentle souls who seem to turn to hard women. My mother; Jennifer. Not Ginny though, I thought. She was different.

'I mean he recovered, of course. He found a job in the city, met your mother and got married. So, he was all right.' I almost felt like crossing my fingers, saying this.

Roderick was quiet. Then he said, 'Was he, though?'

His sharpness shamed me. We had all told ourselves Hughie had recovered. He got some job in a firm in London, went into banking, did all the things that sounded like the right story to tell. But how had I ever helped Hugh, in all those years? I was afraid of him, hurt by his distance from me. The only person he could ever turn to was Persi.

And at the time when Hugh was carted off to the asylum, I had problems of my own, looming large enough to block out the light that might have directed my eyes towards my brother or anyone else.

10

Bombay to Calcutta, June 1921, mail train

All night the rocking and jolting has held me, my heart answering the train's plaintive whistle as it calls out to the night. Now, in the early morning, I lie with my faced turned to the wall of the Ladies' compartment. Something feels different, quieter. Mrs Gaitskill, the fretting, small-faced, puritanical woman sharing the compartment, must have turned the fan off, bother her! I'm drenched in sweat even in my slip and it will soon be like an oven in here.

Comes a light knock on the door.

'*Chai, memsahib.*'

'Yes.' Mrs Gaitskill swathes herself primly in a cardigan to make herself presentable. 'Yes – come!'

I screw my eyes closed, extend my arms away from me, trying to cool down. If only everyone would just go away. All I want, all I have to hold on to is to lie and dream of *him*. Until these moments I have kept up a half-waking dream where Bill and I are together. We are lying naked together, warm and comfortable, laughing, talking. There is that sense with him of absolute comfort and security, of being free and loved as never before. We start to make love, his face all I can see, both of us losing ourselves, his ample body, thick thighs, my body responding ...

'Are you awake, dear?'

Her silly, fussing little voice. As if she's got anything to worry about! My dreams are all I have left of him, can't you see? Must respond, must be polite.

Pretending to wake, I tug something of a smile to my lips and roll over, pulling the narrow sheet over me.

'Some tea, dear.' Mrs Gaitskill holds out a cup and saucer. She smiles in her tight, nervous, way. For a second. Until her eyes move over me. Her mind works, visibly, and something seeps through her face – blood rising, any number of things sinking in. And the look in her eyes as they fasten on my belly, which does not fit with the thinner woman who – apart from that – I have become.

Mother never noticed. I believe she had actually given up looking at me altogether. She had taken to glancing up from a magazine or a meal, allowing me only into the side of her vision as if I was something she'd really rather wasn't there. The only time our eyes met, that I remember, was a couple of months earlier. It was April, one of the hottest days of the year, and I had come down to breakfast still feeling like hell. Mother was at the table with a couple of slices of toast and a jar of marmalade, dressed in white broderie anglaise, her face moist with perspiration even with the fan beside her.

'Letter from Hughie.' She held it up with a strange casualness, somewhere near her left ear. 'It seems he's finally gone back to Cambridge.'

'That's good,' I said.

It was of course. He was so far removed from me in every way, but I knew that was what he had wanted. It seemed we could just forget where he had spent the last year or more. And I had just thrown up my morning tea. The sight of it disappearing, tan and curdled, down the lavatory pan was becoming routine. I reached for a slice of bread and forced myself to say, 'Any more news?'

'Oh,' she said as if indifferent. 'It seems he's playing a little cricket.'

If my mother knew that Hughie had spent the last year and a half locked up in an asylum, she never once mentioned it. I only knew via Persi. And then the Mynah came in, wearing tennis shorts which displayed far more than one wanted to see of his ginger-hairy thighs.

'Morning, girlies!' he trilled and reached for two bananas. None of this helped settle my churning stomach.

My mother seemed to have given up on me entirely. Before, she was forever prodding at my body – too this, too that. Now, when I lost over a stone in those two months, able to keep very little down, it passed her by completely. My clothes hung on me, which was a blessing as of course my belly then started to expand. She didn't notice that either.

I didn't realize myself at first. Not for sure, until I'd missed the curse twice and then all the sickness started. But it wasn't just being sick that caused me to lose weight.

Eventually, dear Jessie Bell had asked me, as kindly as she knew how, to go home. Even once Betty Ashton had come back from England after delivering her boys, Bill and I just couldn't stop. We were completely wrapped up in each other. It was as if we had started a whole new life that didn't – couldn't – take much account of anyone else.

'We so enjoy having you here,' Jessie said. She found it so difficult, poor dear. In normal circumstances, having been in Assam for more than two months I would have been sharper about having outstayed my welcome. But this was not normal. It was ecstatic, undeniable love. The love of my life. I could not say no to it and neither could he.

We had spent that week up-country together in a house that offered nothing but four walls and a roof, two *charpoys* and a couple of braziers for cooking. We had to take everything we needed with us in Bill's truck. I didn't even ask what he had told them at the garden. The little house, looking over the river, had been built for people to come out holidaying and fishing and after driving to a certain point, we had to park and carry everything up a track.

We caught our own fish and cooked the catch on the braziers – fire buckets fuelled by a handful of coal. We walked and climbed, we made love and slept, we cuddled like pups. And we talked and talked. Sometimes we were like children: what's your favourite colour, food, pastime? Me: orange, mutton curry, swimming. Bill: green, mutton curry, cricket, golf, fishing, any sport.

'At least I've always been pretty good at knocking a ball around,' he said, one afternoon when we were lying in each other's arms, 'if not at much else. It's always saved me. You can always get along with other chaps if you can make a reasonable fist of that.'

'I've always been hopeless.' I laughed at the memory. 'We played tennis at school and spent half the time running outside the court because I whacked the ball so hard it wouldn't stay inside the lines! "*There's no need to be so forceful, Eleanora! It's not ladylike!*" My poor teachers – it took years before I could mangle any sort of game together.'

'I suppose you *have* to be able to play tennis!'

'You do,' I said seriously. 'Social outcast otherwise. But I seem to do everything wrong. Hands won't do as I tell them.'

He took hold of my hands, opened them in front of him like a book. 'They're very strong, capable-looking hands.' His eyes smiled into mine. 'As if you play the piano for hours every day.' Which was something I had to own up to be hopeless at as well.

'You know, old girl –' This was Bill's nickname for me, being so much younger than he. He rolled over, propping himself on his elbow to look down at me. 'I've never known this before – not like this.' Those big grey eyes were full of tenderness. 'Nella.' He stroked my hair. 'My Nella.'

I lay looking up at him, naked as a babe. At this man who loved me, loved my much-criticized body. This miracle who flooded me with tenderness. I rested my hand on his solid flank. He was lovely – like a wall beside me, my big, bearded bear.

'Nor me, my love. Never.'

I saw Bill open, become someone free and full of joy and that was how I felt – like a lotus in flower, all that had been waiting to be. By the end of that week, we were different people.

The last night we built a fire outside and sat in the glowing dusk watching the smoke curl into the branches. Night birds called in the trees, leaves shifted in the breeze and the air burred with insects. A flock of ducks flew over and landed nearby, not seeming to mind us. Our great river flowed on below, like a wheel of time, tugging this precious interval away from us as we sat holding hands. Bill's was so big and warm. Every so often we turned and looked at each other. Neither of us could say the unbearable. *We can't ...*

We went back, of course. Jessie could see I was in a dreadful state. Bill and I scarcely managed to see each other once a week after Betty came back, and even then it was a snatched few moments, hungry and shameful, somewhere at the dark edge of the Club grounds. All we could do was to stand holding each other, full of desperation. Both of us knew it was hopeless. He was a married man and that was that. And, even more to the point, a father. I knew what it was to grow up with a father gone. Not to mention my being over a decade younger than he was. It was all just unthinkable.

Except that we thought it, longed for it. We were both so howlingly in love that we couldn't seem to get past it. Bill's big, generous body, his hands, his voice, were all imprinted on me. I never fully succeeded in undoing this, even when all the years and distance had been placed between. But of course, there was this other reason which marked him as mine.

During that week upriver, when we made love, we left the rubber horrors out of it. God knows what we were thinking. I shared all Bill's joy at making love freely. In fact, that last day, when I tore myself away from Jorhat and started the long journey across to Bombay, was the first morning I felt groggy. On the steamer I thought it must just be the motion as I was sick into the brown water churning at the stern. But on it went, from that day. All across the country, being sick into those train lavs, seeing the ground racing past below. I told myself it was something I had eaten – not unusual in India. At the time I was so crazed at the thought of my journey taking me further from Bill that I felt as if I was being torn apart with every passing mile.

He wrote me one letter, soon after, facing up to the fact that this had to be the end. He had said he was hopeless with a pen in his hand. It was not true.

All I can do is thank you, my darling Nella. I had to write to you, but if we keep this up, someone will find out, sooner or later – sooner I would imagine. And you know how that would be. It would bring on us a different kind of hell, one way or another. I love you so very much, my own darling girl. I believe I always will. All I can think at present is, why has life given this to me, given you, the matching piece of my heart, when none of it can be? It makes no sense. Perhaps it will one day. I'm not a religious man so I have no fear of the church or any of its threats towards my soul. It's just basic human decency not to run out on Betty. But all I can feel now is torn away from you, and can only wonder where you are and how you are until I'm really half mad …

I must stop. If this keeps on it will be the worse for both of us.

His final words looked hurried:

Thank you, my dearest love, for all you have given me. These days, thanks to your fresh, sweet love, have been the happiest of my life.
Yours – truly, Bill.

I was screaming crazy for a few days, but what with the sickness and the journey I had to hold myself together. Despite telling myself it was gippy tummy, my second period was late. I knew, really. Bill and I had been gloriously careless and there had been too many conversations among mother's friends, mentions of feeling 'none too well in the mornings' and all that followed.

One morning, back in the Mynah's house, in which, at least, thank heaven, I had my own bathroom, I had drunk my morning tea and felt my stomach buckle immediately. I knelt, retching over the lavatory until I was wrung out. After washing my mouth out I sat, doubled over in the cane chair, my head in my hands, staring down at the cork floor.

'Oh Bill, my Bill.'

Never had I wanted him more, here with me now. At the same time, I felt embarrassed and ashamed at having let this happen. I had truly let the side down, been a stupid, silly little fool. Bill was a married man. I could hardly turn to him and go crashing into his life with this news. Just for a glimmer I felt rage, a bolt of white, deadly rage. Here I am, my life ruined, while his will just go on, undisturbed. He doesn't really love me. He just used me and threw me away … But even in my anger that felt like a lie. He loved me. I loved him, truly loved him. I felt about him the way I had never felt about anyone else – as if I'd grown up into someone open and fearless, who could pour love on to someone else. I knew he felt the same and it was an agony. And if I loved him, I must leave him alone.

And then I felt … nothing.

I sat up, breathing in. That sense in me of a receding tide, all feeling withdrawing. Numbness. This had to be lived through, somehow. That was all.

It was June and the very worst of the heat. I was getting on for six months gone and I knew I had to go. Mother's obliviousness would have its limits and I knew I must leave before the rains, when the east side of Bengal might become impassable. Mother thought I was going to see Jessie Bell again.

I slept for as much of the journey to Calcutta as I could, despite Mrs Gaitskill's blatant nosiness when I showed signs of being awake. Sitting fanning herself in her pale-green dress as we ate vegetable cutlets (I had to wake up sometimes), she told me about her daughter and her two model children and model husband who was a solicitor in Hitchin. Following which she looked brightly across at me and said, 'How very modern, to choose not to wear a wedding ring!'

I kept my eyes on my fork, scooping up a mouthful of rice. It wasn't 'modern'. It was unheard of.

'My fingers get so swollen,' I said carelessly. 'I was afraid I'd have to have it cut off.' As a last resort I looked up at her with a smile and said, 'Do tell me some more about your family.' While thinking, *No, for God's sake don't.*

As we finally escaped our baking railway carriage in Calcutta's Howrah Station, she said in a motherly way, 'Perhaps you might buy yourself a cheap band of a bigger size while you're … You know. It would look better, dear – avoid misunderstandings.'

I sat in the Ladies Waiting Room of the east-bound station, Sealdah, steeling myself for the next leg of my journey. Avoiding the eyes of the other first class passengers, English ladies and wealthy Indians, my mind set out on an alternative journey. From here I could get on the train east to Assam, following our great river north until I reached Jorhat. I saw Bill's arms opening, pulling me close the way he did, as if I was the most dear, precious thing. The ache in my chest felt ready to break open, but I couldn't let go there, in the waiting room, with all these people bustling in and out. I felt the same as I had when I first went to England and school: possessed by the sickness of grief.

I forced myself to my feet. I must stop this – never think these thoughts again. Going to a stall, I bought tea and glucose biscuits and a newspaper, trying to look like a carefree girl, not someone half out of her mind with fear and sorrow.

On the steamer down to the delta, I sat in the shade, watching the square, coloured sails of the jute boats. 'The most beautiful place in the world,' Persi called East Bengal. We chugged noisily along the river, in some places so wide that the land was hardly visible. Then the banks would close in again, all edged with alluvial fertility: greenest green jungle of banana and palm, and all the other brilliant colours, saris and fruits and sails, against the milky brown of the water. At sunset, the sky and water burned orange, faded softly to pink and finally the soft, breezy caress of night in darkening blues.

We docked in Barisal sometime in the small hours. A tonga took me and my few possessions through a leafy darkness alive with crickets, a barking dog here and there and the smells of dung fires, of spice and incense. The town buildings dwindled about us as we reached a more open area on the fringe of the town. Before too long we turned through the gates into the compound and I saw the dark bulk of the convent chapel, bigger and more imposing than I had expected. Just as I climbed down, I felt a motion inside me again, of the insistent personality now growing in there, as if to say, 'Come on then!'

The tonga's pony clopped away into the night. The door of the convent swung open and there, in the light of the Tilly lamp she held, stood a tall, unmistakable figure, dressed in white habit and veil. Her voice came to me, low, through the darkness.

'El-e-a-nora?'

She stayed where she was, setting the lamp down on the floor at the last moment as I walked towards her with my little bag. When I came face to face with her, the string with which I had tightly held myself in all these weeks, began to fray and unravel.

'Oh Persi!' And with a hiccough like a little child, I stepped, sobbing, into her arms.

That first night, even at three in the morning, she took me to my room and put me to bed like an infant. There was nothing I could hide from Persi once in her presence and I blurted out the plain facts of the matter straightaway.

'Get some sleep. We'll have a proper chinwag tomorrow.'

Her words were lightly spoken, but before she went out, carrying her lamp, she bent and kissed my forehead, gently, solemnly. As she left the room in darkness, I really understood how those men at Scutari felt whenever Florence Nightingale wandered past.

Over the next few days, I watched Persi among her sisters. She was the tallest by far. It was strange to me not to see her hair. Yes, she told me, she had had it cut off. It was what you did, as a nun. 'Much cooler too,' she said. 'It's practical.' Without her hair her face looked different; plainer, but still striking, with its long boniness, those narrow, but life-full eyes. I looked for any sign of strain, or forcing herself to this life, but she honestly seemed happy.

As soon as we had a chance, we sat, late that first afternoon, at a little table in the shade of the cloister, which ran along one side of the convent and gave a view of the water tank and the lilies. The lowering sun's light rippled on its surface. We had only been there for a few moments when one of the younger nuns, Sister Sushila, came along, a beautiful, soft-cheeked young woman with dancing eyes. She smiled, putting her hands together in greeting.

'Would you like to take tea, Sister Marguerite?'

'That would be lovely,' Persi said. 'Thank you, Sister Sushila.' I saw their eyes meet, a fondness between them.

'You sit – I will ask Bolu.' Sister Sushila moved away with a neat, purposeful walk to instruct the kitchen boy.

Persi looked out across the wide tank, with its water-lilies, to the tangle of jungle beyond. I could feel her steeling herself. There was so much to talk about – me, my troubles and shame. But I said, 'You're happy. You like it here.'

Persi carried on looking out. An egret lifted into flight from the serene surface of the water.

'I do. I love it.' She spoke gently, but surely. 'Every stick and stone of it. Every bamboo and every leaf.' She turned to me then, smiling. 'And my sisters of course. I've found my *bari*.'

Bari. House. Home.

I smiled at her. 'You're lucky.' I almost blurted, 'You're *my bari*.' I felt so lost, as if she was all I had.

She reached out, then – I felt she could hear my words without my saying them – and laid her hand over mine.

'Tell me then, sweetie,' she said.

I stayed in that dusty delta town for five months. At least, it was dusty when I first arrived.

Away from the splendid mosques and the heart of the town, the convent had stood, for fifty years now, in its own compound, its chapel the biggest and most imposing building for miles around. This burnt umber-coloured edifice was red and womb-like inside, with gracious colonnades running the length of it towards the altar. It rose up out of a garden of extraordinary greenness. Not far from the chapel was the tank, lilies floating serenely at its edges, and all around grew the dazzling leaves of banana and papaya and a tangle of jungle, which had to be beaten back so that it did not take over again.

The convent was a British outpost. Mother Ruth, a compact, competent woman in her late forties, was round-faced, with a ruddy complexion. While she looked like someone who had just hiked across the Pennines in a howling wind, she had also, in fact, done something fearfully brainy at Oxford University. She had an inner stillness that I envied. She was kind, in a detached way, and I could sense her decision not to judge me. Besides which, she had enough on her mind with overseeing the running of a convent of twenty-six women, a clinic, an orphanage and an elementary school, without concerning herself overmuch with some careless young strumpet who had turned up in their midst.

No one said anything to me about my shameful condition – except Persi, who naturally had a certain amount to say, but not in condemnation. What was done was done. The only one who I thought showed an edge of disgust – or of *something* – in her manner, was old Mother Winifred, who had previously been in charge. She was elderly and frail, posh and formidable, peering at me over her half-moon specs as if at something toad-like and distasteful. But even she never actually *said* anything. I saw a Christian kindness and forbearance in action, even if some of them were finding it a bit of a struggle.

There were a few other sisters from Britain, but the rest were locals, most of whom were the younger novices or those who had recently taken vows, like Sister Sushila. Only Sister Mira, a plump, busy little woman, was over forty. The others were young, fresh-faced girls in their white veils, eager and smiling and each of them sweet to me as ripe mangoes.

In a strange way, that place gave me one of life's more benign lessons. The places where kindness is found – especially if you are expecting condemnation – are rare and priceless. As well as the injunction to Christian forgiveness, those women had seen so many things, so much of the outcomes of desperation, that they had apparently grown past judgement.

I was given the sort of room I had come to expect when in Persi's orbit – a white-washed cell at the end of a corridor, containing a metal-framed bed, a small table and a chair. For those months, apart from when I was unwell or needing to rest, I lived a religious life with these women who had taken me in. I've never actually been religious. I'm not a deep sort of person and like most members of the Church of England of my type, it was mostly form and a sort of uncomprehending boredom. For company, if nothing else, I went to many of the offices they kept, coming in from work, the sweat pouring off them, to pray at regular intervals throughout the day. The sight of them, gliding barefoot through the immense, red body of that building, kneeling before the great Meaning to which they had given their lives – well, that moved me, and I envied them.

In my spare time I went to the bazaar, bought cheap lengths of cotton to stitch little clothes and napkins for the child. There was no point in knitting – it was far too hot for wool. I found a fine, white, embroidered shawl and bought that, imagining that he or she might be baptized in it.

They also put me to work. I was sent to the orphanage. No one said a word, but I knew why. At that time there were twelve children housed in a building close to the convent, although it was outside the compound. Once past the age of sixteen, the inmates were expected to move on and helped to find work. That summer, most of them were under ten. None of the children were European of course, but you could not fail to see that a goodly number were *chi-chi* – that is to say, half-caste, or Anglo-Indian.

It was obvious that they had this home in mind for my child. If a girl, perhaps she might even graduate into convent life? She might stand out in the orphanage – though thanks to Pa, my own skin colouring is so dark people have wondered about me. If a boy – what would his fate be? To travel the roads like Kipling's *Kim*? To be adopted? The priesthood possibly? Perhaps I sound detached, but it is true to say that at the time none of it felt real to me. I was in a strange state, finding it hard to believe in the reality of the child, despite its inner prodding, or that I would give birth to it or what would happen afterwards. The thought of any life beyond the next few weeks was more than I could contend with.

I spent the last morning before I had my baby helping in the orphanage. In the long room where the children played, I held a little girl called Ayeesha. She was four years old and thought it very funny to poke at my mountain of a stomach, giggling as she looked up into my eyes.

'Now, now, young lady,' I said, in English. 'You need to be careful.'

She didn't understand my words, but she chuckled at this strange woman in a baggy mauve frock, swollen ankles spilling over her ugly brown sandals. I looked into her bright eyes, this little child. In four years' time, my own would be this size. Would she be looking into my eyes like that and laughing? For a second my well-worn dream came to me again: my travelling north, following the course of all the branching rivers until the Padma met the Brahmaputra, his river, and all the way along to him. Bill, oh Bill. He would run and take me in his arms and nothing would ever matter again, him, me, *our child*.

'Auntie?' the little girl insisted.

I looked down at her, jogging her bird-like lightness on my lap and hoping she would not notice the tears threatening to spill from my eyes. How was I to leave my child here, as a lone white orphan, even under the eye of Persi? What would its life be? Always waiting, hoping to be adopted by some childless missionary couple?

No. I pressed my hand to my swollen body. This child, flesh of Bill's and mine. I simply could not part with her, even if it meant somehow that I had to stay here for ever. I must keep her – or him – whatever it took and whatever it cost me.

My pains began during the evening meal, so sudden and strong so that I bent, panting, over the refectory table.

'Do I need a doctor?' I gasped, as Mother Ruth and Persi helped me along the dark corridor, to a small, white room in the infirmary.

'Healthy lump like you? I doubt it,' Persi said. She was probably more worried than she sounded.

Mother Ruth leaned down once they had eased me on to the side of the bed and spoke to me carefully in her refined voice, as if I were deaf or slightly half-witted.

'Only if it turns into an emergency. And everything is looking very promising, dear – all right? Sister Marguerite,' she went on, straightening up. 'I am needed elsewhere. I'll send Sister Sushila to you. She is very experienced.'

It was a strange thing: one of the very few times in my life when, despite the pain and the unknown path facing me, I knew this was something I could do. This was mine, no one else could do it for me, and my body rose to the occasion with an awesome force. It was an instrument I could play, this new, labouring body, and as I bent, groaning, over that narrow bed, I felt something certain and strong. Before dawn broke on the new day, I had pushed her out, screaming and jubilant.

Persi remained quiet throughout, though I knew she was there. It was Sister Sushila's calm voice I heard, making me feel that all was well and that I was doing things right, and for that I bless her eternally. It was her round face, her head half-encircled by the white veil, her dark eyes beaming up at me from the bloody birth-stream between my legs, saying,

'You have a girl, *didi* – a beautiful little girl.'

In moments, she was sheet-wrapped in my arms and I took in her solid, fleshy looks and quizzical blue eyes. I saw him in her. She was part of him and I knew then that I had done the best and most precious thing in my life. She was mine – and his. I felt battered and strong and joyful.

Persi came and put her arms round me then and kissed me, and there were tears pouring down her cheeks. Sister Sushila waited beside us, smiling. I saw her stroke her hand down Persi's back.

'We look like the Holy Family in the stable,' I said.

Persi wiped her eyes and gave me a satirical smile. 'I see the religious life is making its mark on you,' she said. And then she looked at Sushila and the two of them, side by side, leaned close and put an arm round each other.

154

'I think I'll call her Louise,' I said. It was Persi's second name. 'And since she was born here, her second name can be Mary. Louise Mary Storr-Mayfield.'

Persi's face paled. Sister Sushila stepped away from her, seeing that she needed to leave us alone. Quietly, slipping from the room, she said, 'We will take some tea.'

'I am going to keep her,' I said, defiant in the face of Persi's shock. My arms would be around Louise for ever, I was utterly certain. The strength of her sucking on me was my tie to the world. 'I don't give a damn what I have to do or what anyone says.'

11

1965

'I'm sorry. I really don't think I can go.' Ginny groaned. 'I'm sure if I do, I shall end up being sick in a flowerpot again. It's all the smoke – makes me feel awful. No, I don't mean you, Auntie,' she added hastily, as I moved my ciggie away from her. 'It's a whole roomful that does it.'

It was Club night. Roderick had proposed that we all go into town for the evening, but Ginny looked green-tinged and Persi seemed reluctant, said she was just as happy to stay here. After all, she had no past attachment to Assam or the Gymkhana Club.

Roderick reached across and topped up my glass. I must say, I was impressed by the boy's instincts. My private supply was almost untouched.

'No matter,' I said. Relief was coursing through me at this postponement. I was not sure how I was going to cope with the Club. All those memories, those little corners and textures of memory that would be contained in that place, of my early days and even more, of Bill. 'We can always pop in next week? Tell you what,' I added jovially, holding up my glass of JW. 'When I've downed this, I think I'll go off for my evening stroll.'

'How about Ginny and I coming with you?' Roderick said.

156

'Think you could manage that, Pickle?'

'I think so,' she agreed hesitantly. 'At least if I chuck up under a tea bush, I don't suppose it will matter too much.'

I had taken to going for a little walk before dinner, as the sun was going down. Usually I would walk alone, greeting and greeted by estate workers on the road, making their way home to their lines for the night, and by children and dogs, until my face had creaked into a permanent smile. I would go as far as the point where the reddish-brown, corrugated roof of the processing factory came into view, and there I would turn back. Nothing much was going on there at this time of year other than maintenance of the machines.

On these walks, I allowed memories to flow through me in a way I had not done for years. The walks I had taken with Pa at this time of day along paths in the Panchcotta tea estate, the feel of Jingles' strong back under my thighs, games on the lawn in the late afternoons with Shonu and Akbar, Shonu's bony little hand in mine as we ran along together. Hours which then felt as if we could stretch them into eternity.

It was strange and joyful to be there, like the joining of two electric wires severed long ago. Sometimes it brought me quietly to tears, along with a sense of bemusement at how and where all those years had gone. Turning back into the bungalow garden each time in the rosy evening light, I would have to hand myself back to the present.

Ginny seemed to pick up a bit once we were outside. We strolled towards the factory, as I always did, then took a side turning along a track between parcels of tea bushes. The ground rose and fell gently, interspersed with low-lying tracts of land which, tending to flood and therefore being no good for tea, were given to the workers as land to cultivate their own rice.

Roderick started explaining this to me, then stopped himself.

'Of course, you know all this, Auntie.'

The evening air was full of the herby vegetation, with smoke and cooking smells from the workers' lines and with the richness of scents that makes up the air of India, whether in town or country.

'Oh look, Pod,' Ginny said. They stood, arm in arm, and we all watched two lads who, on a rough tract of ground, were trying to round up the family cow for the night. The animal, a brown creature with fine dark eyes and nose, was apparently not enthused by this arrangement and kept skipping smartly away in the wrong direction. The boys, eleven or twelve years old, one with a long bamboo in hand, clicked their tongues and called to her, trying to get round behind her.

'She's a real naughty one.' Ginny giggled.

At last the boys, more skilled than they appeared, circled round the mischievous cow, who trotted past us, nostrils flaring.

'*Namashkar!*' they called, we called.

I wondered what they made of us, the dumpling man, his pale-faced wife and the crop-haired, tweedy old lady who accompanied them. Perhaps they accepted that all Europeans were odd in the extreme.

'That was lovely!' This seemed to have made Ginny happy and I realized I felt the same. I smiled at her. I seemed to be doing that a great deal more often. 'You should write poems about it, Pod! He writes lovely poems,' she said, turning to me.

'Your father wrote poetry at one time,' I told him, as we

ambled back along the track. The light was becoming uncertain and one had to watch one's feet.

'Really?' Roderick sounded amazed. 'Do you have any of them?'

'I'm afraid not. He started after the war – the first war I mean. I remember reading one that was about the flies that plagued him in Mesopotamia. That was the only thing he ever really talked about.'

'Did he?' Roderick's voice sounded strained. He turned his head to look away across the garden. In a moment I realized he was weeping. Good Lord, was my first thought. The boy seemed to start blubbing at the drop of a hat!

'Oh Pod, my dearest!' Ginny put her arm about his back with tenderness; God, what tenderness, such that my own eyes prickled as well. And how vile I was, how hard and derisive in the face of someone who could in fact *feel* something. Shame on me, I thought, and shame on all those who made me that way.

'Sorry.' He broke down for a moment as Ginny caressed his shoulder, then wiped his face. 'I've so little of him. It was as if he disappeared into thin air.'

He did, I thought, old, bitter feelings rushing up inside me, though unlike Roderick, I was not able to weep. That's just what he did.

'A poem – that's marvellous,' Roderick said, trying to gather himself. 'About the Great War as well!'

Of course, everyone seemed to be writing poems then: poppies, homesickness, mud and carnage. But perhaps Hughie went on with it, I don't know. 'It's something Storr men seem to do,' I said. 'My Pa wrote them too from time to time.'

'Storr?' Ginny said, as we walked slowly on. 'Remind me – it was your mother who was the Mayfield?'

I felt it my duty then to give her the history of the Mayfield Crappers' ceramic products.

'No!' Ginny stopped on the path. 'Lavatories? Is that true?'

'Perfectly, I'm afraid,' I said. 'And hand basins.'

She burst into a stream of giggles, which turned into a wholehearted laugh. Roderick was laughing too.

'Well, what an inheritance!' he said. 'Mother never told me that one.'

'No, I don't suppose she did,' I said. 'I never heard the end of it at school, I can tell you.'

'I'm not surprised!' Ginny said, wiping her eyes. 'Oh, Pod – this is marvellous!'

It was the first time we had managed to break out of 'best behaviour'. After this cross-current of emotions, we talked more easily and I was able to regale them with a few more stories about the three Mayfield siblings. Mother's sister, Aunt Frances, and her titled husband in their country pile in Suffolk seemed to have arrived in the world with a superior sneer on their faces. It was they who ended up inheriting the ceramics business, since their brother, the only boy, was our sweet-natured, utterly unworldly Uncle Hat, heaven bless him. Roderick and Ginny drank all this in and their laughter was gratifying. I think it helped us all.

On the way back through the smoke-tinged dusk, I walked behind the two of them on a narrow section of track, tea bushes on either side of us. For a moment I paused, watching them move away from me, feeling fond, gratified. Could I believe that they might actually be beginning to like me – just a little?

They walked, hand in hand, Roderick in his loose shirt and trousers, Ginny in her mint-green dress, which took on a glow in

160

the uncertain light. Pod and Pickle, for goodness sake! The two of them were married, a child on the way – the simple, universal path of such couples all over the world. Couples, unlike Persi and unlike me, for whom things are straightforward. A child would be born, a life celebrated. Simple, ordinary. For a moment I ached with my old, unrecountable anguish. Bill. Louise.

I put my head back and breathed in deeply, looking at the sky where the first stars were appearing over the shade trees.

Bill, where are you now? I wondered. Was he even still alive? He would be somewhere in the south of England, Surrey, the last I heard, a grandfather, perhaps even great-grandfather by now?

I had long ago choked off all the things that were not to be for me – had only been mine for a glimpse. This was their time now, these two young waifs on the path – for even Roderick, solid as he was, seemed waif-like – who had called me here out of need of their own. Their time, and my chance perhaps to matter to someone, at least a little. Slowly I walked on, following them, my seized-up heart giving thanks.

12

October 1921

Louise's cry, robust and demanding, woke me at dawn. She was then fifteen days old. I drew her to me and sat feeding her, hearing the garden birds and, more distantly, the sombre call of muezzins announcing daybreak from the town mosques. Light seeped slowly through the room. Louise was beginning to plump up. She was a strong baby, round faced, with a cap of light brown hair all over her head.

'My darling,' I whispered, again and again, stroking her cheek with my finger. 'My dearest, beautiful one.'

As she fed, her lips like a bud, she looked up at me, clear-eyed and alert. She seemed strong, so much herself for a being so young – and I saw him in her every time I looked at her. She was the link that bound us.

The wind began at midday. By late afternoon, the usually glassy surface of the tank outside was like a choppy sea. Trees bent right over, doors were snatched from your grip and walking outside became a battle even to stand. People started pouring in from the area around to take shelter in the convent church, the biggest and most solid building for many miles. Everyone knew what was coming; the only question was how bad it would be this time.

'I'm going to be in there all night,' Persi told me that evening, standing at the door of my room. 'You'll be all right if you want to stay in here. Up to you.' We had battened down the shutters and it already felt like night.

'Is everyone else going into the church?' I looked up from changing Louise's napkin.

'Other than the two in the infirmary. There'll be a lot to do. We're getting set up.'

'I'll come. I'll help if I can.'

I was frightened by the idea of being almost the only one left in the convent while the storm howled and beat at us and I struggled across the compound with Persi. Something was banging loudly with the force of it and sharp, stinging things hit us, leaves and splinters of bamboo. I had Louise clutched to me, wrapped in a blanket and leaning forward to shelter her with my body, terrified that something big and lethal would come crashing into us. The wind felt like a raucous, buffeting enemy, terrifyingly stronger than all of us.

Inside, the great red and white cave of the church looked like one of the busiest of Brueghel paintings. The sisters had lit candles and placed them on the ledges of most of the columns along each side, and on the altar. Their light threw gyrating, devilish shadows of the throng, who by now filled nearly all the space. I stopped just inside, momentarily appalled. Was I really going to have to spend the night in here? The stench was enough to turn you up. Some people from the surrounding villages had driven their precious family cow into the church and the beasts were corralled in the back left-hand corner, hemmed in with little tables and chairs. The sisters had also arranged a screen to give some privacy to a number of metal pails in the other back corner, close to where I was standing, and the stink of human ordure was so overwhelming I found myself almost gagging.

'Find somewhere to sit,' Persi urged me. 'I'll let you know if there's anything you can do.' She hurried away, beckoned by Mother Ruth, and I was left standing at the edge of this great agglomeration of humanity.

'Miss Ellie?' Sister Sushila appeared out of the throng, a figure of calm, just as I was close to fleeing out through the door again. 'Come. We will settle you somewhere.' She stroked Louise's head and gave me a reassuring smile. I controlled my breathing, trying to take in air only through my mouth.

'Thank you,' I murmured, as she took me by the arm.

The feel of her strong, fleshy arm, and her calm, soothed me. The shadows no longer looked devilish and I felt ashamed of my first reaction. In the circumstances, the place was surprisingly orderly, the atmosphere hushed and frightened. All I could hear in the high, echoing space was the murmur of voices, the cry of an infant.

There were no pews or anything of that sort. Everyone settled on the floor. We wandered about the densely packed church in search of a space, picking our way round squatting family groups, thin people whose own houses could be blown to matchwood, who looked up at us with scared, wondering eyes.

A young mother was sitting with her back against one of the columns with her family, a baby in her arms and three boys about her. She saw Sister Sushila and me carrying Louise, no doubt looking a bit lost, and shyly beckoned to me, indicating that I should sit beside her.

'Here,' I said to Sister Sushila, who nodded and smiled at the young woman. 'Go. Sit, Ellie,' she said.

The young woman shifted along a bit so that I too could lean against the column. Her young husband, in a ragged shirt and white *dhoti*, sat cross-legged nearby, looking up bashfully at me. They both seemed so very young. I could smell the aromatic scent of oil in their hair. The girl smiled at me and we looked at each other's babies and made admiring noises. And so began the night.

Gradually, people settled, though to start with the doors were hauled open every few minutes to admit another battered-looking family, before slamming shut again. We sat in the red, flickering light, backs pressed against the cold stone, grateful for its solidity, listening to the roaring assault of the wind. Soon, the smells barely troubled me. The press of bodies all around became reassuring. I held Louise close, clinging to her solid little body and gazing into her face, sleeping serenely through most of the turmoil and only stirring now and then to feed.

I only saw Persi from time to time in passing as she and some of the other sisters came round, gliding, gentle figures offering, '*Pani? Biskit?*' They had filled metal churns with water and somehow marshalled large numbers of glucose biscuits like loaves and fishes. A couple of the young novices collected a group of children into one corner and sang songs with them. I marvelled at all of them.

Through the continuous thrum of noise, I became gradually aware of a rhythmic half-singing, half-murmuring, growing more insistent. The young woman next to me and I exchanged looks. Not far from us, a very thin old man was squatting on his haunches, a white cloth twisted roughly round his head. He kept rocking back and forth, apparently in prayer and growing

165

anguish. When Mother Ruth appeared, bringing round a canteen of water, I saw her take in his distress and she sat herself right down on the floor beside him, listening, as he poured out his woes. Persi noticed this and handed him a blanket she'd found from somewhere as Mother Ruth, fluent in Bengali, tried to comfort him.

Later Persi came and squatted close to me for a while. She smiled down at my sleeping little girl. In the candlelight her long face showed little signs of tiredness.

'Someone's sleeping the sleep of the just,' she said.

'What's wrong?' I nodded towards the man, who had now settled back on his haunches, but was still quietly muttering.

Persi leaned close to me, speaking softly. 'He's one of the few who survived the cyclone of 1876. It was one of the worst anyone can remember. It centred right here in Barisal – a tidal wave came after it and there was famine afterwards. He lost all his family – he was about sixteen. His wife's here, at least, but their children are grown up and he's not sure where any of them are.'

I took in the tiny, grey-haired woman who was beside the man, sharing the blanket. Her face was very still and she stared ahead of her. Beneath that unflinching calm, what turmoil must reign in her. God, I marvelled, and I thought *we* were brought up not to show our emotions.

The wind shrieked and raged, unearthly, filling one with a sense of horror. Water thundered from the sky, all night. But we were safe. The dark, solid church rode the storm like a great liner in the darkness. There was no question of sleep. I was glad when Louise woke needing me. She was my anchor, my reason to look after someone else, her comfort and safety weighing heavier than mine. She held me steady through what felt like more hours than a night should properly contain. And, at last, its fiercest raging began, hour by hour, to die away.

The morning light when it came filtered, pewter dull, through two filigree windows each side of the main door, while the rain continued to fall steadily outside. Cows were milked, the sisters set up two braziers in the lady chapel, brewed tea, and brewed tea again, until there had been some for everyone. If I had not fully known it before, I knew it then: they were the most extraordinary women. I have often wished I had the strength of character – not to mention faith – to join them and stay on, living the way they did. All I could do that night was sit among all the other waifs sheltering from the storm and accept one of the little clay cups of tea from Sister Sushila, who, handing it to me, smiled gently and laid a hand for a moment on Louise's sleeping head.

Afterwards, everything was broken and humbled by the storm. We came out of the stinking air of the church at last, single strays and family groups; the bent, limping elderly, children skipping with joy at being let out and the sisters and me, with my little girl who needed her nappy changing. We gulped in the water-swollen air, finding ourselves greeted by a strange stillness now that the turmoil of wind had passed. Everyone paused, taking in what was around us, our survival, before going on our way to whatever remained.

It seemed it had not been the worst of cyclones, but it was bad enough, as we saw over the following days. Crops, encrusted with salt, lay ruined; boats were lost, houses destroyed and trees snapped off. Our human life felt reduced to a carnival of silliness. Wind-seized objects appeared in fairytale places: clothes snagged on buildings, a rickshaw rammed into a stand of bamboo, boats hurled to the ground streets away from the river. And there were the dead, many of them, who had not had our privileged place of shelter, some lying in the streets. The force of it, leaving us all so helpless, altered our minds for a time and made us more afraid.

Water lay stagnant across the fields. Infections were on the march and people fell sick. And so, less than three days after the storm had passed, did my darling Louise.

'She's burning,' I wept helplessly, to Persi. Either she or Sister Sushila always seemed to be there. Two days and nights of holding her, beside myself, this new, small body which had seemed so robust. 'And she can't keep anything inside her!'

I tried spooning cooled, boiled water into her mouth. We slept in the infirmary, along with two of the Indian sisters, both delirious with fever. Louise had diarrhoea and a roaring temperature which reduced her to a pathetic, limp little thing, her breathing quick and shallow like that of a trapped bird. She kept her eyes closed, only surfacing when her face creased and a high mewl of pain came from her.

My mother had sometimes referred to Hughie and me as 'my young', as if we were deer or hounds. In those days as I held Louise's struggling little body, I thought, really for the first time, about Mother's dead son, her firstborn. And I understood then that little David's death had shut off something in her for ever – a capacity for love, its burning vulnerability, that I had only just discovered in myself and which makes us more than animals.

We all tried to pour ourselves into my little one, Persi, Sushila and I. We kept her naked, cooling her by bathing her wasting limbs. We each tried to get her to drink. My breasts were sore and bursting with milk but that did not seem to be the right thing. Sometimes she managed a little water: soon she coughed it back up again until she had no strength to vomit.

'What's wrong with her?' I wept, as Sister Sushila and I bathed her once again. 'What else can I do?'

Sushila put her arm round me and drew me close. She felt fleshy, comforting, but her round face was solemn and exhausted.

'The main thing is to get her through the fever. And we must pray, Ellie. We must baptize her. She is in God's hands.'

Our eyes met for a moment. Sister Sushila's were full of kindness, but dread and fear curdled in me. She must think it enough of an emergency not to call one of the Fathers from town to do it.

'Will you help me?'

Sister Sushila went away and came back with a little clay bowl of water, I suppose from the chapel, and a teaspoon. Gently, she lifted Louise in her arms. I had wrapped her in the special, embroidered shawl, white and beautiful. This was not how I had imagined her baptism, but I could not think of anyone better to do it.

'I baptize you' – Sister Sushila leaned her close to the little bowl, spooning the water over her head – 'Louise Mary. In the name of the Father and of the Son and of the Holy Ghost.' Water trickled over Louise's head. I wished she would scream as so many infants do. But she seemed almost lifeless. However, after a moment she opened her eyes and stared intently at Sister Sushila, who looked up at me and smiled.

'She is listening,' she said, holding her out to me. 'She is blessed now by God. Here, take her.'

*   *   *

A doctor came, soon after. Everyone did everything they could, and there is no more to be done than that. Afterwards, as Sushila said, it is up to God, for whom I had little time before and have had even less since those days, begging as I did at his stone-deaf door.

On the fourth night, I knew she was fading. I lay on the bed with her on my stomach, trying to will every shred of my life-force, my love, into her. But she was leaving me. I could sense the draining of her life. It had been more than a day since she had opened her eyes. She was so floppy and still, so much not my little girl any more. We could not rouse her, even to drink. That night, held close in my arms, the tide of her breathing ebbed away, breath by faint breath, until it was no more.

Persi and I, just the two of us. No coffin, I said. Nothing boxed in, no priests and falseness. I wanted to give her back to my country, as people there gave back the souls of their dead.

I found a little mat and folded it lengthways, sewing the two ends together to make a bier for her, like a straw boat. There were a few flowers lifting their heads after the storm; a pink rosebud like my girl's lips, strands of pink bougainvillea and some yellow daisies, and I wound them about her as she lay wrapped in a piece of white muslin. In the late afternoon, Persi and I took her by tonga to the swollen river, still over-spilling its banks, downstream from the town. The tonga driver drove slowly and treated us with reverence; he could see what we were about.

The two of us walked in the lowering sun along the muddy ridge at the edge of a flooded paddy full of ruined plants. It felt as if everything in the world was broken. It was hard to distinguish the river from the land and we had to search for a tongue of firm ground where we could get closer to the main body of water. The mud squelched under our feet and the water lapped close by. A little further out we could see swirling eddies in the milky brown water. We could go no further and we looked at each other. Here.

I'm not even sure whether we were allowed to do what we did. But we did it. It had to be done and had to be borne. As I held Louise, encased in her little boat, Persi read from the Book of Common Prayer: '*We brought nothing into this world and we take nothing out …* 'And then I was to recite Tagore's beautiful lines with her, but I could not speak: *Day after day, oh Lord of my life, shall I stand before thee face to face …*'

Persi turned to me then, and so carefully, said, 'Come, she has to begin her new life now – back in the everlasting, loving arms whence she came.'

I let Persi take charge. She took Louise from me and waded a short way into the river. But instantly it was unbearable.

'Wait!' I rushed in after her. 'Don't let her go!' I needed more moments with her, snatched seconds with her physically here, her body which I had clasped to me for twenty-two days of life.

Together, Persi and I lowered the little boat to the water. As Persi was murmuring more prayers, I bent to stroke her tiny head and brush my lips over her forehead one last time. She was cold. Gone from me. Together, we gave the frail thing a gentle push further out into the swollen body of the river, having to let go at last. My eyes followed for every second, seeing it glide away until it reached a side eddy that tugged at it and began to turn it. The little barque stayed upright for a few moments, listing, before tilting slowly on to its side, drifting further and further downstream.

Persi silently put her arm about my shoulders. We stood in

the floodwater shallows, watching that pale, disappearing speck which held the flowering of my heart, as she navigated the great river which joined me to her father and her to the human family of souls.

13

Mother's letter finally drove me to go and see Hughie. So that I found myself at the door of a large riverside house in Maidenhead. By then, in the summer of 1938, he had been married to Jennifer for four years and had a little son, whom I had never met.

The house was one of those voluptuary places, all gables and turrets. Jennifer, as Mother never ceased to remind us, came, as she had done, from Money. Even the hall was the size of a generous room, the parquet muffled with Persian rugs and the high ceiling dwarfing the happy couple.

Hughie, looking as rumpled as ever in open-necked shirt and corduroy trousers, seemed to have become rather comfortable round the tummy. Jennifer, sleekly made up and slender – despite childbirth, how marvellous! – wore a dress of dusty-pink silk and cream patent shoes with just the right amount of heel, her hands adorned with just the right number of expensive rings. The honey-blonde hair was pin-curled and arranged to look as if a tornado wouldn't shift it. This was the only occasion on which I spent time with her apart from at the wedding, the sort of event when, strictly speaking, you don't spend time with anyone. I disliked her thoroughly from the moment I met her. In contrast to my sister-in-law, I always felt like something that has been washed ashore on some flotsam-laden, post-storm tide – this being almost true, though she was not to know that.

Hugh greeted me enthusiastically enough, though in the voice of a jovial impostor. 'Hello, Ellie old girl! Good to see you. It's been far too long.'

I made similar social noises. Neither of us was blaming the other. After I had kissed him, the plumper, older cheek of my brother, our eyes met in merciful understanding of all the things we did not know about each other. That moment is something I still hold in my heart.

'You're looking very prosperous,' I said. 'Married life seems to be suiting you.' In fact, he looked sluggish, I thought. Or something. It was hard to tell.

I was introduced to Roderick, for whom I produced a box of little chocolate teddy bears. He was chubby and shy and seemed sweet enough. I could see little sign of Hugh in his make-up – he was pale with wide grey eyes like Jennifer. Nor was he in evidence for long, because the nanny whisked him away for lunch and left us to eat leg of lamb with mint and new potatoes. It was the best meal I had had in ages and we made light, tinkling conversation and drank coffee on the balcony looking over the boat-busy river. Jennifer made catty remarks about the neighbours: to one side 'The most appalling décor – one would have to go about with one's eyes shut!' and on the other, the woman's dress sense 'looks as if she's been through a hedge backwards,' at which I laughed obediently.

It was not until the end that I made my big announcement. First, I simply said that in a few months I would be going back to India. Jennifer stiffened at this. She did not like references to a life I had shared with Hugh in a country of which she had no idea, except for the usual superior cartoon version.

'Oh,' she said, with a strychnine-edged sweetness, 'we thought there must be *some* reason for your visit.'

So I socked it to them, and told them why.

I remember nothing in Hugh's expression through that vaguely amiable blandness into which his features seemed to have settled. Nothing that would have told me that six months after I sailed for Bombay Hugh would walk out of his house one day, leaving behind his wife and son. They would never see him again.

Such sad, wasted years. I had never been able to settle anywhere.

When I left the convent and turned up in Bombay, just a few weeks after Louise's death, even Mother could see that something had happened. I was thin as a rake and half-mad underneath the social mask. Cyclone, I told her. Such terrible things. She never asked. It was intolerable being there with the Mynah wittering about golf and I soon shipped myself off to Calcutta for secretarial training, always the thing for a woman to 'fall back on', a phrase that seemed to fit my situation perfectly.

It was soothingly dull and equipped me for the drugging repetition of office jobs. I came to feel an even greater affection for Calcutta, that rambling old city, and yet it was still too close, too raw. The Hooghly flowed through it, another of the veins of her river, and his. I could not bear to go back to Barisal and see Persi, though we wrote, of course. I tried to recover, drugged myself with tedium for three years. But the smallest thing, the way the light fell, a scent on the air, could bring back Bill or Louise. In the end I needed somewhere foreign and far. I returned to London with its black walls and cheerless little river.

It was easier for not being home. I lived in digs in smut-darkened, cold-water flats. I worked in jobs of supreme tedium: a sugar factory, a building firm, a hospital (a little less tedious). The men in the 1920s, the war-wracked survivors my age, were mostly as deranged as I was and I went to dances and had flings with a few of them. They came and went. We were all trying to get by, to find some way to live, to find all the happiness and celebration that winning a war and still being alive was supposed to confer. But I could not love or form any real attachment to them – nor they to me.

In the early thirties, I met Freddie. He played the piano in a club in Knightsbridge where I'd gone with a few people I worked with. During one of his breaks, this extraordinarily thin and long-limbed, highly charged presence wound up sitting chatting at our table. He looked young, was in fact almost a year my junior, with brown curly hair and a big wonky nose and was foul-mouthed and irreverent. The first time I heard him give a toast, he leapt to his feet, held his glass high and yelled to his – until then unknown – drinking companions:

'Here you are, you sodding bastards – good health and happiness!'

We drank and laughed, drank and laughed some more. We swapped family stories – he had caught the end of the war and come home in 1919 to find his mother dead of Spanish influenza and father off his head and in an asylum. I provided a sprinkling of brutal and carefully chosen details about my own heritage until we were each hysterical and I went home with him that night. Why not?

Freddie did some sort of work in swanky offices, money work, though I never quite fathomed what. He was electrically energetic, with a darting grin and a wicked sense of humour. He was up or down, seldom in between. He was a crazed risk taker.

And a drinker. Especially a drinker.

In bed, his whole body felt highly charged, his long spine quivering under my hands.

'You're a great girl,' he'd say, lying in my arms. 'Not many girls can cope with me. I'm too much for them.'

He could be thoughtful, tender. His piano playing moved me to tears. And every so often, he would sink into a place so dark that he could not speak for days. I didn't tell him anything much – certainly not about Bill or Louise. We were surface-skating friends, sometimes lovers, sometimes estranged for days or weeks, depending on Freddie's state of mind. We were together, then not, then on again for about six years, while I played at being a gay London girl – the outfits and hairdos, the dances. Living as if there had been no yesterday.

I never truly knew Freddie nor he me. I was going through the motions, speaking in a second – third, even – language not my own. But we could soothe each other. He was a port in a storm, though either of us making it to shore was a close-run thing. I drank. You drank. He drank. She drank. We drank. We'd try to cut back, then off it would all start again. We'd ignore each other, fight in his Pimlico flat, be apart again, come together. He hit me, but only twice, ever, and towards the end when he was not really Freddie any more.

Those years are a smashed-up blur, remembered between drinks. Somehow, I worked. I seldom ate sensibly. Freddie and I woke up in Hyde Park one morning, drenched in dew. What larks! He bought a car and we crashed it into a wall in Steeple Aston. A hoot! We shared a bed, off and on, in a sort of sexual companionship. But drunk as I often was, I was never, ever too drunk not to make him be careful – my God, I was careful about

179

sex.

'You're not going to get me up the duff, Freddie,' I'd say to him. 'Not ever – you're not father material.'

I saw Hugh sometimes during those years. Strained, pale, impenetrable Hugh. He worked for a shipping company to begin with. There were a few girlfriends, none whose names I remember. Then Jennifer got her claws into him and turned him into a sleek county banker in a riverside villa. At the time, I had to admit, she may have saved him.

Things went bad with Freddie. It got so that I would turn up at the flat and be unable to wake him. The last time was a real fright; ambulance, hospital. It's got to stop, I said. I don't think he could by then. And I could not keep up my brittle, pretending life. The coming war didn't help. Unsettled everyone. And then Mother's letter arrived late that summer of 1938. A stray baronet, aged forty-two, had passed through Bombay and was in search of a wife. Baronets did not pass through Bombay, or indeed India at all, very often. What about it? I thought. What else is there to do? Might as well. It was my free ticket. Finally, I could step off the crazed London wheel and go home.

14

The wedding of Eleanora Agnes Lucinda Storr-Mayfield to Archibald Arthur Rodney Loverage Byngh (Sir Arthur Byngh, Bart, of Aston Byngh, Shropshire) was announced in the society papers in May 1939. It did not take place in St Thomas's Cathedral, Bombay as Mother would once have preferred – an orange blossom idyll. We were married as quietly as she seemed to think fitting for the ancient creatures we were, in the parish church closer to Marine Drive.

I had known Archie for just over three weeks – long enough to get the banns read. On first acquaintance, he seemed pleasant enough. He was a dark-haired, solidly built fellow, with a moustache waxed into sharp little points, and wore a railway uniform. We were to live in Nagpur, a major junction right in the middle of the country. He was quite high up in the railways, apparently, though I never really asked. He was neither handsome nor ugly. He was a man. He seemed to be able to conduct a civil if stilted conversation about nothing very much. There was a house and a job to go back to. And he was a baronet. This was all that was required. He certainly wasn't pushy. He turned up at the house every two or three days and we had tea or went for a little walk. I honestly couldn't say what we talked about. Nothing much. I was in a trance and he seemed reasonably jovial.

He kissed me very chastely a few times. In for a penny, I thought when he proposed. I seemed to have done something right for once, even though I was over the hill.

Archie decreed that we had to travel to Nagpur on the night of the wedding – a journey of about fifteen hours even with no delays.

'Nagpur's a fine old place,' Archie told me. 'You'll soon settle in. Tennis and – you know, all the usual.'

The fact that the place was such a long way from Mother and the Mynah seemed an advantage. When I met Archie, I was still very shaken up after Freddie. I felt a heel leaving him really, but it was the only way to save myself. I was still barely coping with not drinking and being back in India. I just let it all go by me. There was no pretence of love from either of us. He didn't harp on about his baronetcy, which made me like him well enough. He seemed hardly aware of it. He was going through the social motions – little jokes, the courtesies and small-talk one would expect. As chaps went, he seemed all right. He would be out working a lot of the time. I'd just go and do the things women did. I didn't consider any of it very deeply.

On our wedding night we climbed into a first-class railway compartment – all very swish, with a proper wash hand basin. Our berths were at opposite sides with a table between, fixed to the wall, and whirring fans. Archie spent a great deal of time arranging his belongings, his back to me as if I was not there. I put this down to shyness. The day had been a strain for both of us, the heat, dealing with my family – Archie apparently had none in the country – and of course we barely knew each other. I was quite glad of the quiet. I watched him, the slender back of his neck, the carefully clipped black hair.

I was bemused by this activity though. With extraordinary precision, he lined up his few portable possessions: shaving brush, hairbrush, a little silver tooth-mug, notebook with two well-sharpened pencils and a small, cast-iron model of a railway loco. He stepped back as if to make sure everything was positioned correctly. Then he took off his jacket and arranged it very carefully on a hanger before vanishing into the bathroom.

Whistles blew, there was all the usual shouting and hoohah and the train eased its way out of Victoria Terminus and began to pick up speed. It was very hot and I was worn out from my weeks of whirlwind marriage contracting, not to mention dealing with Mother and buying frocks – she in a mood of mixed triumph and disparagement of me, her beetle-browed bride of thirty-nine.

All of it, those weeks and our wedding day, slid over me like oil. I was barely there. Now, as I stood to remove my pink satin travelling frock in the rocking carriage, while my husband of but hours hid – since anyone who, with no previous signs of anything tummy-ish wrong with them, remains ensconced for almost forty-five minutes in a bathroom is surely hiding? – I was still not quite there. It was as if I was looking out from somewhere behind my own eyes, in the trance I had gone into on the day I found Freddie's unconscious body, and since Mother's letter. And we had been drinking champagne, which always sends me into a rather odd state. So I lay down in my slip, pulled the sheet over me and received comfort from the train's gentle rocking.

Bearing in mind that it was our wedding night, I had, not unreasonably, expected Archie to make a move to some sort of consummation. Up until then some polite kisses had been exchanged – none fully on the lips. He would put his hands on my shoulders and carefully lean to kiss my cheek, almost as if I was a wall that he was worried might fall on him. I have no idea what Archie assumed about my past, but I certainly was not going to tell him.

He slept through the entire journey. I woke first and sat up, on the edge of my berth. I had pretended to be asleep when he emerged from the bathroom so perhaps he had been considerate. I pulled the sheet round my shoulders and sat gazing at this person to whom I had just promised my life, love and obedience.

His face was relaxed in sleep, the moustache drooping now. It was not a bad face: a pointed nose, weak chin, the precisely clipped hair. He lay on his back under a sheet that outlined his slender body, one hand resting on his ribcage, the other out of sight, the slight bulge at the V of his legs. I could hear his breathing. My husband. This was so preposterous that I had a fit of giggles. Archibald Arthur Rodney Loverage Byngh. Baronet. I had to go into the bathroom so that I didn't wake him, snorting at the thought.

I stood for some time staring into the dull looking glass. My shoulder-length hair was still half-pinned up from my bridal experience, the rest of it collapsed down on one side. My face was the face I had always had yet it seemed to belong to someone else. Life was strange – and I was a stranger to myself.

'You've done it now, old girl,' I whispered. 'This is it: Lady Byngh!' Another fit of hysteria took over. A title! How Mother loved it. 'You'll just have to make the best of it now.'

Archie slept his endless sleep. Then, as if those journeying hours had been spent inside a magic lamp from which our arrival in

Nagpur released him, he woke when tea was brought round as we approached the city's outskirts – and appeared to have transformed into a different person.

'I say!' He leapt up from the berth and peered out. 'We're here!'

I assumed this jollity was addressed to me and I was momentarily encouraged. Mine had been a joyless sort of awakening.

'Good morning,' I said, smiling at him. 'You slept very well.'

Archie looked at me. 'Yes,' he said. 'Always do, on trains, don't you find?'

We had all the turmoil of Nagpur station to face, coolies and bags and a car. Archie and I sat side by side, smartly dressed and silent. He seemed somehow agitated.

'Is it far?' I ventured.

'Oh, no,' Archie said, suddenly cheerful again. 'It's in the railway lines.'

It was one of the bungalows built for railway officials: the street lined with trees, a garden, a servant who opened the door to us smiling at me – sympathetically, I later realized. Setting foot into this dark house, in a city strange to me, I quickly came to realize that the Archie I had met, at polite intervals in Bombay, had been a man enacting a once in a lifetime performance. He did confess to me later that his railways colleagues, even his servants, had urged him to find a wife. Now in his early forties and with sentimental thoughts of his long-dead mother, he had indulged in this aberration in a last effort to fit, to be as other men.

I soon realized that the poor fellow was completely off his head.

The moment we entered the house, he pushed past the

servant, who gave me an apologetic glance, along the hall to a door opening into the back of the house, through which he disappeared, closing it behind him. Thinking he would be back in a moment, I waited there, in the brown gloom. As my eyes adjusted, I began to make out a number of painted lengths of something red and white, some crossing each other diagonally; there were other, bigger ones, one reading LAHORE and the same in Hindi, Urdu and Punjabi, another AMBALA.

'Your room, *Memsahib*?' the servant said as I was deciphering all these railway signs. He spoke kindly. 'I am Ahmed, *Memsahib*, at your service.'

'Where has the *sahib* gone?' I did feel something then, a chill of misery. Was my husband not supposed to show *some* interest in and concern for me? And how gloomy and miserable was this house to which he had brought me.

'*Sahib* will be out shortly,' Ahmed said, with that Indian optimism that in saying something you might will it into being.

The bedroom was in fact two adjoining rooms, their single beds pushed against the walls furthest from each other. The window in my part faced the street, a young peepal tree outside. The room was clean and adequate. It was brown and masculine. Then I turned and saw a tiny nosegay of flowers left on the table.

'I hope you like, *Memsahib*?' Ahmed spoke bashfully.

'Yes. I do. Thank you.' I could hardly speak, my throat was so tight with tears. 'You're very kind.'

Ahmed retreated. Once more I was left sitting on the side of a bed. For a moment I thought about unpacking.

'Well, bother this.'

I got up and marched downstairs towards the room into which Archie had disappeared, past a dithering Ahmed, and pushed open the door, stopping at the threshold – since there was little room for me to do anything else – of my new husband's lair.

The entire, large room was taken up by a table, or platform, on which was arrayed the most extensive, involved toy railway system I had – or have since – ever seen. In that glimpse I saw viaducts, bridges, hills and tunnels. A train was clattering across the middle of it.

On the opposite side, in his uniform, worn at all times and now complete with a railwayman's cap, glancing up at me and wreathed in such smiles as I had never seen on him before, stood the man who I had, quite voluntarily, elected to marry.

Archie was not a homosexual. I was no innocent about such things having known some of Freddie's associates. Conjugal relations were entered into, sparingly, between us. They were fondly requested by Archie asking me, well in advance, whether I fancied 'a spot of shunting'. (I'm really not making this up.)

I have nothing against trains. Hughie had a modest train set and I sometimes played with him. I could even tolerate intermittent sexual relations in which I was regarded, with a kind of displaced affection, as a piece of rolling stock. He seemed quite happy to 'be careful'. Children were of no interest to him. Archie was never cruel (he was never exciting to me either, but I had not expected that). I learned of his sweet, oppressed mother, harried to an early death by his tin-pot tyrant of a father. I could pity him. The trouble was, I was lonely and bored and he was absolutely bonkers.

In our dining room, every piece of cutlery at the table, every glass and dish, had to be arranged at a precise geometrical angle. Meals began – we had to pick up our cutlery – on the sixth stroke of a gong, which entailed a fairly athletic progress to the room to get in position once the gong had first sounded. (Dear Ahmed had got the hang of all this nonsense long ago, however, and paced his bonging according to our speed of arrival.) Every item in the house, vase, hairbrush or stool, had its exact position and outbreaks of peevish fury would break out if these habits were not kept.

'Everything's ruined!' he would cry, pacing in small circles. 'Today can't be mended – it's all gone to waste!'

Even I had to sit at a particular angle according to Archie's protocols. The first evening he took me into another room full of brown leather chairs and dark rugs. (Where he had found such dismal things in India I couldn't imagine.) This, I gathered, was our sitting room, its windows shrouded in nets as if we were trapped in a meat safe.

'Now,' he said – he spoke quite kindly – 'when we are in here, you are to sit here.' He pointed to a leather chair opposite his own. I obeyed. I sat. I crossed my legs. A small yelp came from Archie.

'No, *no*. Never cross your legs like that, d'you hear? That's it, knees together. Elbows on the arms.'

As I followed his instructions, he relaxed and smiled. 'That's it, marvellous! We'll get along famously.'

'But what if I need to move?' This was early on and I was humouring him. I still couldn't believe any of this was serious. He might as well have had a statue made, not married a flesh and blood woman. 'I might want to scratch my nose – or do some knitting.'

Archie stared at me. The fact that I might have requirements of my own seemed to baffle him.

'Just make it quick then,' he replied. After a moment's pondering he added, 'I think knitting might be all right.'

He worked long, seemingly unpredictable hours on the railway. For those hours I was free to scratch my nose or position my fork or myself as I pleased.

'Has he always been like this?' I asked Ahmed during that first week.

'I am only working three years for *Sahib*,' he said, adding with diplomatic flair, 'The *sahib* has his own way of doing things and I am his servant. I am accommodating him.'

Apart from Ahmed, an elderly cook and the *mali* who never ventured into the house, there were no other servants. During those early days I explored a little. But I knew no one and had little idea where to go. Whenever Archie came home, the first thing he did was to disappear into his railway room. If, sometimes in desperation for some sort of human company, I joined him there, sometimes he would babble happily to me about trains. Other times, when I opened the door, he leapt up, yelling, 'No! Get out! You can't be here!' I retreated and sat alone again all evening, the one compensation being that I could at least cross my legs if I so wished.

By this time, I had begun to come back to myself. The odd, careless state in which I had married Archie – so careless that I had not even told Persi I was married – was shrinking back. Here I was, shackled to a lunatic in a city whose only advantage to me now was that it was halfway across the country to Calcutta.

After six weeks of shunting in various forms, I packed a small bag. Into it, with my other basic needs, went the little white embroidered shawl which had been folded in my bag and stayed with me everywhere I had been since Barisal. I told Ahmed I was just popping out to the European bazaar. I closed the door and left him, Nagpur and my marriage to Archie gratefully behind me.

15

One sweltering afternoon in the summer of 1941 I found my way to the door of a rain-stained white villa in Ballygunge, one of Calcutta's mainly European southern suburbs. There were beds of wilting pink oleanders each side of the green door. I thought I heard a dog barking, but it could have come from a neighbouring house.

Every living thing was gasping for the monsoon to break. The sky was heaped with gun-metal clouds, everything seeming to have gone quiet, waiting. My temples pulsed. Although I had come in a taxi I was dripping with sweat and still trying to smooth the creases out of my cotton frock when the door was opened by a barefoot, drowsy servant.

'Mrs Savory is waiting.' Her face woke suddenly into a sweet expression and I thought she seemed happy in her work, which was a good sign.

As I walked into a sitting room full of chintz-covered chairs, Mrs Savory stood up. I guessed her to be in her early fifties, a faded redhead, one of those women whom India shrinks stick-thin, wearing a neatly belted shirtwaister frock in pink, also faded, which clashed abominably with her hair. Her face was terribly wrinkled, another thing the climate inflicts on some women of that complexion. For a moment she looked anxious, but then her worn features lifted into a smile which was genuine, not just social. We exchanged moist handshakes.

'Eleanor Byngh? I'm Deidre Savory. I gather you know Charlie Fox?'

'Yes,' I said. 'We both work at Imperial Tobacco.'

Charlie was one of those steady sorts of chap it was safe to dance with because you knew he wouldn't develop Wandering Hand Trouble. It was he who had mentioned that he knew someone looking for a paying guest. The fact that he was one of their church congregation seemed to be enormously reassuring to Deidre Savory.

We perched on the edges of chairs and Mrs Savory offered me water. 'So *terribly* hot today ...' Her voice was soft, a northern English accent, I thought, though I've never been very good with all that. Through long windows behind her, in the weird, stormy light, I could see a parched lawn edged with flowers.

'I've been working in the city,' I explained. 'The main Post Office. But recently I moved down to Imperial and it's really too far to my other lodgings.'

'Of course,' she agreed. 'How sensible. I'll take you up and show you the room and you can see whether you like it. It's all very clean.'

As I followed her skinny form up the stairs, Mrs Savory blossomed into a chatterbox. At full tilt she explained that she and her husband James, who worked at Brooke Bond and was also a lay preacher, were now alone, that their girls Lucy and Jane were settled, which I took to mean married, at home, which I took to mean somewhere in the north of England – and by which time we had reached the landing and were walking into a spacious, white, high-ceilinged bedroom.

Like the sitting room, it looked out over the garden at the back. I saw teak furniture, powder-blue curtains, mozzy nets. It even had a small, private bathroom.

'It can't be long now ...' Deidre said, going to the window. The sky had turned even darker. She raised her arms to pull down the top sash, the underarms of her dress showing salty rings of sweat. Lowering them again, wearily, she said, 'I don't know how people live here.'

'But you live here,' I said, wondering for a moment whether she was odder than she seemed.

'Yes, of course. ' She gave a little laugh, turning away from the window. 'I don't mean *us*, in our comfortable houses,' she went on earnestly. 'I mean the Indians. How they all *manage*, some of them in such poor conditions. I find this country completely *exhausting*. I just don't know how they do it.'

I liked this, her being someone who tried to see things from another person's point of view.

'Mind you, I wouldn't be at home now either. All the bombing – it's been awful, constantly waiting for news.'

'Oh, yes,' I said. I had been in my own little world all this time. I had no immediate relatives in England so the fact that the Germans had been bombing the hell out of it had all but passed me by. 'I hope your people are not in the worst hit places?'

'My sister – in Hull. Terrible. My mother, of course, but she lives further into the country. Wicked, that's what it is.' She was moving towards the cupboard.

'We live rather quietly now, James and I.' She looked girlish from behind as she pulled the cupboard doors wide open, as if to demonstrate that all was above board with nothing sinister lurking within, then moved on to the chest of drawers. I saw the

193

bones move in her freckled arms as she opened and closed a stiff drawer. There was something generous in her manner from the start, as if she wanted to be honest and open with me. Sadly, it was something I never fully achieved in return.

'Oh!' She straightened up next to the chest of drawers. 'Dogs! I hope you don't mind dogs?'

This was more like it. I beamed at her.

'Not in the least.'

Just as I spoke there was a flash followed by an almighty clap of thunder from outside.

Deidre started, clutched her chest, then beamed at me. 'Thank heavens. At last!'

When I washed up in Calcutta I was not in a good state. What with all those years of Freddie and the booze and putting up with London and its damnably miserable weather, I was a wreck. And then my lunatic marriage. I looked ten years older than my real age.

Once back in Cal, with all hope of anything much knocked out of me, I actually began to recover. Archie had not been much of a drinker, so I had already had to cut right back. I was determined. I had seen quite enough dipsomaniac *memsahibs* stumbling about, making shrill fools of themselves, to know that I damn well didn't want to be one of them. It felt like my last chance.

I dried out, lost weight, got a new hairstyle, a neat, jaw-length pageboy. To begin with, I moved from one gloomy room in a shared lodging-house to another. One landlady, Mrs D'Cunha, a widow and mournfully devout Goan Catholic, kept pleading for my company, whereupon she drank herself into snoring slumber.

I had to get out of there. I had my secretarial work to survive on, first at a paper mill across the river in Howrah, then the GPO, before I moved south to Imperial Tobacco's spanking new offices. And following from this, the Savorys in Ballygunge, where I fell on my feet.

Deidre and James Savory were good to me and for me. As staunch Methodists, they stayed away from the Demon Drink. They welcomed me into their home as Jesus instructed them to welcome the stranger – in my case a wild-haired (the hairdo didn't retain control for long) and not entirely sane spectacle, who arrived at the door of 42 Cowper Road.

The Savorys lived a quiet, routine life, doing what they saw as their Christian Best. Life revolved round James's work, their church and charitable deeds. In fact, Deidre was charitable in a way I had never formerly realized was possible, even having grown up with Persi. She was bafflingly disposed to see the best in everyone – even me. Mind you, she knew next to nothing about me.

I told Deidre I had returned from England after an unhappy love affair. She could see I was not in a good way. No one else knew where I was except for Persi, who I was sure would never shop me to Mother. As for my developing into a bolter, on top of everything else, Persi was naturally shocked when I finally Confessed All, but other than a letter telling me she thought me quite mad to have married some man I had known barely a month in the first place, so what did I expect? – she said little else.

In Cowper Road, in that high, airy house, I had a peaceful room, regular, if unexciting meals prefaced by prayers, a calm atmosphere and the company of both Deidre and the maid,

Leela, who was a sweet girl. To my additional pleasure there were the two dogs, Spot, a black and white Jack Russell, and Pepper, a brown, terrier-ish thing with rather longer legs, both of whom seemed to be doing their best to stand in for absent daughters, Lucy and Jane. For my part they stood in for affection in general and dog-devotion in particular. Deidre let them sleep in my room and soon I woke every day to find Pepper, who grew a particular attachment to me, curled up on my bed.

When I was not at work I could sit on the back verandah and read, sheltering from the sun or watching the rain. Everything was orderly, calm. James Savory was a softly spoken Yorkshireman, with mousy hair and solemn grey eyes, who left a pause before his every utterance. He always asked after me, my day, and appeared to listen to the answer. Only once, on stopping to exchange a few words with me outside, did he gently suggest that working for a company producing tobacco might not be the most wholesome use of my energy.

'You may well be right,' I said, stubbing out my own cigarette. 'But as I smoke myself ...'

He smiled tolerantly at me. 'You know Deidre's always glad of a hand with the Sunday School?'

I made a non-committal sound and James Savory gave up on me and walked off along the lawn in his grey flannel trousers, sleeves rolled up, to attend to one of the plants. The *mali* in Cowper Road had an easy ride as the Savorys liked to do most of the gardening themselves.

16

'Eleanor, if you're going to the bazaar would you bring back a couple of dress lengths for me?'

Deidre came to find me as I wheeled her pushbike round from the back of the house.

'Of course.' I put my bag across me diagonally, ready for cycling. I was looking forward to going into town – life was rather quiet down here. 'What sort of thing are you after?'

'For England, for my girls.' Deidre scrabbled in her purse and handed me Rs 20. 'They're so short of everything – it'll be a nice surprise. In fact, if the money stretches to it, bring me a piece for the little one as well. Something she can grow into.' She smiled. I could see her jaw moving under the skin. Deidre seemed to get thinner every month. 'You've such a good eye, much better than me.'

'Oh, that's not true!' I laughed. Though it was. I've scarcely ever met anyone with a worse eye for colour. But I was pleased by the compliment. Deidre was generous in that way.

'I know you like to get into Cal, into all the hurly-burly,' she said.

'There's plenty of that these days,' I said, re-fastening the

197

buckles on my bag.

'I know. I can't face it. Now you go carefully on that bike.'

For over a year now – my *purdah* year, I called it – I had lived here in Ballygunge with the Savorys. I went to my secretarial job at Imperial, where the European employees, many of them British, behaved so far as possible as if they were all still living back on their small, chilly island. I returned home to the Savorys' sparing though wholesome food – odd approximations of English dishes, or very mild curries – the home-made fruit cordials and exceptionally weak tea.

Eventually I felt compelled to help Deidre out at the Methodist Sunday School. I seemed destined to be with religious people without ever quite learning how to join in. (School had stamped all that sort of thing out of me.)

Now and again, someone suggested going to a film at the Lighthouse Cinema, or a dance. Chaps like Charlie Fox and a small group of others, of mixed ages, would pile into a car and go to Spence's Hotels or the Grand and have a reasonably jolly evening.

And I suppose I can't be an out and out dipso, because I hardly drank that year. I could go out, get a bit tight – then stop. It had been a sober year. We heard a lot about the war in Europe, but it hardly affected us in India. Until Pearl Harbor. Then Singapore fell to the Japs. Then Burma. And suddenly, it did.

By that May morning, when I cycled into Cal, fighting was in full spate in Arakan. Calcutta had become the centre for everything in the Eastern war, people and equipment pouring into the city from every side. The poor refugees were crawling in from the east and the place was filling up with allied troops, our lot and the Americans. There was so much traffic, Jeeps and trucks roaring about trying to get through Calcutta with its trams and carts, rickshaws and dispatch riders, not to mention people and cows, that the police had a full-time job just trying to keep the place moving. The *maidan*, Calcutta's long, central area of parkland, filled up with trucks and ammunition. The Red Road, which runs through it, north to south, was converted into an airstrip.

Troops were being put up in hostels all over the place and needed feeding, nursing and, of course, entertaining. The hotels we danced in were of the sort reserved for officers, which really made things hot up and there was always a jolly evening on offer. I was old enough not to attract too much attention, though one or two officers tried it on. Stolen kisses, but no one ever stole my heart – nowhere near.

I wove through the crazed traffic, braced for potholes, breathing in clouds of fumes as I cycled through the old business district with its pillared and porticoed buildings housing businesses and banks, and along into Bow Bazar Street, where I hauled the bike off the road. Deidre knew I preferred that sort of shopping to the big European stores like Whiteway Laidlaw and the Army and Navy, of which there were a good many in Calcutta in those days. But give me a good market any day.

I managed to struggle through the throng to the filthy wall of a building adorned with peeling film advertisements, where I could lean my bike. The crowds pouring past me were a fascinatingly mixed crew from all over the world: servicemen and women in various coloured uniforms, British and Indian secretarial staff and innumerable Indian male clerks in their muslin *dhotis* ... And there was all the clamour of the city – the bells of the trams and rickshaws, the honking of car horns, raised voices, scraping cries of crows. And the stink of exhaust and ordure, of incense and crushed marigolds, dung-smoke and sewage.

The heat was intense. I was running with sweat, my face gritty with filth. It was good to rest in the shade. I stood there letting the life of the city, my city, sink into me. In that moment, I felt a sudden lifting sense of happiness.

Out of the latest pool of passing faces, the Armenian secretaries, the pink, sweating Europeans and office peons in bright red and yellow turbans, one face settled itself into familiarity. I struggled to make sense of it – the uniform, jacket and skirt, the specs … She spotted me at the same moment.

'*Ellie!* It *is* you!'

'Oh, my heavens – *Jessie!*'

Though we had written, I had not seen Jessie Bell – and she was still Jessie Bell – for twenty years.

'You look just the same!' Her round face was grinning at me in delight.

How could I look the same? I felt I had lived a thousand years since I last saw Jessie. And while she looked basically unchanged, the curvaceous body, round face, glasses, she was – we were – definitely middle aged. The strands of hair I could see beneath her cap were faded, her skin lined and tired looking. But the uniform lent her a femininity that I had seldom seen in Jessie in all these years. And now so much time had passed, it seemed long enough to overcome the embarrassing way I had had to leave her parents' house in Assam.

'You're in uniform! Red Cross?'

'Yes, just along here.' She looped her arm through mine –

such comfort – to stay close in the throng. 'Come and see. Oh!' She loosed my arm again. 'Best bring the bike – you can prop it inside.' She almost had to shout over the mayhem. 'It's quite dreadful near the border,' she went on as I wheeled the bicycle beside her. 'The tea gardens are all mucking in to help the refugees of course – everyone who's not gone into the army. But that mainly leaves the older ones running the show and Pa's not at all well. We decided to throw in the towel and come to Cal while we could still manage the journey. Poor Pa ...'

Her face wore a look of real distress.

'He completely overdid it. But it's ...' She shook her head. 'You see sights up there you'd never believe, Ellie.' She steered through a grand, arched doorway. 'Now, here we are. Red Cross Central Supply Depot. You have to see this.'

We entered the vast, grey-painted building, echoing with the sound of hurrying footsteps, clacking typewriters and trundling trolleys. From somewhere further off I could hear hammering. Indian coolies in grey-blue overalls hurried to and fro along wide, shadowy corridors.

'Packing Department.' We peeped through a door – smells of glue and hessian, long tables piled with items, some overflowing on to the floor.

'There's everything in there to be sent out to the troops, from ciggies to gramophones,' Jessie said as we hurried on. 'Apparently the West African soldiers are mad for games of Snakes and Ladders! Now, here's Hospital Supplies.' A sea of lint and gauze and sheeting. Another door read 'Rolling and Tying'.

'Ah, "Wool Section",' Jessie read as we passed. 'All those socks and balaclavas – although never enough, by all accounts.'

'I'd better get knitting,' I said.

'This is one room I'm glad not to be in.' We walked by the 'Post and Cable Section'. 'It's full of people desperate to find their people who are trying to get out of Burma – it can take weeks on end and then as often as not, it's not good news. Now, this is us: Duty Free Parcels.'

We entered a room that looked like a gigantic drapers' shop. At one end, dextrous young Indian men and women were sewing parcels into white calico wraps and these were piled all about them like giant sugar cubes. To one side, long tables were stacked with towels, flannels, boxes of soaps. The rest of the space was lined with shelves and cupboards, stuffed and spilling with one of the items India produces so expertly and in such abundance: coloured fabric. Bolts and bolts of it, all around me, piled or hung, or slithering to the floor, all brilliantly coloured. The sight of this profusion lifted my spirits.

And sprinkled round the room, heads bent over various samples of cloth strewn across long tables, were servicemen and a few women.

'My God, Jessie, what a treasure trove! Where do all these go?'

'We run it with the Joint War Committee. All the troops can come in, send parcels of this stuff home. Everything's so short with the war on. It's something they can do for their families – helps keep up morale.'

For a moment I imagined the door of some little house in that cold island opening one morning to greet an unexpected white parcel – grubby by then, no doubt – from which would spill all this vivid splendour.

'I've come in to buy cloth,' I said. 'Can I get it here?'

'Sorry.' Jessie grimaced apologetically. 'No can do. Forces

only.' She looked directly at me then, this middle-aged Jessie, with a hint of a different kind of apology. I had never told her about all that had happened, about Louise, but I know that she still felt somehow that she had let me down, back in 1921. 'It's very good to see you, Ellie. I'll have to get to work now but we must catch up properly. Look, here's our address.' She wrote on a scrap of paper. 'Come and see us soon, when you can?'

'She must come here and visit!' Deidre exclaimed, when I told her what had happened.

I had returned from the bazaar with various lengths of floral-sprigged cotton, in colours safe enough not to clash with the hair of anyone at all. The smallest, pale blue with white daisies on it, was for the little girl. Deidre seemed genuinely delighted with them.

But before Jessie made any visit to us, I went to see Dr and Mrs Bell. They had a room in a modest Church of Scotland guesthouse in one of the little roads off Park Street; very plain, very efficient.

The sight of Mrs Bell came as a shock. Strangely, it was the thing that conveyed to me almost more than anything else just how terrible things had been near the border in Assam. She always was wispy-haired and eccentric, but now she was shrunken, an old woman, seeming much more than her sixty-eight years. But her face lit up when I walked in.

'It's a tonic to see you, dear!' Her voice scarcely rose above a whisper the whole time I was there. We met downstairs in the guesthouse sitting room – rather a chairs-all-about-the-walls sort of place – and Mrs Bell said her husband was 'not to be disturbed'. I saw the troubled look in Jessie's eyes as she said it, though both of them were trying to be cheerful.

When the tea arrived, we all moved chairs close to the one small table, marooned in the middle of the room. At the centre of it, on a white cloth, was a skinny pink rose in a tiny glass.

'Robert likes to think he has a heart condition,' Mrs Bell announced, as Jessie laid a white cup and saucer in front of her. I had to lean closer to hear her. 'But really, his nerves gave way. Exhausted through and through, the poor dear.'

She began to weep, a hand to her face. I think this was something that happened several times a day. It seemed unforced, as if her emotions were forever shimmering at the surface. Her own nerves were clearly not in much better a state. Jessie did not say anything. I was rather appalled, but she must have been used to it.

'I'm sorry.' She recovered, pulling a hanky from her sleeve to blow her nose vigorously, before looking at me with her pale, watery eyes. 'I never thought we should see times like these, Ellie. We tried to help as many of those people as we could, we really did. There were so many. Good people – they'd all been in Burma, just trying to do their jobs …' Her eye wandered and she drifted into silence. She reached for my hand and took it in both of hers, as if I was a source of new strength, and she sat holding it for a time. Her hands were trembling.

Jessie visited us a few days later. Out of uniform, she looked a more matronly figure, in a tight, pale green shirtwaister dress, her hair plaited and coiled into a little bun above each ear. But I could see that her quaint appearance sat comfortably with Deidre Savory. In fact, she seemed relieved. Goodness knows what she had been expecting of a friend of mine.

The four of us sat over a watery stew, which would have been better altogether had it been a curry. James and Deidre listened with great attention as Jessie described the situation in Assam.

'The ITA started to get everyone organizing, pulling together ...' She saw their baffled expressions. 'Sorry – India Tea Association. A lot of the younger chaps have gone into the forces of course. There are empty bungalows all over the hills. But there are still quite a few people, and my father wanted to do everything he could. The gardens have suddenly found themselves on the frontline.'

'They must be terrified of an invasion,' Deidre said, as Jessie took a sip of her drink. Seeing her plump lips on the edge of the glass took me right back to school, across all Jessie's years and mine. It was comforting.

'Oh, they are,' she said. 'Though of course, it hasn't happened yet. But there are all sorts of odd bods up there, helping out, spying on the Japs. There's a very unusual Englishwoman up in the wilds organizing the Naga hill people, they say. The Nagas are about the only ones in Burma who've sided with us and not gone over to the other side.'

'But the refugees,' James Savory said, sitting with his elbows on the table, hands clasped, listening intently to Jessie. 'You hear terrible things ...'

Jessie nodded, her face very sober.

'Days, weeks in the jungle with the Jap army breathing down their necks. They're all very sick – those who made it. Living skeletons, some ...' She shook her head but could not seem to go on.

Deidre gave a little outbreath of distress, shaking her head. James lowered his head, as if perhaps praying. The silence

205

lengthened.

'There's pink shape to follow,' Deidre said, eventually.

Jessie and I sat out in the garden afterwards, with tea and, in my case, some smokes. The light was fading and the gloaming lent a soft glow to the white of lilies in a nearby flowerbed and to Spot's white patches of fur as he lay close to us. Insects came and went and we could hear soft voices from the garden beyond ours.

'So, Ellie, how've you been?' Jessie began. She sounded so tired. Jessie carried her family on her back at all times. I thought for a second of my own mother, over in Bombay. We exchanged brief, cursory letters barely once a month.

I looked at her and we both started laughing at the impossibility of answering this question spanning twenty years.

'All right, in the main,' I said. 'You know – ups and downs. I was in England for a stretch. It's good to be back.'

'Oh, England,' Jessie said, with a dismissive gesture which made me laugh. '"That other Eden, demi-paradise ..."'

We both laughed, then were silent for a moment.

'That chap,' Jessie said cautiously. 'The one you were so keen on – Bill?'

'The *married* one I was so keen on.'

'So?'

I looked ahead into the dusk, my heart beginning to thud so hard I could hear the blood in my ears. Ridiculous, I told myself. Stop it.

'He stayed married. As you must surely know.'

'Umm,' Jessie said.

I fastened my eyes on the flickering fireflies at the far end of the garden, trying to compose myself. It was hearing his name.

Even being able to mention him after all these years, being with someone who had actually known Bill, made him real again. The great lake of sorrow in me that had frozen for so long, felt as if a sudden scalding desert wind had passed over it, filling me with meltwater that had no escape.

'I presume they're still over there, in the gardens?' I said, casually lighting a cigarette, as if Bill was a dalliance, yet another man in a chain of affairs I might have had in all these years; nothing more than a mad, youthful moment.

'I believe they went to a garden in Darjeeling for a time – something of a fresh start, I think. But so far as I know they're back in Assam now – or were, before the war. Working for a different company, I think.'

I nodded. They. He and Betty. Still there. Their children must be grown up by now. I tried to calm my thoughts by imagining how Bill would look these days, and Betty who I had never seen. Bill might be bald and podgy, perhaps with that grog blossom that European men develop after years out here. Would we even have anything to say to each other now? And Betty, once perhaps fair and pretty, now one of those stringy English women with her lips set in a permanent line of discontent. I realized Jessie had said something else.

'Sorry, what?'

'I said, so there's been no one else?' She sounded awkward asking.

'Oh, yes' I said breezily. I bent down for a second to stub out my ciggy in the tin ashtray. 'Quite a few. I even married at one time.'

I explained that my name, these days, was technically Lady Byngh. Archie and I had never formally divorced.

After recounting the bizarre interlude of my marriage, and after we had stopped laughing hysterically, I said, 'Well, I thought I might as well get something out of it. So I have a title, when needs be, which of course my mother thinks frightfully useful. And what about you, Jess – anyone?'

'Still Jessie Bell.' She nodded in her quaint, considering way. 'One or two nibbles. No bites.' She straightened the skirt of her dress. 'Honestly, it's never really bothered me. I've found my life pretty interesting as it is.'

Doing all the things Duncan might have done, I thought.

'And now,' she added cheerfully, 'there's so much to *do*. What are *you* doing, Ellie?'

Deidre, having grown used to my entrenched lack of altruism, seemed taken aback when I said I thought I ought to 'volunteer for something'.

By then, women were swarming into helpfulness, at First Aid posts, the ARP, entertaining troops at the YWCA or running troop canteens at the railway stations.

Which is how I found myself working at the racecourse nearby in Ballygunge, otherwise known as the Royal Calcutta Turf Club. Calcutta was filling up with service accommodation. The grand Clocktower building had been converted into a hostel with hundreds of beds for forces men to spend time on leave or recuperate after leaving hospital.

The place was being run, for the time being, by a middle-aged Mancunian lady called Mrs Martyn – full of zip and with a warmth that seemed to leave each of the many lads who passed through with the impression that she was his personal friend.

The lads had a good billet in the Turf Club. The vast, cream building with its clocktower had a wide, shaded balcony along the upper floor looking out over the stands. Between them and the curve of the racetrack itself was a generous sward of green, usually dotted with sprawling young men, the sound of their talk and laughter and their cigarette smoke all floating into the building. When it was hot, the balcony was lined with beds – 'No throwing beer bottles over the side!' Beer at Rs 1 a bottle, meals, rest and entertainment, the occasional horse race – even an ice-cream parlour! Everywhere you looked there were chaps lounging about or playing cards or billiards, all glad to eat hearty food and sleep between sheets, miles from the heat and horror of the front.

My job, three shifts a week, was to do anything Mrs Martyn required of me, from spending the evening at the reception desk, to tackling the very temperamental Bengali cook ('Since you speak the lingo, dear'). I had to deal with the day's and often the day before's post, organize laundry, talk to the men and so on. Occasionally I would go when I was not even on duty for some entertainment or other and Jessie often came with me, glad of the company.

I really began to feel my age, working there. When one of the lads chatting to me at the reception desk told me his age, his birthday, I realized he was born two days before Louise.

'Are you all right?' he said sweetly. I must have been gawping at him oddly.

'Yes!' I laughed. 'Of course.'

Many of them, except the few older officers, treated me like a sort of mother or auntie and it was a role I began to settle into. Middle-aged woman that I had become, any feelings about men were well damped down in me, I thought.

17

Of all the other Sunday afternoons I worked at the racecourse, I have forgotten almost everything. Yet that one afternoon … I can even recall conversations that were mundane in the extreme, engraved on my memory. I remember what I was wearing: a burnt-orange button-up dress with a red tie belt and slender red lapels and some comfortable brown leather sandals.

Being August, it was tremendously hot and muggy. We were all like a bunch of wet lettuces and there was an electric fan on the desk where I was working. Mrs Martyn seemed unusually tired that afternoon. She came dragging along out of the main sitting room, her face sagging with weariness. Some young homesick lad had no doubt been swamping her with eager tales. Her hair and her pale lilac dress hung limp in the humid air and she really was not at her best. I wondered if she was going down with something.

'Eleanora dear, could you stay on the desk for a while? I really am fit to drop.'

'Of course.' I was pretty happy doing any of the work there. None of it was too taxing – aside from dealing with the cook – and it was all rather chummy, made one feel useful. Mrs Martyn looked as if she would be better served by lying down with a good book. She had been to university and was married to one of the 'heaven born' of the Indian Civil Service. I knew that most

English socializing, centred round dogs and the marvels of other people's children, bored her to death.

'Oh, and see if you can finish off the post, would you please?' she asked, disappearing wiltingly towards the stairs. 'I've got rather behind.'

The entrance where I sat was in the middle of the building and inevitably a place of passage between the downstairs rooms. People roamed to and fro, needing to ask something or, being at a loose end, stopping for a chat with the motherly figure that I had now apparently become.

A soft, unsoldierly looking lad with hedge-hoggish hair ambled into view almost immediately. I looked up amiably.

'Where are you off to?'

'Me? To get me some coffin nails. Then I thought I'd look in on the barbers. I'll have to get shipshape for when they send me back.'

'Oh dear. Will that be soon?'

'Horribly.'

And so on.

The *dhobi*, a wiry, hardworking man, arrived with a barrowful of laundry and I tipped him from my own purse. Two more chaps stopped by to talk, both looking like fair-haired innocents.

'That Magnolia ice cream, Eleanora! I'm gunna be *dreaming* of that when we leave here!'

Where were they from? I asked. Northampton and near Skegness. Not that this meant a great deal to me, but I did my best, smiling and playing interested. They were sweet boys, only twenty-one or so, both wanting to tell me about their girlfriends at home. Gwen, who was a *real peach*.

211

In a lull, when they had gone off in search of ice cream, I was about to tackle the post. One of the *malis* came in to say crossly that beer bottles were flying off the balcony. I climbed up to admonish three rather tight, mischievous lads who looked barely old enough to be let out on their own.

Settling back behind the desk on the slippery leather seat of Mrs Martyn's chair, I pulled the pile of post towards me: an anxious note from a lad in the Lincs Battalion, 'I'm afraid I may have left my raincape behind.' Another, recently departed from the Turf Club, still banging on about the ice cream (though I must admit it was delicious). A man who had been a cook in Burma asking for a job. But of course, we had a cook. Unfortunately.

Someone started up on the piano in the main sitting room and strains of 'Apple Blossom Time' floated to me, the sound of it making me soppy.

Come along, Eleanora.

'Private Concern Please,' the next letter said on the envelope in a curling hand, large and careful as a child's. The letter was from the wife of one of the bearers in our employ:

'He has got a KEPT in Calcutta and spends all his earnings for her sake.' She was, she said, a woman with five children, a baby included. 'It is a year since we are enduring these troubles and now, owing to unspeakable dearness in every commodity, we are absolutely starving.'

I stared at the desperate little note, taken aback by the extent of my rage at this. I could picture the poor, cringing, abandoned woman in a threadbare cotton sari, a babe at her breast and the others all whining round her with hunger. Trying to picture the faces of our bearers, I thought, I'll set Mrs Martyn on this one – she'll make mincemeat of the miserable little sod, whoever he is.

I was holding the letter, so seething with fury that I only half registered the wheelchair which appeared through the side door, the person in it half-twisted round to speak to whoever was pushing it. I was sliding the letter back in its cheap envelope to lay it aside when I realized the men were approaching the desk. I looked up to greet the fellow in the wheelchair, an older officer, thin and slightly jaundiced, his right leg in plaster.

'*Nella?*'

It was said quietly, but it was a voice I would have known anywhere. It was like entering a dream. My eyes, my brain adjusted to the sight of the big man pushing the wheelchair. The loose white shirt, sleeves rolled to the elbow, the hair, clipped shorter now and just a little receded at the temples, the large eyes, the face. His face.

'Bill?'

There was another moment's silence as each of us came to terms with the space of twenty years between us, which, in that pause, became both so vast as to be unchartable yet also, all at once, to be nothing. I became very aware of myself, how I must look, my unusually bright frock, whether I looked like an old woman to him now.

'You know each other, do you?' the sick-looking man in the wheelchair said, obviously prone to speaking the obvious. Counter to this intelligence he then introduced us as if we had never set eyes on each other in our lives before.

'Bill, Bill Ashton, and this is Eleanora – she works here with the heroic Mrs Martyn. Where is the lady today, by the way?'

'She's resting,' I said with a polite smile.

This was all so impossible. What was Bill Ashton to me now? And yet, the moment was so charged that neither of us seemed to have any idea how to proceed from here. I became grateful for the other man, who, since we were both apparently struck dumb, chattered on, introducing himself as Tony.

'I just came to ask if the barber might be about today?' he said. 'Bill very kindly said he'd wheel me about. Course it is Sunday so might not be a good time?'

'I think I saw him arrive.' I pointed, glad to be able to take refuge in my job. 'Through there and keep going to the end.'

'Splendid. Let's go along and see,' Tony said, looking up at Bill. 'While I've got my personal bearer!'

'All right,' Bill said.

'Thanks, Eleanora!' Tony cried cheerfully as Bill wheeled the chair round. I pointed the way again because I could not think what else to do. There was Bill, just some man from my past who had arrived, another woman's husband. But there also walked a part of my heart. As he swivelled it round, Bill looked back at me for a second. I already knew he would come back.

I sat paralysed; thrown into utter turmoil. Bill still looked much the same. Older of course, but not greatly changed. In a way I did not want him to return. I could feel all those memories and feelings flooding back – the first times we were together, those days up in the little house by the river, making love, the precious hours lying together. There was Louise and all that happened afterwards that he knew nothing about. Sitting in Mrs Martyn's chair, I straightened my spine, trying to breathe.

And then I numbed myself. I tried to summon something in my defence. Bill would see me just as an old flame – of a brief, mistaken time. He knew nothing of what happened, of what I had endured on his account. And I didn't want him to know. I didn't want to feel. I wanted to greet him, cool as marble, because all that was in the past, and … I heard footsteps coming nearer and I already knew they were his, and my heart …

No one was around. Both of us knew this might not last for long. He hurried over to me. I saw that his face was thinner, that he was truly older. I stayed behind the desk.

'My God. *Nella!*'

His nerves seemed to leave him and he laughed suddenly, seeming delighted.

'Well, well,' I said, and started to laugh as well. 'What on earth are you doing here?'

'That chap in the chair – he joined up from one of the gardens and had a bad do of it, so I came to see him while I was here. I've had to bring Betty to Cal. It's no life over there at the moment. No one's safe.'

'So you're staying in Cal?' This felt like chit-chat – easy enough.

'No, not me.' He became tense again and I really saw then how exhausted he looked, how drained. 'I'll be going back – in the morning, in fact. Can't just stay here, while … Well, you know.'

We looked at each other. There was a moment of some sort of frankness.

'God, Nella,' he said, again. We stood, then he said, 'You really look just the same.'

After all of it, the absence, the not-being-the-wife, after Louise, after everything, I wanted to feel cold and angry. Angry with Bill for doing the decent thing and staying with Betty. Or to feel nothing. Yet, there we were. It would have been so simple just to walk into his arms. I know he would have been happy if I had, because it was still there – still and again, already – something essential between us.

There were footsteps, voices. Time running out like water.

'Well, I suppose I'd better get on,' I found myself saying, indicating the pile of letters on the desk.

'Yes,' he said. 'Of course. Lovely to see you, Nella.'

He moved away and the voices drew closer. Halfway across the foyer, Bill turned as I looked up and our eyes met, just as two young servicemen appeared from my left, laughing and chatting.

Bill raised his hand, briefly, and went through the other door.

'Eleanor?'

I didn't hear her at first. A week had passed since Bill. I was sitting out in the shade at Cowper Road, drenched in sweat in the steaming cauldron the garden became between the rains. The lawn was parrot green, the grass patched with mud and with puddles reflecting the light. Each fat-leafed plant was letting out hot, moist breaths and berries, previously shrivelled in the heat, now lay on the ground swollen and bursting.

My hair was more frizzy than usual, as any damp caused it to be. I was sitting at the bleached wooden table, my legs spread wide under the full skirt of my frock, little trickles of sweat wandering down between my breasts and down my sides, soaking my dress.

All that week I had felt strange, as if I was not quite there. Bill, there in front of me. It was like a wave picking me up, tumbling me over and over, stealing my breath. The reality of him, still in the world. Logically of course, this was obvious. But I still found myself wondering if I had dreamed it. And now, there was nothing to be done except settle down again.

Afterwards, when he had gone, I had rushed into the bathroom. It was a long time before I could stop shaking.

A crow landed on the grass, flapping and ungainly. It wore its usual suit of dark grey but with a black face, which, like all our house crows, made them look as if on some impulse they had plunged their heads into a heap of soot. It pecked at the ground, glanced at me as if I had caused it some offence and flew away.

I sipped my glass of tepid *nimbopani*, feeling foolish. For the last few weeks I had been out on a few dates with a quite pleasant army officer called John Brennan, which I saw now, almost with a sense of despair, was a ludicrous waste of both of our time.

Only once had I ever had those feelings, of opening, of letting yourself fall with complete trust into the love of another, something so whole and complete, that –

'Eleanor!'

Deidre was beside me suddenly, scrawnier than ever, in a limp, prawn-pink frock, her forehead shining with moisture.

'Are you all right, dear? You seem a bit out of sorts.'

I smiled, vaguely. 'Yes, thanks. Just a bit weary.'

'There's a letter for you.'

She put the pale blue envelope in my hand, with no nosiness – Deidre was very good like that. Handwriting I had not seen in many years.

'Have you heard?' Deidre was saying, wiping the insides of her elbows with a hanky. 'They've arrested all of them – that Mr Gandhi and the other Congress-*wallahs*. I mean, I know they want to make their point, but they could wait until we're not in the middle of this terrible war. Causing all this trouble. "Do or die!" I mean, what a thing to say – so extreme!'

I laid the letter casually on the table and fixed my face into a smile, waiting for her to leave.

Dear Nella,

My turning up like that must have been a bit of a shock – I'm sorry about that.

In the heat of the moment I did not think to tell you that I had run into your brother Hugh, about a month ago. The resemblance between you was so striking – even behind his large beard – that I asked him whether he was indeed another Storr-Mayfield!

He is doing relief work along the border. I must say he did not seem eager to fall into conversation or to talk about his family. But it seems, from another chap I met, that he has quite a reputation up there – has done some pretty heroic work, crossing back and forth to help get people out. I thought you would like to know I had met him – and that he seemed in good health.

It was very good to see you, Nella.

My very kindest regards,

Bill Ashton.

I stared at the letter for a very long time. It was so disappointing, so decent and so just the right thing for the situation we were in – which was no situation at all. A thoughtful, harmless note; a scrap of communication floating between us on a sea of feeling into which we must never again dive.

18

The envelope was addressed, to my huge irritation, to:

'LADY BYNGH, 42 COWPER ROAD, BALLYGUNGE, CALCUTTA'

Why had Persi taken it in to her head to do that? My elevated social status was not a detail I had previously mentioned to my landlady, who was hovering.

'You're not *Lady* Byngh, are you?' Deidre said, sounding perturbed, as if she had been shielding some sort of impostor in her house for the past year.

'In some respects, I am,' I said enigmatically as I tore open the envelope, thinking, damn Persi – now I'm going to have to explain about Archie and Deidre will think me a most dreadful strumpet. By this time, she was making no bones about peering over my shoulder at the telegram:

BARISAL 19 AUG 1942. 'RETURNING CAL STOP PERSI.'

'She's certainly economical,' Deidre remarked. 'This is your nun friend?'

She was looking at me now almost as if at a stranger. A baronet's estranged wife and a laconic nun all in one go were a bit much for a down-to-earth Methodist.

'Yes, Persi. Her real name is Marguerite Persimmon.' I was

smiling. It was so like Persi to include so little information.

'Travelling in the monsoon from all the way over there!' Deidre went to the hall table and hoiked a bunch of wilted flowers from a vase, then stood with them dripping in her hand as if wondering what she was intending to do with them. 'That won't be easy, will it? I do hope she'll be all right.'

'Knowing Persi, she'll most likely already be on her way. They have a house here in Calcutta.' I folded the pithy missive and suddenly grinned at Deidre. 'And those women are really quite something.'

In all the time I had been back in Calcutta, Persi had not been here. Though there had been regular letters, I had not seen her for years. I felt a rush of excitement, of the sort you might feel about coming home for Christmas, I suppose, had you a home to call your own and any affection for the Christmas season.

The Calcutta house of the Sisters of the Mission of St Agatha was an austere grey building on noisy Lower Circular Road, its upper windows flung open to let in a breath of air laden with the sounds of truck gears crunching and groaning, of engines and car horns and rickshaw bells. The front door was tucked in at the side and, above it, a little alcove contained a white statue of Mary – something that seemed rather Catholic, even though these nuns were staunch members of the Anglican Communion.

I had never visited the convent before because my only contact with the sisters, apart from Persi, had been at the Mother House in Barisal.

The bell tinkled somewhere inside and suddenly I felt like a child, waiting for admittance on a front doorstep in my orange frock and sodden sandals. It had rained, cooling the air a fraction, and in some sections of the road the rickshaw pullers were wading up to their shins.

When the door opened, I saw a reserved-looking Indian face peering out from under the white veil.

'Hello,' I said, already feeling foolish. There was something about nuns. 'I've come to see Sister Marguerite. I believe she's just arrived – from Barisal?'

'Oh …' I saw the penny drop and a gentle smile appear. 'Yes, come in.'

She glided ahead of me; white habit, sandals. The corridors were all painted a deep red, making me feel as if I was moving along inside the blood vessel of some large creature. We turned a corner, then the young sister stopped in a doorway.

She waited for the occupants to notice her, then said, 'Sister Marguerite, a visitor for you.'

Persi was already standing when I went into the room. At first glimpse she looked exactly the same as she had twenty years earlier.

'El-e-a-nor-a!' She held out her arms, beaming. Full of happiness, I hugged her back.

'Oh, Persi. It's been far, far too long!'

We drew back to look at each other. In fact, Persi, now fifty-four, did look very much the same. The skin was perhaps a little tighter on her face, giving it a hollowed-out look; there were more lines, a tiredness about her, but she had just completed a long and no doubt gruelling journey. Essentially, she was still the same old Persi. She did not comment on how I was looking all this time later, so perhaps the same was true of me.

It was only then that I took in the person standing just behind her, waiting to greet me. A warm sense of joy passed through me, of instantly reconnecting with my younger self.

'Oh, Sister Sushila! How wonderful – I didn't know you were here too!'

We held out our arms and she stepped in, laughing, to join the huddle.

'Hello, Miss Ellie – bless you. How are you?'

Sister Sushila had matured, her rounded cheeks and big eyes even more accentuated now she was in her forties. How beautiful she was! She had gained a little weight and was more curvaceous. As we stood, fondly taking each other in, I suddenly felt tearful. I was with the people who had known me longest and most fully in all the world. As Sushila's hand rested on my back, I thought, That hand helped deliver Louise, held her, nursed her … She saw my tears and stroked me, her eyes speaking with no need to say anything more.

'Now,' Persi said, breaking away. There were two other sisters in the room, one European and one Indian. 'This is Sister Joan, who is in charge here in Calcutta.'

A thin, middle-aged Englishwoman with a long, rather noble face, smiled at me, though with more politeness than warmth. I wondered if it was the light, or were her eyes of two different colours? I didn't dare look too hard.

'And this is Sister Martha who has come from Barisal with us.'

The young Indian sister gave a shy smile and tilt of her head.

'Sister Frances?' Persi said to the sister still lingering in the doorway. 'Might we please provide some tea?'

'There's trouble on the way,' Persi said as we drank the tea. 'That's why we're here – appalling time to travel but we made it in the

222

end.'

I felt myself tense with misgiving. Trouble here usually meant trouble on a huge scale.

'You may not have noticed,' Persi said. 'But there's a famine coming. It's already beginning out in the *mofussil* – and it's getting worse. Mother Ruth said that when it really bites, everyone will head for Calcutta and Sister Joan will need reinforcements.' She held her arms out. 'So, here we are. Sisters Sushila, Martha and I – the shock troops!'

There was a period of almost a month during which my family, all the family that really mattered, were in Calcutta. I was able, at last, to introduce Jessie Bell to Persi and Sister Sushila on a visit to the convent, when we took tea in a side room as before.

Neither of them said, 'I've heard so much about you,' which personally I always find one of the more worrying social platitudes.

Persi said, 'So I hear you're working for the Red Cross?'

And Jessie, in another of her shirtwaister frocks, sitting with her hands in her lap, looked much as she did during the interminable school prayer sessions. She talked a little about her work, then said, 'My mother has remarked on it – that there are more destitutes here in Cal than before. I wasn't sure if it was just her nerves making things seem worse. Do tell us more about what is happening in East Bengal.'

And they were off, two practical people always concerned for others, talking about the catastrophe that was looming in the east like another tidal wave.

Two weeks after Persi arrived, Jessie turned up one evening at 42 Cowper Road.

'Do come in, my dear.' I heard Deidre down in the hall, then the sound of sobbing. 'Eleanor!' Deidre shouted.

Robert Bell had seemed to be gently recovering, but that afternoon Mrs Bell had found him on the bathroom floor, already past help. I took Jessie's weeping form in my arms.

The funeral was such a small, sad occasion, with, apart from the minister, only Jessie, her mother and myself and a couple of kindly supporters from the Church of Scotland hostel present.

'I can't stay on here with mother,' Jessie said, only a couple of days later at Cowper Road. 'She's in such a state. I'll have to get her back up to Mussoorie.'

'But it's a hell of a way, Jessie,' I said. You had to travel all the way to Delhi and then an overnight north. 'Is this a good idea? There's trouble everywhere, riots and so forth – and your mother … How will you manage?'

Jessie shrugged in a defeated way. There would be nothing much for her in Mussoorie. Her Red Cross work would be over.

'Going up there is all she talks about. I'll just have to manage somehow.'

Within days, Jessie's active participation in the war effort was over. She and Ellen Bell boarded a train to Delhi and made their way up to the foothills of the Himalayas to wait out the war. For many more years – other than in letters – Jessie left my life, just as I was about to witness the unfolding of the most painful part of Persi's.

19

We went to the Club in Jorhat, finally – Roderick, Ginny and I. Persi said she would stay behind. She had no special attachment to the place. It was not her scene and she was good at being in her own company.

'I'll have a quiet evening,' she said, adding with a smirk, 'I can't stand the pace.' She was settled in a chair with the book about temples on her knees, a cinnamon-coloured shawl draped stylishly round her shoulders.

I was not sure if I was imagining that Persi seemed unusually quiet.

'Are you all right?' I asked stiffly. Being a caring soul did not come easily to me. There were any number of things that might be preying on her mind.

She looked up at me, one hand resting on the book. It was a curious look, a testing look, more than just a glance.

'What is it?' My heart started racing. Was there something she needed to say? Was she ill?

She looked away then, across the verandah to the night drawing softly in across the gardens. 'You go along,' she said. 'I'll be fine and dandy here. Does my heart good just looking at it.'

*   *   *

I sat in the back of the car, looking out as we bumped our way over the railway track near the gate of the tea estate, watching the smoky light of evening come down over the land.

'All right, Auntie Eleanora?' Roderick peered solicitously at me in the Ambassador's mirror as we thumped down particularly hard and Ginny squeaked, 'Lord, Pod, do be careful!'

'I'm quite all right,' I said.

And it was true. Looking at the two of them from behind, Roderick's disorderly hair, Virginia's neatly brushed, the top layer pulled back into a tortoiseshell hairclip in the style she favoured, I realized that I *was* all right. I felt more relaxed and of a piece than I had in years. It was as if something was beginning to shift in me. The child sheltered in Ginny's womb was not something I had to try and forget, to push away. Somehow, in filling myself with my own memories, taking them in and looking at them, I could separate things out better. I had what I had, in my time, albeit for such a brief time. I did not need to envy them.

The days had passed doing nothing of great note except for the paths I was re-treading inside me. Persi was quiet, perhaps tired, or if not tired, *something*. Ginny was easily worn out as well. There had been a drive to the river at Nimati Ghat – oh, the memories! Other than that, a wander round Jorhat Town, strolls round the estate, evenings spent quietly, the odd drink, games of Snakes and Ladders or cards. I discovered, to my surprise, that Persi was a demon bridge-player. So that was what they got up to in those convents.

What was so touching about these two young fools here was that they seemed to accept me. I suppose they had heard nothing much about me to put them off. They needed family and the fact that I was what had arrived did not appear to disappoint them, even if Ginny was wary of me. Every so often, whenever there was a chance and especially when he and I were alone together, Roderick would ask me about Hughie. What was he like, did he resemble him in any way, not looks, but *essentially*? It was touching to see how eager the dear boy was. Eventually, just a few nights ago, he had worked his way round to the question I least wanted to deal with and about which I hardly knew how to be truthful – Hughie's death.

'Sadly, we never knew exactly,' I told him. 'He was on the border in '42, that I know for certain.' Thanks to Bill. 'He was helping refugees coming out of Burma. A lot of the tea planters got involved since they were on the spot, and other odd bods who were around – I suppose you could say Hughie was one of them. Very dangerous work. Heroic, you might say. That was the last we ever heard. Mother waited until long after it was all over, but ...'

I felt certain muscles starting to clench within me and I had to control my voice. Didn't want to be a tearful old trout, embarrass the boy. And this seemed the best version to present to him.

'Mother was getting ready to decamp to England, in the early weeks of '47. So, it was a case of now or never. She decided to have a memorial service for him before they left. It would have felt odd to do it in England. So – it was February '47. February the fifteenth. It was ...'

I drew in a breath. I had been about to say 'bloody'. Because it was. It was harrowing, emotional, in the most zipped-up British way. In fact, what was so terrible about it was going through the form, the church words, which can be comforting, I do appreciate. But it was in the church in Bombay, miles from Assam and done by a vicar who didn't know Hugh or any of us. He had

227

seen it all before, but it really meant nothing to him. I stood there in a hat and coat and we could have been in some village church anywhere. None of it had anything whatsoever to do with Hughie. The Hughie who I had not seen since 1938, in England, looking wrong there. Then Bill's letter, saying he was in good health. All I could hope was that even if it had been the death of him, returning home to India had somehow brought him back to himself. Because at that time, I really did believe he was dead.

Roderick was waiting.

'It was – well, you know how these things are.'

'Nothing much to do with the actual person who's died?' Roderick said.

I gave him a grateful look.

'Mother wanted to draw a line. Accept that he really had died, and we had to go on. In a way it did help. We were leaving and Hughie was staying here.'

'I suppose he died near here somewhere?' Roderick said. His round face crumpled for a second, but there were no tears this time.

'Didn't your mother tell you *any* of this?' I asked, as gently as I could manage, since I felt pretty furious with Jennifer.

Roderick shook his head. His eyes were like round pools and I was reminded of the little lad I met, briefly, that last day in Maidenhead when I ate lunch with Hughie and Jennifer.

'She simply refused to talk about him – ever. Or about any of your side of the family. I never really knew anything, hardly even that you existed. I could remember you coming, once, like a sort of shadow.'

Which, I thought but did not say, might have been just as well.

'I do remember that you gave me those chocolate teddy bears though.'

We both laughed.

'Children remember the important things,' I said.

But as we drove along in the dusk, I thought of Persi, sitting in the bungalow, the way she had looked at me. Should I be asking her whether she wants to – dread words – *talk about it*? After all, when did Persi and I talk about anything? When had we ever? Persi was a doer. *Why dig it all up?* she'd say.

Jorhat was so familiar, even now. The straggling outskirts of the little town, still half country. There were some new buildings of course, but the drive out along Club Road was much the same, the bungalows with their neat gardens on each side. Every corner of the place gave me back memories of my young life. And of him.

JORHAT GYMKHANA CLUB – the old brass plaque on the wall as you came in. It all looked so much the same and yet, as the car stopped, something in me loosened – my feelings really did keep surprising me – and a warm sense of peace went through me, almost like a snifter of Scotch.

It was all so long ago now, Bill and I. And it was good while it lasted. I might even say it was beautiful. Good God, what was happening to me? But to know, for certain, that even if it was all wrong and at the most inappropriate time, I knew that at least once in my life I had loved someone and been loved in return. I had that. It was truly something. And what's more, Persi had had it too. I felt a great wash of tenderness for all of us – him, Persi, me, so that I fear I must have been sitting there with a half-soaked, soppy kind of expression on my face.

'Ready, Auntie?'

Roderick was standing by the car door. I looked up at him and really smiled then, and saw him register something in my face, something he would never fully understand. But he seemed to comprehend this sudden joy in me and he smiled back.

'Time for a drink,' I said, grunting a little as I climbed out of the car.

It had scarcely changed. We drank sitting on the old cane chairs in the cosy gloom of the bar downstairs because outside, the night was growing chilly. And I was relieved. Upstairs, in the half-light of the balcony, I might have had to sit with the ghost of a large, bear-like man sitting close to the balustrade, watching me in that quiet way of his.

But I did tell Roderick I wanted a quick walk round for old times' sake. I climbed up to the deserted balcony. The lights were off, every table quiet. I stood breathing in the night smells, the grass, threads of cigarette smoke, a hint of Scotch; smells which I was not even sure were from now or from then. There, over there, was where I first saw him. White shirt, sleeves rolled up. There, by the balcony, where we had leaned, our shoulders grazing each other's, on a night much like this. A tender feeling round my heart. Those stolen days upriver. *But he didn't love you enough to leave her* ...

He did love me, though. He was guilty, afraid and decent and he loved his young sons. He took everyone home to live somewhere near Reigate.

And he loved me. He did.

It was all a long time ago.

*   *   *

230

'I got you a Scotch,' Roderick said, raising his own glass to me as I joined them down in the bar.

'You're a dear boy.' I twinkled at him, full of my new buoyancy, which they could sense. Ginny was on *nimbopani*. Alcohol made her sick, she said.

'Does it look the same?' she asked.

'Just the same.' I sat back, crossing my legs, feeling strangely younger for a moment.

They introduced me to a couple of other planters, but it was not the main Club night and there was only a scattering of people in the place. The three of us chatted, Roderick bemoaning his lack of sporting prowess.

'I've never been any good at golf or cricket,' he said apologetically. 'So I feel a bit of a spare part around here.'

'Yes, it can certainly be a passport to a social life,' I said. Bill had described it as his salvation.

'Well, I don't mind,' Ginny said. 'Quite honestly I can't think of anything more boring than having to sit through games of cricket. Do you like sport, Auntie?'

'Depends who's playing,' I said. 'And whether there's a decent drink to go with it.'

'Isn't it usually tea with cricket?' Virginia frowned.

'Ah, well – there's always the noble hip flask.' I winked at her. With my first pegs warming my insides, I was feeling relaxed.

'You're very naughty, Auntie,' she giggled.

They chattered on a bit about this and that. The room felt cosy. Roderick fetched more drinks. I sat back, warm and hazy and, increasingly, was overcome by a loose, nothing-to-lose, now-or-never feeling. I wanted to be known.

'D'you know,' I said, tipsily, when there was a lull in the

conversation. 'I met the love of my life here – in the bar upstairs.'

That got their attention of course. I didn't tell all – not my style. Only that he was married, doomed love and so on. They were startled. No one imagines older people ever to have done or felt anything.

Then Ginny, in her frowning, good-girl way, said, 'But you *were* married, weren't you – I thought?' She looked uncertainly at her husband as if she might have put her foot in it.

So I told them about Archie. Some of it, anyway. I didn't mention shunting. Not as such. Their faces – wondering if they were allowed to laugh.

'I know,' I said, laughing first. 'That's why it only lasted six weeks.'

20

1942-43

Thus began one of the most distressing periods of my life – of all our lives.

Persi and the others arrived in Calcutta just before another great cyclone in October '42, which ravaged East Bengal, wrecking the crops, impregnating everything with salt and making everything many times worse. But the sisters there were already well aware what was coming.

Winston Churchill and the British Government had already, in the spring of that year, ordered the Rice Denial Scheme, exporting rice out of the area, both to feed the war effort and to remove it in case the Japanese invaded, denying them supplies to feed their armies. No consideration was given to feeding the local population who had grown it. Hoarding began. Prices rocketed. The Viceroy, Linlithgow, played down the whole situation.

'Even if they find any rice for sale it's unaffordable,' Persi had told us that afternoon when she arrived back in Calcutta. She spoke calmly, but I have never, before or since, seen her so quietly charged with rage. 'And on top of that, they started rounding up the boats all along the coast – to stop the Japanese getting their hands on them as well. So fishing, transport – all wiped out in one fell swoop. There was scarcely any food before. There's nothing coming across from Burma these days.'

That famine was coming was obvious to Mother Ruth, in charge of the Mother House in Barisal. And the convent was an obvious magnet for those among the desperate on the delta who could reach it.

'By the time they came to us, they'd tried everything,' Persi said. 'They'd sell everything first – the doors, windowsills, cooking utensils. When there was nothing left, they would come into the town. They were eating snails and rats by then.' Persi looked straight ahead as she spoke. 'They don't have the energy to bury each other. The vultures aren't going hungry.'

There was a silence.

'How's Mother Ruth going to manage?' I asked Persi, eventually. 'Without you there?'

Persi gave me one of her looks.

'We were only getting people from the surrounding area. Believe me, duckie, most of them are heading in this direction.'

Calcutta had already received many of the gravely sick and other refugees who had poured through Assam from Burma in a most terrible mental and physical state. Now, more harrowing still, came a wave of destitute famine victims from the surrounding countryside, thousands arriving, desperate, to crumple like paper on the streets. The cyclone was the final straw on top of everything that the policies of the British Government and the war raging across our borders combined to visit upon Bengal.

The city was already bursting at the seams with its influx of military personnel and traffic, the roads choked with trucks. We had blackout regulations, the ARP, all the things one heard about from London and other cities in Britain, while we waited for the Japanese to start our own blitz.

Lo and behold: in the December of '42 and again in January we had several nights of bombing – not far from us in fact, since they were aiming for the Kidderpore docks to the south of the city. Rumours circulated that it was all caused by Subhas Chandra Bose and the Indian National Army, the Indian soldiers who had crossed over to fight with the Japanese. Bose was a Bengali and, from the British point of view, he was seen as a terrific traitor. INA propaganda leaflets were found in the rubble afterwards – but no one knew for sure whether they had been planted.

All through that winter, they came. The trickle became a flood. There had always been the poor on the streets, but the numbers swelled. The starving people of Bengal came on foot, on carts, on trains, pouring into Sealdah Station along Lower Circular Road, not too far from the convent. Many of them did not move far from Sealdah – they were already so weak and there were feeding stations set up on the railways.

We had to learn to see what was before us. The family encamped under a tree on the pavement close to the forecourt of Sealdah Station might, at first glimpse, have seemed almost normal – vagrants perhaps. Focus your eyes more intently and you would begin to make out the stick-thin limbs and swollen bellies of the children, or the father lying beside them, who might seem to be just resting. Look yet more closely: the abandoned look of his wasted body, the stretched skin of his jaw, the swollen lower limbs, all betokening something more extreme. Perhaps he was even already dead. You might take note of the hollowed-out face of the mother, the way she squatted, staring ahead as if haunted, her breath coming in shallow, panting gasps. You might see the thin diarrhoea trickling uncontrollably down the legs of one or more of the children. And you would have to take in the horrifying reality that before your eyes was a family who were starving to death.

This was how it was at first, especially if, like me, you were sheltered by living and working in Ballygunge, in an office block untouched by such realities.

More came, and more.

First of all, some of the hungry arriving at Howrah or Sealdah Railway Stations, if they had the energy, would head for the middle of the city, which offered the greatest concentration of restaurants, bins for raiding, shops and people from whom a few *annas* might be begged. Anyone with money could access food at any time throughout the famine, though prices were high. Life continued much as ever for very many people, eating in restaurants, socializing. It was the poor, the rural poor especially, who fell into the chasm of hunger and destitution.

One day, early in '43, when I got home from work, Deidre hurried to meet me as I came through the door. I could see from her face that something was up.

'It's just terrible, what's happening!' she burst out. She seemed shrilly angry and I could not work out what was wrong for a moment. 'I found Leela shooing them away from the door! There were two women with children and a baby.' The words tumbled out of her. 'It was so thin it looked like, I don't know, a mummy, or a little monkey. The women were skin and bone – heaven knows how old they were, they looked *ancient* but they can't have been. They kept putting their hands up to their mouths, you know, the way they do and saying, '*Phan ... phan ...*' That's all they think they can ask for – boiled rice water! I mean, in the name of heaven!'

'What did you do?' I asked her, picturing this dreadful scene.

'Well, I didn't have any rice water,' she said helplessly. 'It was four in the afternoon. I gave them some glucose biscuits and a couple of mangoes – oh, and a banana. And ...' Her voice cracked. 'The children started fighting over the banana, like little animals. It was awful.'

She looked at me, her face stretched, appalled.

'We must do *everything* we can – all of us.'

As the weeks passed we were confronted with the hordes starving on the streets, their very numbers at times defeating any impulse towards charity or helping. The city itself could not keep up. The destitute were reduced to drinking rainwater off the streets, contaminated with God knew what. Diseases broke out, preying on the weakest and most vulnerable: diarrhoea, malaria, cholera all began to spread. The burning *ghats* were at full stretch.

One evening, passing along Park Street, where there were many eating houses, I saw a gaggle of people fighting round the refuse bin belonging to a restaurant. In the half-light, I saw two men beat a woman to the ground and snatch from her the piece of slimy waste she had managed to pick out. Even in the bustle of Chowringee, in front of the most high-class arcade shops, you might almost trip across a skeletal figure lying at the edge of the pavement or in the gutter. You might press a few *annas* into their hand, but it was hard to know what else to do. Often, shameful as it is to admit, I know all of us found ourselves shutting off and walking past, as if we had not seen, as if we did not know we had a sure meal ahead of us, because it was so overwhelming.

The city felt more and more chaotic, but there were attempts to help. Government feeding programmes were set up hastily and all the churches, temples and mosques moved into action to meet the desperation of this ragged, starving tide. Deidre busied herself with the Methodists; the Friends Ambulance had a programme to feed children.

By January, I was working with the sisters. I carried on with two evenings at the Turf Club after work, not wanting to leave Mrs Martyn in the lurch. But for the other evenings and whatever time I could spare at the weekend, I was with Persi, Sushila and the others.

There were difficult conversations in the convent about how best to help. An aspect of the famine that especially upset the sisters was that women, desperate and alone, were being prostituted for food and even sold to the army. There was a long conflab about whether part of the convent could be spared as a refuge for women. In the end, with all the best will, they decided they just could not cope with this.

'So many of us are already working in hospitals,' Sister Joan said. She looked haunted and worn out already. 'There just aren't enough of us to manage here – and the danger of us spreading an epidemic among ourselves …'

'We can go out and offer what help we can,' Sushila pointed out in her steady voice. 'We can't help everyone, but God will guide us to do what we can.'

Groups of sisters would be on the streets at various times of day.

They would go to the feeding stations to offer what medical care they could to those waiting in line. I almost always went out with Persi and Sushila. I wanted to help, of course, felt driven to, but I also just wanted to be with them; it enabled me to keep an eye on Persi. She had such a tendency to give of herself at any cost that I was afraid for her health. She had been a long time in Barisal, which was a cleaner, more rural place. Calcutta was heading towards its hottest months and was already covered in filth and the ordure of the mortally diseased who lined the streets. Yet Persi and Sushila, in doing what their calling entreated them to do – to serve God and serve the poor – both shone with a kind of glorious energy.

Once, in the early days, when we went as far as Sudder Street, I saw Deidre among the Methodists, who were ladling out watery rice along the seemingly endless queues. She looked startled, seeing me there with three women in habits, and I introduced Persi to her.

'Ah,' Persi said breezily, 'you're Eleanora's latest nursemaid, are you?'

'Well, really I'm her landlady,' Deidre said, bemused. I had never fully explained about Persi and realized I might have to now.

'We're doing what we can,' Deirdre said quietly, looking along the lines of emaciated, raggedly clothed people. 'Though God knows it never feels much.'

'Bless you,' Persi said. At last, they smiled at each other.

The little we could really offer was dressing sores, trying to stop infections spreading, administering eye drops if we had any, giving people clean water to drink and sometimes getting someone into one of the overcrowded hospitals. It felt so inadequate, but in fact you could sense that even a crumb of human care was something, at least in mental terms. The sight of nuns seemed to reassure people.

But others came to help in Sudder Street and at the feeding programmes and, after a while, we found it better to stay for almost all the time in Lower Circular Road. We would work our way along the street. As the weeks passed, the sights became worse. Never in my life before had I seen people in such a state of emaciation that they barely seemed human, more like puppets made of wood and string. One had to struggle with feelings of horror.

It was hard to understand how they could still be alive. Women with only flaps of skin as breasts tried to suckle infants who were bony as tiny bags of kindling. And sometimes, of course, they were not alive any more, but still lay in the streets, more and more of them every day.

21

'I take it you have checked it today?'

Persi was inspecting us like a sergeant major as we stood in the corridor of the convent: Sister Sushila, young Sister Martha, who was a newly trained nurse, and me. The wide doors of the chapel were open and even I took reassurance from the sight of the quiet space inside with its silent cross and white-clad altar.

Sister Martha nodded, looking down at the black medical bag on the floor beside her, its handle reinforced with a skein of hairy string. Under my arm I had a length of tough canvas, stinking of the disinfectant with which it was vigorously scrubbed after each venture out into the Calcutta streets.

'*Pani.*' Sister Sushila held up one of the water carriers, a container rather like a small milk churn. She made one of her head gestures, gentle, yet also assertive, towards the door. 'We must go. Let us pray, sisters.'

She looked at Persi, who lowered her head and closed her eyes. Sister Martha and I did the same. I was a 'sister' for the moment. In the background came the sound of someone pumping water out in the covered part of the compound, the clink of cooking vessels and the sound of the endless rain.

'Blessed Lord, Father of mercies and God of all comfort,' Sushila said, 'we beseech thee, look down in mercy and compassion upon the suffering and afflicted of this land, and upon us, your humble servants, who seek to bring them succour …'

Godless as I was, most of the time I was glad of their prayers, because the strength to carry on had to come from somewhere. My days were still spent in the privileged, fan-cooled tedium of office work at Imperial. Ciggies for the troops! The tobacco companies weren't complaining, naturally. The office was full of people shutting out of their minds the other world of the streets below. I always seemed to be happier with the misfits and odd religious types. Even so, sometimes as the summer grew hotter, it was hard not to sink into despair, wondering whether Calcutta might just crumble into a pile of rubble and human sludge under the weight of the war and the thousands of starving incomers bursting its seams.

Full of a dread which had become worse on every such outing, I followed these white-clad women out into the uncertain dusk light, into the swish of August rain falling steadily on Lower Circular Road and the charnel house which this street had, over this year, become.

The four of us walked up the right-hand side of Lower Circular Road, accompanied by the usual mayhem of traffic and fumes, the honking of horns, rickshaw bells and men pushing flat, laden carts, yelling to get people out of their path, their feet sloshing through water up to their ankles.

All of us wore sandals, since a few steps would have soaked leather shoes. Persi walked in front with the medical bag, then Sushila, leaning slightly to one side to balance the weight of the water canteen. I followed her, carrying our makeshift 'stretcher', with little Sister Martha behind with the other metal can of water.

Sushila's hips swaying in front of me in her white habit were a reassuring sight. Being with her and Persi was like coming home: a thread of memory and love extended between us. Sushila, who had brought my little Louise into the world. Once or twice she turned, to make sure we were still keeping up, and we would exchange a smile, each with water running down our faces, our clothes already almost soaked through. We did not bother with umbrellas because we had so many other things to carry.

It was always unnerving as we made our way round the bodies lining the street, like soaked bundles of rags in the dusk, not knowing what new form of wretchedness and distress would meet us each time. And it felt pathetic, being able to do so little except to offer water, to bind a wound, to give a kind word or blessing, before moving on to one of the hundreds more. All we could do was to add a little human – and the sisters no doubt thought, divine – comfort to the work of the feeding stations. The famine hospitals were full to the brim and from what one heard the conditions were little better than being on the streets. We felt our helplessness, but we carried on.

The rain began to let up a little and the sky lightened, even though the sun was going down. Persi pointed into the station forecourt and we followed her, sloshing through the water streaming across it in our sodden clothing. People were huddled under any sort of shelter they could find – the station wall, a tree. Anyone with enough energy watched our arrival with a vague air of expectation. Persi bent over one family, exchanged a few words – nearly everyone spoke Bengali – offered water, examined the man's leg. They stared impassively up at her, made small, acknowledging movements with their heads.

We found Urvashi round at the side of the station building,

243

a place we had taken to checking because people sometimes took refuge there out of sight. Immediately, we saw the outline of a young woman's slender hips as she lay curled on her side, the green of her cotton sari darkened by the wet.

She was thin, though not the thinnest we had seen by a long way. Her arms were bent up next to her head, one supporting it, the other covering her as if she was expecting a blow. There was a train getting up steam in the station behind and she had not heard us approach, so that when Sushila bent and gently touched her arm, saying, '*Didi?*' she jumped, violently recoiling against the wall. She looked frightened out of her wits, but she lacked the strength to get up.

As first Sushila, then Persi, spoke to her kindly, she managed, with their help, to drag herself up to a sitting position. Her face contorted as she moved, pulling her knees in close to her. She was obviously in considerable pain.

Martha and I stood aside, and it was not until later that we found out anything the girl had said. I watched Persi and Sushila as they squatted down in the mud by the smut-covered wall, asking her questions. How in tune they looked, working together. It only came home to me then that in all this time, twenty-three years, they had been working side by side.

Sushila rested a hand gently on the girl's arm. The girl kept moving her head, seemingly in agreement. Martha and I looked at each other. We could already see what would be decided. This was someone we could actually help.

After a time, Sushila stood up and took Persi's hand to pull her upright as well, the way a wife might help her husband.

'She can come with us,' Persi said, coming over to me. 'She doesn't seem to be sick. I'm not sure what's happened. She's injured and I don't think she can walk – let's get the stretcher ready.'

'Persi, why don't we put her in a rickshaw?' I said. 'I'll pay, if you like? It'll be heavy getting her all the way back.'

'No, no …' Persi waved my offer away, the old habit of never spending any money on anything not strictly necessary. I was a bit fed up with her. I was trying to spare her – and all of us.

When we opened out the canvas, laying it on the ground, which was muddy and spotted with shiny coal smuts, the girl looked quite horrified at what we had in mind and immediately began to try to get to her feet.

'I will walk,' she insisted, making a dismissive gesture towards our ideas of how to transport her.

She did manage for a while, leaning on Sushila and Martha while Persi and I followed behind carrying all the other things. I had the medical bag in one hand and a half-full canteen of water in the other and it was heavy going. Halfway along the Lower Circular Road the girl's knees buckled. We struggled to get her on the canvas on the wet, dirty pavement, with people hurrying past us.

A man who looked like an office worker saw our difficulties and came over to help. He seemed kindly enough, but at the sight of him up close to her, the girl started screaming her head off. Persi thanked him and asked him to leave us. Taking a corner each, we lugged the stretcher and all the other things the final stretch to the doors of the convent. Sister Joan opened the door, her face falling into even graver lines at the sight of us all.

'No infection, I'm pretty sure,' Persi said immediately.

Sister Joan called Sister Gertrude, the nurse in charge of the infirmary, and we helped the girl upstairs and into the comfort and care of one of the beds. I wondered, as she lay down, once more curled on her side, if it was the first bed she had ever been in.

We did not find out anything about the girl that evening apart from her name: Urvashi. Sister Gertrude chased us out of the infirmary, ordering, 'Go and get dry all of you!'

I always brought spare clothes with me while the monsoon was in full spate. Once we had all changed, the four of us sat in the kitchen for a cup of tea. Sushila and Martha each wore a kind of white cotton snood over their hair and Persi had put another veil on. It was a long time since I had seen Persi's hair.

The kitchen was a long, quarry-tiled room at the far end of the building, with a range and worktable at one end and a smaller table and chairs where one could sit at the other. Sushila made *chai* at the stove, the gas cylinder hissing comfortingly. There were not many spare moments in any day, but after our rounds I would often sit with them for a little while in the dim electric light, before cycling home.

'Here, take tea.' Sushila brought us each a cup of sweet, milky tea, with a few glucose biscuits in the saucer.

'Thanks, dearie,' Persi said looking up at her, wearily.

Sushila patted her shoulder before sinking on to her chair. Their eyes met for a moment in which I realized fully, for the first time, that what I was seeing was love. I knew that look, knew it from Bill, the frank, warm openness of it. I was moved by it, glad for dear, devoted Persi. How that woman could love, in her odd, backhand way. I blessed Mother Ruth inwardly for allowing her and Sister Sushila to come here together, rather than separating them, trying to kill off every warm and devoted impulse the way the churches often have.

When I had been with them in Barisal, Sushila had not long arrived herself from her training in Calcutta. They had clearly been fond of each other then. But after twenty years, I could see that Persi's heart, wounded all those years ago by the loss of Enid, had long found its home in Sushila and discovered a mutual devotion. The honesty of this love was sweet and warming to see.

'So, what about the girl?' I said.

Persi put her cup down and tucked each of her hands into the sleeves of her habit.

'From what she said' – Persi looked down at the pitted wooden table-top – 'she's been assaulted. Numerous times. There are injuries. That's why she's in such pain. She didn't say much, except that she's a widow.'

'*Widow?* She looked barely old enough to be married, let alone widowed!' I exclaimed.

'I think it is a very bad story,' Sushila said softly. 'Maybe she will say more later on.'

'She's very beautiful,' I said, remembering the girl's face, gaunt, but with huge, soulful eyes.

'She is,' Martha agreed. 'Almost like a film star.'

I heard a faint 'Huh' from Persi and Sushila smiled at me as if to say, Well, we all know what she thinks of *that* sort of thing!

There was silence as we drank our tea. None of us wanted to talk about the streets or dwell on what we knew still to be out there. Martha excused herself and said goodnight. When she had gone, Persi looked at me.

'Heard from Mumsie lately?'

'Oh, she's all right. I had a letter a couple of weeks ago. She says she's learning to knit socks.'

'Huh. That sounds out of character,' Persi said. We all laughed. 'What next? Running a children's crêche?'

'Not everyone can be good with children, like you,' Sushila reproached her.

'*Me?*' Persi retorted. 'I'm lousy with children. Why in heaven's name d'you think I joined an order?'

Sister Sushila made another of her comical faces at me.

'You're very *naughty*,' she said, wagging a finger at Persi and laughing. 'A very bad person.'

'It's true though.' I carried on the teasing. 'She's absolutely terrible with children. And a dreadful influence.'

Sushila's full-flowing laugh poured out of her. Persi looked down her nose at me and spooned sugar into her tea.

'A good deal better than my actual mother though,' I added fondly.

'Huh,' Persi said again, cup to her lips. 'I suppose somebody had to say it.'

'Very bad!' Sushila's cheeks were still dimpling. 'I am surprised you have grown up into such a good person, Ellie.'

'That is debatable,' I said.

I could see both Persi and Sushila stifling yawns, so I drank up my tea and stuffed my rolled-up dress and underwear into my bag.

'Best be off,' I said. 'We all need our beds.'

'You could sleep here,' Sushila offered. With her snood now hanging over one ear, she looked like a sleepy little girl.

'It's fine. It's not that late.' Strangely it never bothered me, cycling home at night, even with the streets blacked out. In fact, I rather liked it. For all that was going on in the city, the ride home was usually peaceful in Ballygunge. And Cowper Road was only ten minutes away.

'All right. Good night then, Ellie,' Sushila said.

'Night, Eleanora,' Persi said through a yawn. 'Go careful.'

I left the two of them sitting there, flagging with exhaustion, but so comfortable in each other's company. It was not the most remarkable of half-hours, not at the time, but with all that happened soon after, I have never forgotten it.

At that time, I felt I was living several separate lives. There was the haven of Cowper Road, insulating us, to a large degree, from the outside. There were Imperial Tobacco and the Turf Club, both the worlds of Europeans. At the Turf Club, working with Mrs Martyn, it was not hard to present a cheerful front. We had at least some idea of the hell the hostel offered a respite from.

But I kept seeing Bill everywhere, expecting him to appear, even though he said he was going back up country. When I walked about the city, if I saw a certain kind of European woman of the right age I wondered, is that Betty Ashton? My mind could be cool and controlled; Bill was married and all that was long behind me. My poor, silly heart, though, had been stirred up again and when I was there at work, half-occupied with sorting the day's post or some other task, it all kept coming back to me.

The other life, though, was the convent and the streets: the hell that was playing out for the poorest Indians across Calcutta and throughout Bengal. If you decided not to close your eyes and ignore it, venturing out each time with Persi, Sushila and the others was like opening a trapdoor and plunging down into the destitute, starving and diseased reality that lay about us. No wonder, most of the time, it felt safer not to let one's mind dwell on it.

*   *   *

The girl, Urvashi, was recovering steadily. Goodness knows exactly what hell she had been put through, but she was young and now, resting in a comfortable bed and being fed well, her health and the wounds soon improved.

I went to see her in the infirmary upstairs in the convent. There was a room with six beds in it and two single side rooms. In the ward with Urvashi, on one of the black metal bedsteads with their neat white bedding, lay two of the nuns, both of them English. Near the door, were a very elderly sister whose eyes twinkled at me as I passed her and another younger sister suffering a dose of some sickness, asleep.

Urvashi was lying quite still with her eyes open. I could see the angles of her face; a longish nose, sharp cheekbones, big eyes. Though very thin, she had not passed into complete starvation and did not seem ill. Injured, hungry and exhausted, but not sick. When she caught sight of me, she jumped nervously and half sat up.

'It's all right,' I said soothingly, gesturing that she should not disturb herself. How old was she, I wondered. Sixteen? Seventeen? No older, surely.

I perched on the chair by her bed and she sat up painfully, bending her knees close to her. I asked if she spoke Bengali and we continued the conversation in that language.

'Are you feeling better?' I asked.

She gazed at me. There was a luminosity about her. It may have been the thin face and huge eyes but she looked somehow exalted, feverish or joyful, as if she had had some kind of revelation. Yes, she inclined her head. Better every day. Everyone is so kind. This place is like heaven. Then, earnestly, she said, 'Tell me about

250

Jesus Christ? He is helping me?'

Oh Lord, I thought.

'He was a very good man, very holy man,' I said. 'But you should ask one of the sisters. Sister Marguerite – does she come to see you?'

Urvashi gave another brilliant smile. Yes, Sister Marguerite, she would ask her. And my name was?

I told her Ellie – it seemed easier to say.

'Ellie,' she repeated.

'I'm happy that you are feeling better,' I said, getting up. I patted her knee. 'You just rest now. I'll see you again.'

I did not see her though, not for some time.

Only a day later, while I was working at the Turf Club, Persi, Sushila and two other sisters set out along Lower Circular Road as usual. I did not find out what had happened until I went to the convent the next evening.

Even when the sister on the door let me in, there was something in the atmosphere. She was a young Indian nun and her face wore a look of quiet dismay. The place was hushed, something more than the usual calm of the convent, and as I went in I glimpsed the slender, white-clad figures of two of the sisters kneeling in the chapel, which was also not normal at this time of day.

'Is that Eleanora?'

Mother Joan heard our voices from her office and came along the corridor so briskly that her veil billowed like a sail behind her. Mother Joan was in her fifties, a plain, unadorned, academic sort of woman. The skin of her thin ankles below the habit looked dry and tired, especially against the brown, monsoon sandals.

'Come to my office a moment, Eleanora.'

'What's happened?' I tried, following her impressive figure along the corridor, but she was plainly not going to speak until we got into her little cell of an office, a dark wood desk squeezed inside and space for little more but the chair.

She turned and in the window's light I could see she looked distraught.

'Sister Sushila was taken ill last night, while they were out on their rounds. Very suddenly. It's cholera.'

My mind reeled. '*Cholera?* Is she … ?'

'She's here.' Mother Joan raised her eyes to indicate the infirmary above us. 'I'm … I mean, I'm in a quandary.'

I could see she was really distressed, that she needed me to say something reassuring. Who else did she have to ask?

'You mean, she perhaps ought to go to the hospital?'

Mother Joan sank down on to the chair behind her desk. For a second, I imagined her as the headmistress of a girls' school in England, in a dull-coloured suit and with tightly curled hair. But no – she had chosen this, a life far from home and faced with difficulties she could never have imagined as a young novice. I wondered if she had had even a wink of sleep the night before.

'We're in the middle of an epidemic,' she said. 'The hospitals are overflowing. There are all the starving who need to be taken in there. I'm just so concerned that … Obviously we're keeping her in complete isolation, so far as … Except …' She looked up at me then. 'Sister Marguerite won't hear of sending her anywhere. She has *insisted* – she wants to nurse her herself.'

Our eyes met, the moment heavy with implications. Horror seeped through me. Dread like a pressure within my chest. Cholera. Sushila. And Persi.

'Are you sure it's cholera?'

Mother Joan nodded. 'I've seen it before. But it's possible she has another infection on top of it. We're taking every precaution we can. But it's bad. She's become very ill very quickly. I really don't know …'

Unable to go on, she looked away, through the window into the compound. Seeing tears in the eyes of this disciplined, reserved woman moved me deeply.

'There's no budging Sister Marguerite. You know what she's like. Whatever I say, there's no answer to obedience, not to anything ...' She shrugged.

'Just to love,' I said.

Our eyes met in silence.

'Just looking in on them should be all right,' Mother Joan said. 'The disease is carried in food and water. I don't know how she's caught it, but …'

I crept, weak with dread, up the stairs to where the two side rooms of the infirmary were, close to the little ward where Urvashi lay. The air was heavy with heat and moisture, the whole city seeming to sweat out the monsoon humidity, and the house felt so silent, as if everyone in it was praying with every fibre.

Sister Martha was sitting on a chair outside the door. She stood up as I appeared, with a tired, sad expression. We moved a short distance along the corridor.

'Can I go in?' I whispered.

Martha made one of those yes–no gestures with her head. 'It is dangerous for you,' she said. 'Sister Marguerite is staying there. We cannot budge her.' Again, she moved her head ambiguously.

'Let me just look in.'

I opened the door, silently. Another small room: a bed, bedside table, chair, and wooden blinds half-covering the window. Although the window was open, the day was suffocating and the room smelled bad, edged with bodily wastes. Sushila lay on the bed, very still, turned towards us. It was a shock to see her with no veil, no snood. Her roughly cropped hair stuck damply to her head and her round face was pinched with agony even in sleep.

Persi, whose back was to me, knelt on the stone floor, her elbows on the bed, forehead resting on her hands. She was wearing her black shoes, the old, scuffed soles facing up at me. I could sense the desperate intensity of her prayers. I stood there feeling terrible and utterly helpless.

'Persi?' I spoke very quietly.

She turned and, seeing me, got painfully to her feet and came nearer, though not too near. We spoke in whispers.

'Mother Joan said she thought it was cholera?'

Persi nodded. Her long face was as I had never seen it before, both stretched and shrunken at once. Old, she seemed suddenly. Not just middle aged – not that I'd ever really thought that of her in any case until then.

'What happened?' I asked.

Persi glanced back at Sushila.

'One minute she said she didn't feel too well – I only wish she'd mentioned it, before we went out.' Persi's face contorted, but for the moment she controlled her tears. 'She must have been feeling terrible. But we set off to come back. A few minutes later she was sick. And then …' She gestured towards the lower half of her body. 'It was pouring out of her. She collapsed …'

She put her hands over her face and I could see her body quivering. I had never, ever seen Persi weep before and it brought me instantly to tears as well.

'Oh God …' I wanted so much to embrace her, but as soon as I took a step forward she shooed me away.

'Don't,' Persi said wildly, almost scraping the tears from her face. 'I've got to get her to drink, to try to keep something more inside her. Just – pray for her. For both of us.'

Sushila stirred then. She gave a dreadful groan and pushed herself up on her elbow and it was only then I noticed the drip in her arm. Persi just got to her as she retched violently over the bowl, moaning with distress.

'Come.' Sister Martha touched my arm. 'We must leave them.'

We left the room and Sister Martha softly closed the door behind us.

I went back the next day and the next. All I could do was to look in through the door. Persi stayed, hardly ever coming out of the room. The nuns did everything they could to assist. Afterwards, they tried to understand why it had not been enough.

When I went in one afternoon at the end of the week the silence in the convent had deepened. At four o'clock that morning, Sushila's soul had left them. She was forty-two, a year younger than me. I was not there when Persi took her leave of Sushila. Her body had had to be carried away, wrapped in a clean white sheet, on the death carts bound for the burning *ghats*.

IV

22

1965

I woke with the sun that morning and looking over at Persi's bed was surprised to see that she had gone. Then, faintly, from outside, I heard her voice.

Wrapping my stiff morning limbs in a shawl, I looked out at the verandah. Persi was sitting with her back to me in one of the cane chairs. Her hair was loosely plaited, its length disappearing under the cinnamon-coloured shawl she wore. Nip, the little dog, was looking up at her. It must have been him she had been talking to. Now she was gazing out at the shine of dew on the grass. I could hear birds. A train whistled in the station and smoke drifted on the air. I wanted to go and sit out there, but something about her stillness made me feel I would be intruding.

She must have sensed me there, though, because she glanced round.

'Morning, dearie!'

'All right if I join you?'

'Why would it not be?' She sounded cheerful. I had imagined her dwelling on sad, grievous thoughts.

I lowered myself on to the other creaking chair with a bit of a grunt. Nip jumped up immediately and settled himself on my lap. I sat stroking his wiry coat.

We watched a couple of chipmunks frolicking past. A gangly young Assamese lad appeared pushing a bicycle, an orange cloth bag hanging from the handlebars. He disappeared behind the house.

'You all right?' I asked, eventually.

'Why d'you keep asking me if I'm all right?' Persi said, testily. 'Why would I not be all right?'

'Sorry,' I said huffily. 'You just seem a bit quiet. For you.' Good God, this was difficult. Why am I such a hopeless old fumbler when it comes to saying any decent, kindly thing that needs to be said?

'What I mean is … I think it was very staunch of you to come back here. To India. Stir up all the old memories and so on.'

Persi gave me a look. 'D'you think I can't remember in England? It's *good* to be here. More than good.'

'Is it?' Of course, she was right. Being here returned us both to the very heart of our lives and tied us back into them again: the joy, love, grief.

'It is,' she said.

We smiled at each other, laughed gently. I was still not certain what it was, exactly, that blew Persi out of the religious life and back to England before 1949 was out. I have the impression it was something to do with the fact that the God she had been raised to believe in was not, as it turned out, on anyone's side in particular. But maybe it wasn't that at all. Maybe it was trying to carry on in Barisal without Sushila. Or that fresh-faced Urvashi vanished one night – it seemed with one of the *malis*, who also disappeared – and never came back. Or Independence, the utter bloodiness of it all. That we were not wanted. Or just that she had had enough.

'Do you actually believe in God?' I asked her.

'Believe?' She was silent for a moment. 'No. Long for? Yes.'

God. Another of her lost loves.

'Well, this is our last week,' I said, after a while. 'The boy said he'd like us to go over to the Club one last time tomorrow. Why don't you come this time?'

'I might.'

A crow hopped into our view, gave its scraping cry and flew off. *Kak*, I thought.

'D'you think you've given him all he needs?' Persi said.

'Roderick? We've had little chats of an informative kind, about Hughie, if that's what you mean.'

'About Hughie.' Persi gave an assenting tilt of her head. 'What does he really *need* to know about Hughie?'

'How d'you mean?'

'I just mean' – she flapped her hand dismissively – 'what does he want? He wants to know that somewhere, in that brief interval in which Hughie hung about long enough to conceive a child and see him grow into something walking about, before he left for ever, never getting in contact again – that somewhere in there, there was love. Now, there's truth and there's cruelty. He wants to feel that he was loved – whether it was true or not.'

'Hughie really was a shocking father,' I said.

Persi looked directly at me then. 'And brother?'

I could not say anything.

'There was really nothing you could have done,' Persi said, with sudden gentleness.

My chest tightened, as if a heavy crate was pressing down on me. 'But there was, wasn't there? I could have got in touch with him. I just left it and left it, until it was too late.'

Persi was silent for a moment. A heavy moment.

'Whose responsibility was it?' I felt her look at me but I could not meet her eye. 'Not just yours, was it? Look, Roderick wants love: from you, me, anyone, the poor lamb. Above all, to think, somehow, that he had it from Hughie. Apart from that, how much does he need to *know*?'

'I wish *I* didn't know,' I said. And then wished desperately that I hadn't. Because none of this was Persi's fault either.

23

The service held by the sisters to say goodbye to Sister Sushila was among the most agonizing of hours I can remember. It was a reserved affair, much like any other Anglican service, in the pale-walled chapel, led by Father Henry Somebody-Or-Other who had to come in to officiate. He was a kindly enough soul and the whole thing was fraught with gentle pain. Sushila's was only one loss amid the mass of suffering and death outside, but they were having to part with someone they had all deeply loved. As had I.

The younger Indian sisters wept, quietly wiping their cheeks. Mother Joan stood in the front row, straight-backed, her anguish chained in with her habitual discipline. I slipped in behind them all, the only woman there not wearing a habit and veil. I was a couple of rows behind Persi so I could not see her face.

We finished by singing 'Lead Us, Heavenly Father, Lead Us' and I was so full of tears I could scarcely sing. All I could think of was the day Louise was born and, so soon after, the day she died, accompanied on both occasions by Sister Sushila and her gentle kindness. I remembered those moments of seeing her eyes meeting Persi's, the obvious love between them. I wanted to howl, but no one else was howling, least of all Persi, so why should I indulge myself?

As we turned to leave, I saw Persi step out into the aisle as

Mother Joan was approaching from the front pew. Their eyes met. Mother Joan's face was tight, like a mask, but I saw her take Persi's hand in both of hers and cradle it against her for a moment as if it was a wounded bird before she released it.

Deidre was fond of saying, 'We've just got to keep going.' And keep going was what we did. For three years.

I carried on at Imperial, lived in Cowper Road and helped Persi and the other sisters for as long as it was needed. The famine and the influx of starving villagers peaked late that summer. But there was always something that needed doing and I had come to love the sisters.

The girl, Urvashi, recovered very well and by the time the community had ministered to her for several weeks, she was mad keen to become a Christian and join the order. Which, by and by, she did. By late 1944, I would meet the young novice Urvashi, or Veronica, as she had chosen to be called (Veronica wiped Jesus's face on the way to Calvary, she told me proudly) in the convent corridors. The veil only emphasized her striking blade-like nose and sharp cheekbones.

'Hello, Miss Ellie!' she would greet me, her big pool eyes shining at me. Never have I known anyone so enthusiastic.

She was devoted to the faith, the order – and above all, as it turned out, to Persi. Persi had been one of the four of us who carried Urvashi to the convent. Urvashi-Veronica latched on to her like a mother – which dear Persi, in deep grief as she was for Sushila, seemed to find highly irritating.

'Oh Lord, it's my little satellite,' she said one day in the kitchen, where we were drinking tea, as Veronica came in and greeted her almost as if she was actually God. Veronica did not yet speak much English and she was bustling about in the store cupboard. She was eager but wayward and not the sharpest knife in the drawer. She had to have everything explained several times over.

'Now, now,' I said. 'That's not very Christian.'

Persi rolled her eyes and took a sip of her tea. She was so thin and worn then. We did not talk about Sushila. I did not know what was going on in Persi's mind and she rebuffed any questions or mention of her. The fact was, with the war still on and the famine raging outside, there was no time to think of anything except the next thing to be done.

August was the month when, whichever year it was, momentous things seemed to happen.

Sushila died in August '43. The war ended in August '45, after they dropped those appalling bombs on the Japanese. All the forces chaps gradually left, so there was no need for me to carry on working at the Turf Club. But from then on, through 1946, there was so much turmoil that making any sort of plans in one's own life was all but impossible. Even though the war was over, 1946 was the year that stands out as one of the very worst.

Negotiations over Independence: what kind of India? Clement Atlee, the British Prime Minister, sent ambassadors over to discuss. The Hindus wanted to be in charge, the Muslims wanted their own country. No one could seem to agree and by August the city was in a horrific state. Soldiers and tanks tried – and failed – to contain the unrest. It became known as the time of the Great Killings, thousands dead and wounded. The north side of Calcutta was the worst – at night especially. Fires, riots, trams set ablaze and corpses all over the streets the next morning, the

265

air rank with smoke. Blood-letting of a most savage kind between Hindus and Muslims. It seemed straightforward killing was not enough – many were savagely mutilated. After seeing bodies dying in slow agony during the famine, this was several degrees worse. It gave you a sense of despair about humanity as a whole.

In the middle of all this, Jessie Bell managed a brief visit all the way from Mussoorie, partly to tell me that she and her mother were going to England. She did not say 'home'. Apparently Mrs Bell was like a lost soul by then, her nerves in shreds. She had lived in India since before the turn of the century when she had followed her husband with baby Duncan, Jessie's brother, in her arms. And now all she could think of was the comfort of the familiar places of her youth.

'Where will you live, Jessie?' I asked, as we sat out in the garden at Cowper Road. 'Do you have anywhere there?'

'With Mother's sister, to begin with, in Aylesbury,' Jessie said. She seemed numb. All she could think of was her duty to her mother. 'We'll manage somehow. Auntie Alice is a kind person.'

She hugged me very tightly when she left – not the casual wave of her usual departure. Jessie: a matronly, resigned figure now.

'Write to me, won't you, Ellie?'

Within a very short time I had a letter, not from Jessie, but from my mother in Bombay, saying that she too was planning to return to England and the family home in Berkshire as soon as things could be arranged. It did not sound as if the Mynah was going with her. I had not seen my mother – or Peter Kelner – for several years by this time. I can't say I felt anything much about it.

That autumn, Persi left Calcutta and went back to the Mother

House in Barisal, taking Urvashi-Veronica with her (though I suspect this was not Persi's idea). However, the upshot of this was that the girl seemed much more at home in the sleepier environment of Barisal (perhaps more like the home she had originally left) and she settled in very well and stopped trailing about after Persi, who of course then decided to become rather fond of her.

By the time she had been there a year, Persi was living in a different country called East Pakistan. I have the abiding memory of grainy newspaper photographs of apparently limitless river meanders of people walking with whatever they could carry towards the borders of east and west: Hindus leaving West and East Pakistan for India; Muslims heading in the opposite directions. Each border was soaked in blood. August 15th, 1947. Independence. Partition.

I could see that soon, my native land, the place that had held my heart all my life, was going to want to evict me too. It felt the most sad, hurtful thing – but it was, as Persi would say, 'How it is, dearie.'

24

1965

We spent the evening after my morning conversation with
Persi pleasantly enough. Ginny seemed distracted at dinner,
but Roderick was on cheerful form, regaling us with tales of
wild elephants rampaging in the gardens – I could recall similar
mayhem but kept quiet – and of his first experience of a *gherao*.
When the workers in the garden had a grievance, a group of them
would surround one of the managers and refuse to let him move
away until their demands were taken seriously.

'It's happened more since Independence,' Roderick said.
'Indianization – that's what they want. Us out and the gardens
run by Indians. It will happen, of course.'

'It's frightening.' Ginny sat hunched in her chair, her hair
hanging loose, which was unusual at dinner. 'One day they might
hurt you. Doesn't it scare you, Pod?'

'It did at first,' he admitted. 'But the thing is, I know them
all now. They're good chaps, most of them at least. It's made me
brush up on my negotiating skills no end!'

I watched Roderick fondly. He still seemed to me absurdly
like an overgrown child, but he was a good man. A kind man.
I could see a lot of Hugh in him and of my own Pa and it felt

soothing to be with him. This conversation brought to mind that morning when the tribal woman, in her bright sari, dared to come right to the threshold of our house with her pleading and how I could see Pa wanted to help her, even though there was nothing he could do.

So I was too caught up in my own thoughts and memories to notice Ginny's paleness and the way she was sitting hunched in on herself.

Persi and I were asleep. The door burst open, letting in dim light. Roderick's voice was scared, urgent.

'Miss Persimmon? I'm so sorry but can you come?'

Persi was like a cat, even then; awake and on her feet in seconds, pulling her shawl over her nightdress as she left the room.

My heart was pounding from being so suddenly awoken. I lay and listened. Low voices, over which rose Ginny's, high and distressed. I didn't know what to do. No one had asked for me – Persi was a nurse; that seemed to be the thing. After a moment I got up, pulled a cardi on and went to look out of the door.

Roderick and Persi, either side of a sobbing Ginny, were guiding her towards the front door. She was in slippers. A smear of blood stood out on the pale skin of her calf.

'Thank you!' Roderick called emotionally, as he and Ginny disappeared. Persi stood at the door and I heard the car starting up. Persi pulled her shawl closer round her and the car drove away.

She turned and came towards me. She had nothing on her feet.

'She's going to be a sad little rabbit when she comes back,' she said.

There was not much sleep to be had after that, though I lay, trying to rest, hearing from her movements that Persi was awake as well.

I had tried so hard to keep my mind from dwelling on the small creature growing inside the girl, not wanting myself to grieve or remember and most of all not to become jealous of all she was to have that had been taken from me. But that tiny being was somehow always with me even so and now, I was surprised by finding the night's developments almost unbearable. Not my child – but someone's. A new life. And now, not. That vivid, brilliant flow into the future had, it seemed, been blocked and was draining away, lifeless.

I thought I heard Roderick come back, though I was not certain if I was dreaming. When I came to the next morning I thought I could hear him moving about. A sense of dread filled me.

Persi seemed to be asleep now, but I got up. I had to try and be some sort of aunt to the boy, even if being comforting was not really my speciality. I felt nauseous – lack of sleep combined with the awfulness of it all. Loss is a dreadful thing to confront, in someone else as much as in oneself.

Roderick was sitting at the table in his pyjamas with a cup of tea.

'Oh, hello, Auntie.' I could see the pup had been crying.

I sat down beside him.

'No baby, then,' he said in a desolate voice.

'Not this time, perhaps,' I said, trying my best to sound gentle. It must have come off all right because he managed a sad little smile. I found my throat aching, my chest so tight that I was struggling for breath.

'The poor girl is terribly cut up about it. She's so longing to have a family – we both are.'

'There'll be other chances.' I touched his shoulder for a moment. 'There will. It's not uncommon, dear. This is just a false start, that's all.'

Roderick gave me a grateful but, I thought, bemused look, as if wondering how someone like myself could know anything at all about it.

'It's *terribly* sad,' I said. 'But there will be sunshine, my boy. Buck up.'

'She wants you,' he said.

'*Me?* Whatever do you mean?'

'They said she would need to be in for a day or two and she said, Please would you come in and see her.'

'Why d'you think she wants to see me?' I asked Roderick, as we drove into town that afternoon. One never wants to show one's underbelly, but this was one of those times when none of us could really help it. I felt nervous as hell.

Roderick glanced at me as we pulled up by the low, tin-roofed hospital building. He stopped the engine and turned to me.

'Ginny hasn't got much family – just her father now.' He spoke shyly. 'She could do with an auntie, you know. We both could.'

A warm feeling crept round my heart, though I could scarcely believe it. These two young pups didn't seem to see what a dreadful wreck I was – in fact they were disposed to like me. I almost felt tears coming on, which wouldn't do at all. I stared down at the old pair of baggy cream slacks I was wearing.

'Well, if you're really that desperate.' I made a kind of barking laugh. 'I'll do my best, old chap.'

'We are.' His voice was lighter for the moment, amused. 'We really are. Look, why don't you pop in and see her? I'll have a wander round outside for a while.'

As I was getting out of the car, he added, 'She really does like you, you know. Even if you don't believe me.'

I rolled my eyes and went into the hospital.

The ward was small – only eight iron bedsteads, four along each side. Ginny was lying with her eyes open, dark rings under them, her cheeks very pale. Seeing me coming, she pulled herself to sit up, wincing, hugging her knees. Her hair was all hanging down and she looked so young, like a little girl. She was the same age I was then, I thought, as I approached. She just looked up at me with big, tragic eyes.

'I'm so sorry, my dear,' I said.

She reached her arms out and I perched on the edge of the bed as this little one leaned into me, weeping. I wrapped my arms round her, something that had not happened to me for a very long time. Her hair was soft against my cheek as she pressed her forehead into my shoulder and sobbed.

'Oh dear, oh dear.' I rocked her gently, stroking her slender back, and damned if I didn't just start myself. Couldn't help it, tears running down my face, chest feeling ready to tear open. God knows, it was nice to be needed for once. And I couldn't stop thoughts flooding in, holding her like that in my arms, of how, had my own daughter lived, my Louise, I would sometimes have held her thus, and how old she would be now – goodness, in her forties – and how sweet it felt that this young thing would put her trust in me in this way.

'I'm sorry,' Ginny said, eventually.

'Whatever for?'

She pulled back, startled by the sound of my voice, I think. Seeing my own tears, she looked utterly astonished.

'Auntie? Are you all right?'

'Of course I'm all right!' I patted the pockets of my long shirt, trying to find a hanky. In the end I had to resort to wiping my nose on the end of my shirt instead and we both laughed.

'Not well prepared,' I said. 'Look, I am *so* sorry about what's happened, dear.'

'You're so *understanding*,' she said, as if my pathetic words had been some sort of revelation. 'I'm so glad you're here.' Her tearful eyes looked into mine, desperate for reassurance. 'I feel as if I'm not ... I mean I've failed Roderick. I know how much he wants a family.'

'My dear ...' I took her hands. 'There will be family. For a start, *you* are his family. And there will be babies – I'm sure there will. It's just an unlucky start.'

'D'you think so? It doesn't mean I'm ... I don't know, *barren*?'

'No. It often happens, the first time.' I had some vague idea that this was true. 'It'll be all right.'

'You would have made a really nice mother,' she said, leaning into me again, as if in relief.

'I –' No, I could not stop. It was time for truth, time to be known. 'I ... had a daughter. She was called Louise.'

Ginny pulled away from me, slowly, looking up into my face with such tender astonishment that more tears coursed down my cheeks.

'What do you mean?'

So, briefly, I told her. Told her my heart, about my girl. The first time I had ever told anyone. She listened with her wet eyes fixed to my face. Her features reacted to every detail and she cried and so did I.

'Oh, Auntie,' she said. 'How sad!'

'Well, I suppose it wasn't to be,' I said. 'But for you it's different – there will be more babies; I'm sure there will.'

We hugged, holding each other tight. Over her head, I saw Roderick appear at the door of the ward. He came towards us, hesitating for a moment when he saw what a heap of emotions we were, both of us, as if he was afraid of intruding. I beckoned him.

'Here's your Pod,' I said to Ginny.

Both of us were inclined to pull ourselves together then. She wiped her cheeks and looked up at him, showing signs of cheer, and Roderick shot me a grateful glance.

'Hello, darling.' He sank down on the chair and took her hand. I saw two people who truly loved each other.

'I'll take myself off,' I said, getting up.

'No, Auntie. There's no need!' Both of them assured me at once.

It seemed that both of them had room in their hearts for me and this was almost too much to take.

'I don't suppose you happen to have a hanky on you, do you Roderick?' I asked.

'Of course you must go!' Ginny had said, quite cheerful now, that afternoon as we left the hospital. 'I'm perfectly all right, Pod. For goodness sake go to the Club. I'm quite all right here and there's no need for you all to sit at home.'

'Shall we risk sitting upstairs?' Roderick said as he, Persi and I stood at the Club's entrance that evening.

'All right. Let's be devils.' I was feeling more jittery than I expected, being there again. It had been an emotional couple of days and I wasn't used to dealing with all this carry-on.

It was early yet and there were few other people there. Roderick went into the bar to fetch drinks while Persi and I climbed the stairs and settled ourselves near the balustrade, looking out over the peaceful green. A chap was just finishing off painting white lines on the grass. Now it was March, the evenings felt warmer every day, but we had still both brought shawls.

As I was taking in the view, gently lit by the setting sun, an extraordinary thought struck me.

'Good God!' I said, before quickly wishing I hadn't.

'What?' Persi was already wrapping herself in her shawl. She sounded peeved, as if I had barged in on her train of thought.

'Nothing,' I said.

'Don't say "Good God" like that if it's nothing after all,' she said.

What I had pictured was the inside of my suitcase, lying forgotten in a corner of our bedroom and still containing three and a half of the four bottles of Scotch I'd brought out here with me. I'd taken one out when we arrived to ensure having the odd nip, not sure how supplies would be in the house. But another of Roderick's loveable qualities was that he was a generous host. Most astonishing was that for all this time I had hardly given those bottles a thought. We were due to fly back again in three days. I'd have to present them to him as a gift.

But now ...

'Oh God, Persi ...'

'What on earth's the matter *now*?' she said irritably.

'Sorry,' I said, with unusual humility. But I was sorry – I was babbling. And what was she thinking of? Her own memories? She had still not said a word about Sushila, who I am quite certain was the real love of her life, however much she had devoted herself to Enid at the end of her days.

Persi softened. 'Go on?'

'We've got to go back,' I said. 'Home.'

The thought of Greenburton House, all those rooms, the ailing roses and wretched weeds pushing up between every stone, seemed utterly hateful. It all seemed to fold in on me, swamping me.

Persi gave me one of her looks. 'Sell it,' she said. 'Just get rid of the whole damn pile.'

Curiously, this had never even occurred to me.

'Here we are, ladies.' Roderick appeared with three glasses bunched somehow in his hands, tongue pushed out in concentration like a little boy. By a miracle, he managed to get them to the table without dropping the bally lot. He sat them down, ice clinking.

'Well,' Persi said to him gently. 'This is a sad day, dear. I'm sorry for what's happened.'

'I know. My poor dear girl,' Roderick said woefully. 'But she's being so brave – saying it'll all be all right in the end.'

'It doesn't mean anything necessarily,' Persi said. 'I've seen many a girl miscarry and go on to have a football team of a family.'

Roderick brightened. 'That would be something, wouldn't it?' He raised his glass to us. 'I'm just glad you were both here – it would have been so much worse if you hadn't. Let's drink to hope for the future, eh?'

'I'm so grateful to both of you,' he went on after our toast. 'Coming all the way out here, being so open about things. If there's one thing I can't stand, it's untruths – secrets and cover-ups. I do rather hold that against my mother. I don't know that she was holding back anything in particular from me, but she wouldn't talk about my father at all. It seems so wrong – I would never do that to my child. If I ever have one.'

He looked very woebegone again for a moment.

'Seeing you has been marvellous, Aunt Eleanora, because you have all those childhood memories. I feel I have so much more idea about my father now. And it does sound as if he died doing something rather heroic, up here on the border.'

Persi's eyes met mine. I thought for a moment she was going to say something, but she looked away again. And I couldn't – not today of all days, especially.

'Poor old Hughie,' I said, avoiding the issue. 'He was a good soul really, like our own Pa – life took its toll on many of the chaps of our generation. And I have to say, our mother really was not a kindly person.'

'But you went to live with her, didn't you?' Roderick said. 'After it was all over, here?'

'Good Lord, no!' I chuckled. 'Wherever did you get that idea? She went to live at Greenburton with dear old Uncle Hat, who had been happily bumbling along on his own. He died soon after, poor soul. Our mother was as the Upas tree – everything that falls under its shadow dies.'

Roderick looked at Persi, a horrified expression on his face.

'True, I'm afraid,' she announced, between two sips of tonic water.

'No, I went where I always went to begin with – battered old London. My secretarial skills saw me through but after a few years I got sick of it all: cold-water flats with rain leaking through the roof, bombsites and soot everywhere. And you couldn't keep a dog. So I went to live in Henley – worked in a rather tiresome little boutique. And eventually Mumsie died and the house came to me.'

My mother had not known, in all that time, that I was even in the country.

'I see,' Roderick said. 'That all sounds rather miserable.'

'As sin.' I twinkled at him, at the understatement of this. Those were the years when Johnny Walker and I became even more closely reacquainted – in fact best friends. The silly woman, Cynthia Marsden, who owned the boutique, eventually cottoned on. I didn't tell Roderick that I had been sacked and on my uppers before Mumsie died. Truth does have some margins of limitation, in my book.

Persi was looking after Enid, who had been widowed and fallen ill shortly afterwards. So I did not see much of her at that time either.

I wanted to get off this subject, so Persi and I regaled him with a few more tales of Calcutta and her nursing in Egypt.

'What extraordinary lives you've led,' he said.

Standing at the top of the Club stairs as we left, I took a last look round. It was dark outside now, the lights under their cane shades drawing clattering insects round them. It still looked so much the same. It struck me that this might be the last time I ever saw this place. I stroked the wooden banister rail on my way down as I used to when I was a child.

Persi followed me slowly down and we drifted out past the bar towards the exit. There was no sign of Roderick.

'He's been waylaid,' Persi said, pulling her shawl close about her. The darkness smoothed away the years. Beside me, with her thick plait of hair over her shoulder, stood the tall Persi of my childhood, of Barisal and Calcutta. Dear, dear Persi.

'He'll be along,' I said. 'Ran into some chum, no doubt.'

We waited. I walked idly about the poorly lit entrance area, peering at the wooden boards on the wall.

JORHAT GYMKHANA CLUB

(EST'D 1896)

GOLF CAPTAINS

Names, dates. I stepped closer. People of the age of my own parents:

D. R. MALINS 1897–1904

C. M. HUTCHINSON 1905–1910

Pa would never have been on one of these boards, I thought, smiling. He was so uninterested in anything that involved hitting a ball. My eye ran down the list:

E. K. WISHART 1911–1922

W. R. H. TEATTIE 1936–1945

And stopped:

W. J. ASHTON 1951–1954

My body seemed to take in this information before my mind could catch up. My blood pumped. *William John Ashton.* Bill. *Bill?* He was supposed to be living somewhere in Surrey ... My breath stopped. Started again.

'Wait there a moment, Persi ...'

There was no clear thought in my mind – except that I had this moment, *now*, when I could ask. I rushed back inside and hurled myself towards the bar. The barman, a middle-aged fellow, gave my no doubt demented-looking person a polite nod.

'What can I get you?'

'Have you been here long?' I demanded.

He was bound to think I was bonkers, but no matter. Actually, when he got sorted out as to what I was on about he was rather a darling.

'Bill Ashton? Oh yes – used to come here a lot. Still does pop up from time to time but he's getting on a bit, of course. Big fellow, marvellous at cricket – good golfer as well. D'you know him?'

'He was in England. I thought he went back?'

'Tried to make a go of it, I gather. I suppose it didn't work out. Anyway, see that fellow over there, Fred Simms? He'll know where you can catch up with him if you want to.'

Catch up with him. I didn't say anything to Persi or Roderick, not then. I sat in the car in complete turmoil. It was too raw and peculiar in my mind. An absurd idea – I must just put it aside. Try to pretend to myself that I have not acquired this information that Bill is only about ten miles away. Ten miles. With Betty?

Calcutta; his face as I stood there next to Mrs Martyn's desk, paralysed.

Don't be such a silly old fool. Don't disturb …

I slept barely a wink. All I could do was lie there, hearing Persi's whispering breaths, my mind fixing on one memory after another. The secret loves of my life that, until this week, I could never disclose to anyone else. Except Persi. And yet now – I did not feel like telling anyone, not even her.

By five in the morning, I was on the verandah, watching light seep over the garden. My whole body felt painful, exposed, as if I were twenty again and fresh from losing him. I wanted it to stop — not to feel, for this not to have happened. I could just go home, continue being the somewhat disagreeable person I had apparently become, the old maid who lived alone with that peculiar friend of hers.

But I had seen. He was here, where I might never be again. How could I go home without ... *I've got to go and see him. How can I not?*

'Are you all right, Eleanora?' Persi said, as we sat sipping tea by the middle of the morning. 'You seem a little sub-dood.' She spoke in a joking fashion.

'Perfectly, thank you.' I smiled. 'Just a little tired. Having said that ...' I put my cup down nonchalantly. 'As Roderick's going to be going into town, I thought I might go along. Have a last look round.' For a moment I was worried she might say she wanted to come as well.

'Why don't you?' she said. 'There won't be time tomorrow.'

Roderick, fortunately, was in far too much of a flap about Ginny coming home again to notice the galloping pulse rate of his maiden aunt.

'I'll find my own way back,' I told him. 'You go and get your girl and look after her. Why don't you put me down at the railway station? I can sort myself out from there.'

It was only once I was alone in a taxi, driving out into the country the other side of Jorhat, that I really started questioning my own sanity. What was I doing, silly old fool, getting all steamed up like this, like some young girl with a pash? Trying to see this man, this person who had ... But he was *here*. *Why* was he here? What did it *mean*?

The emotions were so charged that it might have been yesterday that we parted, here in Assam. I couldn't help it. It felt as if I had been suddenly cut open. However much I kept trying to talk myself out of it, I sat there, in that clapped-out Ambassador car, jittery, as if my blood was going to burst out of my veins. Some things never die, however much you try to make them, however many years lie between: Louise, Barisal – our little girl, floating away like a lily along the great river's flank.

I tried to prepare myself. To stop my ridiculous feelings. Bill's last letter to me, in 1942 (I still had it) had been so polite and impersonal, telling me he had spotted Hughie. Then nothing, for twenty-three years. A stranger ... And Bill was an old man now. It was a shock to think that he was knocking on eighty. He might be quite doolally for all I knew; not even recognize me. And what about Betty? If she was there, I would call in, a breezy old acquaintance, and take my leave as soon as I could. It was perfectly natural to look up an old friend.

We turned through the gate of another tea garden soon after three in the afternoon. Dust rose lazily from the road. The taxi driver, a young Hindu lad, crawled the car along at snail's pace as he and I puzzled over exactly where we needed to go.

'Oh – there,' I soon said. 'That must be it!'

A yellow bungalow was tucked into its own fenced plot not far into the gardens. In the distance I glimpsed the impressive roof of what must have been the garden manager's *burra* bungalow through the trees.

'You can stop here,' I instructed. 'And please wait. I don't know how long I shall be, but I'll pay you.'

'Yes, Madam.' He looked heavy lidded, glad at the prospect

of a nap for which he was to be paid.

The fact that the driver was there, parked in the shade of a tree with a clear view of me walking to the house, helped me contain my nerves. Although I felt as if I was about to explode with the tension of it all – what the hell I was thinking I really don't know – I couldn't just dither about outside.

I opened the gate. There was a rectangle of front garden, roses and lavender in beds around a neat lawn. It was so quiet that I could hear the hum of insects. No one else seemed to be about. The windows were shrouded with blinds against the afternoon sun so I could make out nothing of the inside. It was a terrible time to call on anyone, but it was the time I had.

A green door. A little bell with a rope. I could just walk back to the taxi, say there was no one in.

'Come on, you silly old thing,' I muttered. 'Just get on with it.'

When I pulled the rope, the bell let out a mellow tinkling. Even in the mid-afternoon quiet it sounded feeble. He's probably asleep, I thought, or deaf as a damn post, or both. He had no reason to expect anyone visiting, especially at this ridiculous time of –

The door opened. I expected a servant. Or worse still, Betty. But there was a large man, slightly stooped, a stick in one hand. He wore trousers of some dusty blue, a white shirt, the sleeves rolled to the elbows, over which was a sleeveless woolly, baggy and much darned. A tummy, comforting looking. Beard, grey giving way to white. Those eyes.

We stood face to face, taking each other in. And then he smiled, as if we had only seen each other a few days previously.

'Hello, old girl,' he said.

*　　*　　*

Stepping inside. His house, Bill's house. Bill. Here, now. I felt each one of my steps, felt the present upon me in one of those rare, crystalline moments that only happens at life's best and worst twists in the road.

I followed this man, the complete familiarity of him, the shoulders, the back of his neck, into his sitting room. He turned then, and we stood apart.

'Shall we have some tea?' he said.

I nodded, though hardly aware of what he had said. We stood a moment longer. Then stepped into each other's arms. Silly old things – entwined round each other and hungry as two youths.

We talked for six hours flat in his sitting room. It was a simple, manly place, with just the basic furniture, his books and pictures. There are things one needs to say and others one does not. The knack is working out which is which. That first day was not the time – not for that, for our Louise. Instead, we travelled the years in a grand sweep, recounting what had brought us to here, to now.

Bill did not bother his servant at that hour. He made tea himself and we sat facing each other, he forward in the chair a lot of the time, leaning his arms on his thighs. He seemed full of energy. After the first few minutes, once all the barriers were down, it felt so ordinary, so very comfortable. We were simply back together, he and I, both changed, yet not. An extraordinary thing, simply being able to be oneself and be acceptable, still.

'I did four years in England,' he said. 'Betty was delighted to be back. In theory, I was supposed to be able to retire by then – I was over sixty, just.' He sat back for a moment to take a sip of tea, then leaned forward again. Suddenly he started to laugh, shoulders going up and down in the way I remembered.

'Reigate. Worst place on earth!'

We both laughed our heads off. Personally, I have never had the pleasure of a visit to Reigate, but I knew just what he meant.

'By 1950, the boys were grown up and on their way. Betty and I were going through the motions of being married – outside the house, at least.' He gave me a sad glance. 'Loneliest thing, that. I was going slowly – no, in fact rather rapidly – off my chump. Living in a matchbox, rain, more bloody rain and not of the exhilarating kind. So I thought, well, I either get out of here by shooting myself or I do the sensible thing and call it a day. Go home.'

'Did Betty mind *very* much?' I asked.

'No, I can't say she did.' His shoulders started shaking again. 'God, Nella, it's a treat to see you. You were always the one person I could tell the truth to.' He was serious again. 'I thought of contacting you – so many times. But I'd disturb your life and I imagined you must be settled. That I had no right ...'

There was nothing I could say. I understood. My mind cast back for a moment over those lonely years, the late forties, fifties, in England. How different they might have been. But then, could I have settled down and been a wife, after all this time? I smiled at him.

'Well, maybe you had a lucky escape.'

Bill laughed and reached out to touch my hand.

'God, Nella. You're here.'

Bill's servant came in with supper later – chicken and dal and rice, which we shared. It was only right at the end, as I was about to leave and when things had fully re-grown between us, that we stood up and embraced again.

'Oh, my dearest one …' Bill's huge hand came to rest on the back of my head. I fitted myself into him, feeling the big, warm comfort of him. He was home, for me – he had been for so long.

'So – here we are,' he said, eventually, between kisses, as we held each other. 'Do we have some time, do you think, after all?'

'Well – my dear nephew has invited me back – next winter - for as long as I fancy…'

I reached up and rested my hand on the worn contours of his face. Such unbelievable, unforeseen joy. I had no sense of reproach towards Bill over all that had happened. But being known is part of being loved. And of this, my deepest sadness, of our little girl, I hoped I could speak calmly, when the time was right.

There would be time, for all of it.

25

December 1965

As we drove into the Rungabari gardens, instead of pulling up as before at the assistant's bungalow, Roderick drove past it and turned into the grand sweep of the manager's drive. A moment later the wide, stately *burra* bungalow came into view, with its long verandah, covered balcony and rust-coloured tin roof.

'Oh, my word – promotion!'

'We wanted to surprise you.' Roderick chuckled like an excited child. 'And in fact, it was all rather last minute, the Farleys deciding to up sticks and go home.'

'It's magnificent.'

I had only glimpsed the house during my walks on the last visit. It was a welcoming, settled-looking place. I could already look forward to sitting on that shady balcony at the centre of the house, held up by decorative wrought supports, through which pink and white hibiscus weaved upwards towards the light.

'It's taking a bit of getting used to.' Roderick braked at one end of the house, switched off the engine and turned to me. He seemed much older and more of a piece with himself than when we parted only ten months ago, after his and Ginny's sad loss. In fact, he appeared lit up with happiness, the dear fellow.

'You look tremendously well, Aunt Eleanora.'

'I am.' Not that I was going to tell him this, but my proudest achievement was conquering the gout. 'As do you, dear.'

We were both smiling way like a couple of March hares. A movement caught Roderick's eye. Nip came tearing out of the house, so I opened my car door and the little dog and I had a fond reunion.

Roderick jumped out and went round to hoik my case out of the boot while Nip was jumping at my legs.

'Ah, here she comes!' he said happily.

Ginny came down the verandah steps, and I remembered the scared little rabbit of a girl I had met the first time. What a difference now: hair swept back, rather à la Princess Anne, a primrose-yellow frock, pushed out at the front by the very unmistakable passenger on board.

'Auntie El!' Another name I seem to have acquired.

'Hello, dear!'

There was a good deal of smiling and we exchanged kisses in a way that felt triumphantly natural.

'My, my, someone's making their presence felt!'

She blushed, looking down at the six-month cargo.

'Very much so. Full of beans – kicking me! Come on, let me show you your room. You can have a choice – we're rattling around in here. Oh, did Pod tell you?' She stopped for a moment on the stairs. 'We've got some children coming – for Christmas? In fact, they're due tomorrow.'

'Children?'

Ginny laughed, looking at my startled expression.

'You don't mind children, do you, Auntie? We have so much space here and they were asking the planters if we'd host some children for the holiday, from the orphanage in Kalimpong. Poor dears have no families to go to. And anyway, Pod and I need to get into practice.'

'Very noble of you,' I said.

'Not at all. We're looking forward to it. You don't mind?'

'Why should I mind?' A bit of life about the place was seldom a bad thing, I reasoned. And they could hardly expect me to do too much about it. 'How many are you expecting?'

'Two or three. Girls, I think.'

'That's probably for the best,' I said.

Ginny laughed, leading me into a bedroom. 'Is it? I've no idea! Now – there's this room ...'

'This is perfect. No need for a tour. And look, my case is in here already.'

This first room was of a very generous size. It had the usual white walls chequered with thin wood battens and canvas ceiling, and the windows, through which sunlight slanted in at this time of day, looked out over the drive and front garden. There was a cream bedspread and Ginny had arranged three pink rosebuds in a glass on the dressing table.

'I put flowers in every room, just in case!' She laughed, delightedly.

'It's lovely, dear.'

One of the servants had already placed my case on the stand. With a pang of shame, I remembered the last time, the way I had not wanted to let it out of my craven sight because of its clinking contents, to which I had at the time been virtually married. In the end, I had presented the three remaining bottles to Roderick as we left.

'It's so *lovely* having someone here,' Ginny said, plonking herself down on the edge of the bed. 'I've got used to it all – the heat and the insects and the servants, who are all pretty good sorts. I do like it, in the main. But sometimes it's just so *lonely*. It's heaven to have you back here to talk to.'

I really had no idea what to say to this, not least because it sounded so genuine. I'm afraid I might have let out a 'Huh', as I bent over and unlatched my case.

'And for Christmas,' she went on, 'I want a houseful! It's wonderful that everyone's prepared to come here. I can't wait to meet your friend Jessie.'

I coughed, digging a package out of the case.

'Here we are, as requested.'

'Cheddar cheese – oh, marvellous!' She felt the weight of it. 'That must be a whole pound!'

'There's a bit of Stilton in there as well, as it's Christmas. Heaven knows what my clothes must smell like – we'd better get it into the ice-box. And these ...'

'Chocolate biscuits!' Ginny clutched this booty to her. 'Thank you so much! Now, you must tell me *everything*.'

Everything?

We caught up over dinner, although of course there had been letters. The three of us sat at one end of a vast table. Long windows looked over the garden at the back, all green and splendid trees. I recognized two of the servants who had come from the other house and we *namaskared* each other.

'How are your doggies?' Roderick asked.

'Ah, dear old Honey didn't last the year,' I said. 'Poor old girl. But the Cairns are in fine fettle – they don't seem to mind the kennels the way Honey did.'

'I do wish Miss Persimmon had come too,' Ginny said.

'How is she?' Roderick asked, accepting a plate of some sort of chicken *fricassée*.

I pulled a wry face. 'Let's just say, they're getting used to her!'

'She's a lovely lady,' Ginny said, with such sincerity that I regretted my levity.

'She's very lame at the moment. They're talking about a hip operation, but apart from that, she's perfectly all right. She said, "Nothing'll stop me coming next year, dearie!"' Roderick and Ginny laughed fondly. 'Sent love and *salaams* of course. She's doing well. There are three churches to choose from in town – one just a stone's throw away. She does still go to church, I think, sometimes, anyway.'

Persi's exact religious affiliation these days was rather enigmatic.

'There's a lovely garden to sit in, close to the river. She's made a pal or two. Oh and there's a tiny little lady there, poor old Alice, doesn't know if she's coming or going. She wears a crimson cloak so at least you can spot her and even with her dodgy hip Persi goes careering round the town after her to stop her absent-mindedly falling in the river.'

'Oh, I can just see her!' Ginny giggled. 'Persi in hot pursuit.'

'She's always had lame ducks to look after, me included.' I chuckled.

'She has a real grace about her,' Ginny said, suddenly solemn. 'I love her. I've never met anyone like her.'

'No, nor me,' I conceded.

25

As soon as Persi and I had got back to England in March, both of us knew that we could stand no more. Neither of us wanted to slip back into the state of things before. After India, with all its griefs, all its gifts, we had broken out of the squalid, helpless and, in my case addicted, pit into which we had sunk. Light had poured in and we were not going to shut it out again.

So the question was, what next? The house would sell for a tidy sum, which, I told Persi, who resisted, we were damn well going to share.

'I know you've got your eye on one of those new places in the village,' Persi said.

A new development was going up in Greenbury – small, simple places on one floor with little gardens. I could get rid of almost everything – in fact live with just a few essentials, travelling light as Persi had always done.

'And I'm going for that place by the river.'

I knew where she meant, immediately.

'What? An old folks' home, Persi?'

'I am an old folk, Eleanora. I'm about to turn eighty.'

'But do you have to live with lots of *other* old folks? Don't you want to live with me?'

Persi gave me one of her withering looks, before softening.

'What, because you're the fountain of youth? In case you have forgotten, I am rather fond of living with a number of other people – I have done a good deal of it, dear.'

'Ah, yes, I suppose –'

'And no,' she interrupted. 'I don't want to live with you. I always used to hope I would live long enough to see you grow up and stand on your own two feet. So, d'you think we're there yet?'

'What – at sixty-five?'

She waited, quizzical.

'Maybe. Pretty much.' It was true – it was a relief, the thought of only me and a small place.

'I think, dearie,' she said sweetly, 'you really do have everything you need now.'

'I'll get a company to clear the house,' I said to Persi when, by June, we had firm prospect of a sale.

'No, you won't,' Persi ordered. 'You do it yourself.'

This was over breakfast. We had carried on eating on the card table. There was no point making too many changes: after all, soon everything would be cleared away. But it was the week after I had to put dear old Honey down and I was trying to keep from falling on the booze too much. So I was sensitive. But I knew what she meant, much as it irritated the hell out of me. *Face things, Eleanora.*

I had no excuse. Things were different now. There was India. There was Bill. Letters. I was not at the bottom – nowhere near.

'You had an unloving mother,' Persi announced, scraping burnt toast crusts as she stacked the plates. As if I needed telling. But in fact Persi's witness to the fact was always a help. 'That's the long and short of it.'

'Is that worse than not having one at all?' I enquired, before sticking the marmalade spoon in my mouth.

Persi considered. 'I can *believe* that my mother loved me.'

'Mumsie loved Hugh.'

'Did she? Or was she just sentimental about him?'

Persi was in one of her cutlass moods that morning. There were only so many times one could face being run through by her. I pushed my chair back.

'Well, I'd like to think she loved at least one of her offspring,' I said.

I began at the top of the house, in a far corner, and worked my way round. The task filled me with a kind of energy – a mix of rage and liberation. I lined three old dustbins up at the back and filled them with everything. It didn't matter what. Persi said she could not bear to look – the waste. Mother's papers and books, her face powder and clothing. I found a moth-eaten fox-fur stole, a soft green silk dress also destroyed by moth, and more everyday frocks and skirts. Underwear – horrors – straight in the dustbin. Of her few bits of remaining jewellery (the burglars had made off with the rest) I kept only one silver bracelet, which I remember from India, with leaves engraved around it. To my surprise I found some cheap clip-on earrings she bought here in England in the fifties, round and white with little pink spots painted on – surely too young for her?

It did not take as long as I feared. Mother had moved too many times to leave much of a wake behind her. Whatever it was that finally drove her from the Mynah – perhaps a coupling that had reached the end of its natural – she had come home on the boat with only a couple of trunks.

Persi left me to it as I dragged the full dustbins down the garden, piled it all high and lit a bonfire.

All that time I tried not to dwell on anything. But every so often something brought me up short. A worn album with a deep red cover, thick pages arranged with tiny white-edged pictures: Hughie and me as tots at Panchcotta, standing in front of Mother, who was wearing a long, pale dress and a smile. In the picture we looked like a family.

I stared at both their faces for some time. My brother. Hughie, Hughie … And what happened, along the way, to that beautiful, angry woman who was my mother? It became unbearable and I closed the album, dust puffing out from its pages. But I did not burn it. It was all that remained. And there was a picture of Pa, with his horse, Minto, with the white blaze down his face.

All the time, amid the purge, I was searching. For something, for her to have at least left me some trifle other than money. A twist of paper containing a silver ring, especially for me; a note telling me – vain hope! – that she loved me. Of course, I didn't find any such thing.

By the height of summer, we were left with only the most basic pieces of furniture, many of the rooms standing completely empty. At the bottom of the garden lay a heap of greying ash. The place echoed with emptiness and we were cleansed. My life could be seen now. Looked at in a stream of light. With everything laid bare, I saw who had mattered and I started writing letters.

When I finally left Calcutta in '47, we were all terrified there would be an all-out civil war. I travelled home on the boat with the Savorys from 42 Cowper Road, and it wasn't until we docked in Southampton that we said goodbye. I had shared a life now for six years with James and Deidre. It had been a good berth: calm, kind, lacking in fireworks. I was grateful.

'Do keep in touch, won't you?' Deidre said, buttoning her thin coat round her as we all shivered in what was supposedly a summer breeze. Her eyes filled with tears and she and I hugged each other. 'I'd hate to lose touch after all this time.'

But we had lost touch and it was largely my fault. I'm not sure I had even remembered to send a Christmas card. I wrote a long, and so far as I could manage it, honest letter, telling her I had been rather out of sorts but was now much better. I told her about Roderick and Ginny. Not Bill. She never knew about Bill.

And Jessie. After five years in Aylesbury, Mrs Bell died. There was no place in England for Jessie and she went home again. India was always home. She had kept on the house in Mussoorie, in the hills, and settled there. I had thought several times of writing to Jessie and telling her everything – all that had happened since I left her house in Assam in 1920. But somehow, I never got round to it.

One balmy afternoon come four o'clock, Persi and I were sitting on the baking terrace behind the house. The garden was wild and there were weeds growing all along the cracks between the paving stones, but we made the best of it, with a table and a couple of weather-worn wooden chairs.

Persi wore a bright blue summer frock and a white, embroidered shawl, her snowy plait emerging from under a straw hat. Her long arms were white and stringy, but she looked elegant enough in her flat sandals. A lifetime of sensible shoes had left her with straight, bunion-less feet. Suddenly, she got up and went slappety-slapping into the house.

Returning, she plonked the tray down, teapot, cups and saucers, biscuits, and said, 'Right, El-e-a-nor-a. I think we need a conversation.'

'Oh God, really?' I said. I could guess what was coming. What we had long avoided – with each other, with Roderick.

Persi stayed standing to pour the tea. Our one remaining silver pot gleamed in the sun. I saw a tremor in her hand and her face was set, very solemn. As she sat, smoothing her skirt under her, I thought, she's nervous, which made me nervous as well.

Teacups at the ready, we sat back, looking out over the tangle of bushes and weeds that now occupied the garden, the neglected beds and wayward rose bushes. Soon, this would all be someone else's problem.

'Come on then, Persi, spit it out.'

She took a sip of her tea, then stared ahead of her.

'Of course, I gave him my word.'

'And broke it, almost straight away,' I said. 'Which was the right thing to do.'

'Was it?' She looked sadly at me for a moment. 'Does the truth always *help*? I've never known, then or now.'

We had all managed, in so far as we could, to settle into life in England. By 1951, Mother was here in the house, I had moved to Henley, to work in that silly little boutique, and Persi was working her last year as a nurse in a small London hospital. I got a letter from her, sometime in early summer. She was coming over to see me – alone.

I managed a certain amount of pulling myself together that day, not wanting Persi to see that how much I was on the sauce bottle. She arrived in a loose, dusty-blue dress – a bit of a sack in fact but it looked stylish on her. And I needn't have worried. She was in no mood to give me a dressing down. We went to sit by the river on what passed for a warm day. As we settled on a bench, swans gliding about in front of us, I saw she looked very tired and I thought, She needs to retire – it's all getting too much. But I realized she was nervous as well.

'Look, El-e-a-nor-a,' she said with no further ado. 'I'm in a rotten position. Breaking a confidence. But I feel I must.'

I looked at her in bewilderment. Knowing how honorable Persi was, I could tell this was something big. But what had it to do with me?

She reached into her bag and took out a worn, brown envelope, on which I could see a number of foreign stamps, much franked. Persi seemed on the point of handing it to me, but she changed her mind and, instead, put her hand inside and drew out a letter, holding it on the flat of her hand.

The envelope was addressed to the Mother House in Barisal. Instantly, although I had not seen it for many years, I knew that handwriting. It was Hugh's. She and I looked at each other as seconds passed. I shook my head, straining to see the date franked on the stamps. It was impossible to make out, but I knew, already.

'He's alive?' I held my hand out for the letter, but Persi shook her head.

'Better if you don't.' She sounded distraught. 'There's nothing unkind – nothing like that. But he asked me to promise not to tell anyone. Your mother, you, Jennifer …' She stopped, shaking her head. I could see that she was absolutely strung up. Not tearful, just in a terrible state. Now, in her face, I read sleepless nights.

I sat, stunned. We had the memorial service for him early in '47, shortly before mother left India. Nearly two years after the war had ended. And yet ... There had never been any notification, but the times were chaotic, the countryside at the border vast and wild. And who would have notified us? Hugh had not been in the army. I had wondered, of course. After all, he had left his family once. But I always dismissed the possibility. Hughie, somewhere out there, still alive – no. He would not do that. He would surely have got in touch – with his mother, at least. With me? But no, he chose Persi. The old jealousy flared in me for a moment. Always Persi.

'Were we all *so* unbearable to him?'

'He wanted to spare everyone. Jennifer – Roderick, especially.'

'Oh Lord – yes, of course.'

'Where is he?' I managed to say.

'Calcutta. He's all right. Some sort of academic work.' She lowered her head. 'Whatever he wanted me to promise, I thought you should know.'

She broke down then, for a moment, really broke down in a way I had not seen for many years. Only once, after Sushila. It was awful to behold. Our family had always asked too much of her and time and again she had given it.

For me, the real pain of this had barely begun.

'What about Mother? And Jennifer?'

Our eyes met. No. Sleeping dogs. At least keep some part of the promise.

'I don't even know if I should have told you,' she said.

I stared ahead of me. 'No. Nor do I.'

'We never faced up to it last time,' Persi said, holding her teacup, her face shaded by the brim of her hat. 'But what about next time – with Roderick?'

This was before Persi's hip got so bad and she had thought she would be coming back to India that winter.

'I don't want to face up to it,' I said petulantly.

Even Persi was silenced by that. No one came out well from this – not Hugh, not Persi, nor I.

In those years after 1951, I must have thought about writing to Hugh every day. I even began, a number of times. But he did not want to hear from me. That was clear. Did not want a sister, a mother – even a wife or child. Every time I got close to trying to do something about mending this rupture, I was so overcome by the hurt, the rage I felt towards him – how callous, how cruel and irresponsible he was! – by my fear of being rejected, that I gave up. I was a mess myself, a scrap of flotsam again, this time floating about the English counties, drinking too much, barely holding down a job. My brother did not want me. So be it. The many ruptures of our lives – including two wars – had broken our family. That was hardly unusual. I let it go.

Persi wrote to me when he died. By then Enid was sick and she could not get away. A fellow academic wrote to her, in 1959, to say that Hugh had been out in the Bengal countryside involved in a piece of research and there had been floods. He had been overcome by some sort of waterborne infection.

So – too late to get in touch with him now.

'There's something else,' Persi said.

I looked at her. *Now* what?

'Remember when we were at Roderick and Ginny's, there was that book, the one about temples?'

'The terracotta ones?' Temples scattered about the Bengal

302

countryside, in small villages. Persi had seemed rather taken by it.

'It was by two men: a scholar called Mohandas Dutt and another called David Carterton.'

I waited.

'In his letter Hugh said he had changed his name. He didn't keep in touch with me after that, as I've told you. I had no idea what "David Carterton" had been doing all that time until I suddenly spotted that book. It took them years to put it together – going about on trains and bicycles. The most extraordinary thing was that Roderick had a copy of it. That he had seen it in Calcutta and felt drawn to it, wanted to buy it. Not knowing ...' Her hands went to her face.

'That it was written by his father?'

Persi nodded, wiping her cheeks.

26

One night, after I had moved into my new little dwelling, I stood naked in front of the looking glass.

I was alone, apart from the two doggies, who were shut up for the night in the kitchen. Persi was in the early days of settling into her new home. My furniture had been too big and dark for this house: I had bought a lighter, more modest wardrobe, with a long glass behind one of the doors. In the normal run of things, I would take barely more than a passing glance at it, and even that would definitely have been when fully clothed.

In four months' time, I would be back in Assam, if the fighting going on between India and Pakistan did not make it impossible. They were fighting over Jammu and Kashmir but everyone was worried that the Chinese would get involved and invade again the way they had in '62. That had involved evacuating women and children from the tea gardens and all sorts of carry on. But it would have taken a great deal to prevent me going back and in the event, thankfully it was all over by the autumn.

Bill wrote to me every week, straightforward about his sense of longing. *I know I'm hopelessly over the hill now, Nella. But it's funny how little that changes things. My longing for you is like an old ache that has woken and never leaves me. Do hurry home again – my dearest one. You always have been the very dearest of my life ...* We both knew we were to be lovers and sooner or later, I would be seen. *He* would see me, heaven help me. What a thought!

Now, I decided, it was time for the full horror show of my long-neglected frame.

Sitting on the edge of the bed, I peeled off my cardigan, started to unbutton my blouse. Distracted, I slipped off my misshapen shoes to look at my feet.

'Oh, dear.' Bunions. The left foot worse than the right. I found myself wondering if bunions, strictly speaking, counted as anything that *mattered*? My ankles were still pretty good, considering – legs from the knee down, in fact. And best of all now, there was no gout.

The temptation of my old pal the bottle was always there, like a sea of oblivion always available and beckoning to me. But I did not welcome oblivion now – there was life on offer. I still drank, of course. I wasn't going to spend my remaining days sipping tonic water or some such other ghastly concoction like Persi. But I had put myself on the wagon a few times and cut right back to a state that might just be construed as moderation. No booze before six in the evening and then only a couple of pegs. Though 'couple' was open to interpretation at times.

Stockings off – feet didn't look much better for that. Dreadfully dry. Put something on them, I thought. Suspender belt off; blouse off. Cotton skirt unzipped, dropped to the floor, stepped out of. Bit of a grunt as I picked it up. Petticoat and brassiere – gosh, yes, I still had really quite generous breasts. Did that cancel out bunions? Those breasts, which had fed my Louise … I cancelled this thought quickly, a road I did not want my mind to travel, not now.

'Right, come on, let's get on with it.'

I peeled everything, even my pants - those elasticated ones that hold one in rather – all in a rush so's not to dwell. And I stood, eyes closed, arranging myself in front of the looking glass. Last time Bill saw me naked, I was twenty – and probably looked a great deal better than I gave myself credit for at the time.

Eyes open again, braced for awfulness.

'Well, the hairdo's all right.' My hair was still quite dark, salt and pepper, neatly cropped. It suited me well like that, I could see.

And the body? I am not a thin lady. I am sallow-skinned. There were lumps and bumps about my narrow hips, the faint worms of old stretch marks down my belly, which I also chose not to dwell on, my top-heavy breasts. My skin looked old and neglected – saggy bits on my arms and thighs, a small varicose vein wiggling down my left calf. My face ... It was hardest of all to look at my face. A sixty-five-year-old woman stared back at me with a pathetically hopeful expression. The body could have been worse – it showed the scars and war wounds of a life. It was lived in and I could live with that. But what I did not want was a face that looked boozy, forbidding and *cross*.

Lines of discontent settle. Gravity pulls on one's face and the emotions of years, however well one attempts to hide them, become set there. The losses and disappointments. I did not want to end my life the barking, disgruntled person I had become. The person whom others regard with ridicule, fear even; whom they avoid.

This was the miracle of Roderick and Ginny. They needed family. They needed me. And they were determined to see past the appearance of old trout and find out who I was. Or at least that was how it seemed.

And Bill, his letters, week by week, the vibration I had in me now of hope and expectation.

'*All I long for now is to have you here with me, Nella. You do know that however much we have all tried to do our best, keep our promises and so on – that I have always loved you. Ever since.*'

I lifted my chin to stare into my own dark eyes. Bill – look back at me, my love. And I smiled.

'Not too bad really, old girl,' I said, hearing him as I spoke.

That was in August, in the summer warmth.

The other letter arrived in September.

27

December 1965

'Roderick's off to town to pick up the children from the Home.' Ginny appeared on the top balcony where I was sitting the next afternoon. She giggled. 'I think he's a bit nervous – two little girls! I want to have a bit of a rest before they get here. He wondered if you'd like to go along as well?'

'Why not?'

As I got to my feet, Ginny put her head on one side.

'You're looking very spry these days, Auntie.'

I gave her a bow, smiling. I was practising the smiling efforts really quite hard.

'Thank you, my dear.'

And I did feel pretty good, I thought, as I made my way down the cool stone stairs. Considering it all. I had had three months to come to terms with things.

'Apparently,' Roderick was having almost to shout as the car windows were open, he driving in a lazy style, his right arm resting on the window frame, 'Dr Graham's Home isn't just an orphanage – it's a school and some of the great and good send their children there. It's one of those Scots missionary places and they clear it out for Christmas. I suppose it gives the staff a – Whoa!'

A cow faced us, chewing unconcernedly, plum in the middle of the road as we turned a bend, and Roderick swerved mightily, almost landing us in the ditch, which was all rather entertaining.

'Daft creature,' he mumbled, swerving back on course again. 'Anyway, when they clear the place out for the holidays – two thousand kids, more or less! – they pile them all on buses to get down from Kalimpong to the station at Siliguri.' He chuckled. 'Evidently most of the town keeps out of the way that day. Must be absolute bedlam! Some get on buses to Darjeeling. But the rest all climb on to the trains and go off to Calcutta, some as far as Madras. The others, who travel east, come out here to the gardens.'

'Astonishing,' I said. We were coming into Jorhat now, nearly there. 'Do they have teachers with them?'

'I don't know. Doubt it.'

'It's a hell of a way, out here.'

'Four days by train from Siliguri to here. On average.'

'Poor little souls. So, two of them, you say?'

Roderick glanced at me, in the middle of turning right at a junction, amid a muddle of bullock carts, bicycles and cars.

'Two girls. We had a letter – they're called Meena Lal and Tashi Tsering.'

He saw my questioning expression.

'Tibetan. Some of the refugees are here now – came out with the Dalai Lama, after the uprising in Lhasa in '59.' We pulled into the road to the railway station. 'Quite a story, I should think.'

'Not bad – only an hour or so late,' Roderick said with a grin, emerging from the station master's office.

We sat waiting on the sunny station platform, chatting intermittently. It was three in the afternoon and there was a heavy, somnolent feel to the place. Bodies lay sleeping in patches of shade. A few people wandered about. A woman in a turmeric-coloured sari crossed the track, barefoot, carrying a small child. Monkeys scampered along the opposite platform, dogs dozed or scratched themselves, crows cawed in the trees behind us. Every so often we heard the splash of water from somewhere. Otherwise, it was quiet enough to hear the hum of insects.

At last came the distant whistle of the train. A plume of smoke appeared, moving gradually closer.

'Here we go,' Roderick said.

The station took on new life. The *pi* dogs scrambled to their feet. Vendors unravelled their limbs and appeared out of the shade with baskets of nuts or tangerines, bananas and guavas. Railway employees emerged muzzily from offices and a couple of white-clad coolies in red turbans came forward.

The rusty-red carriages clattered slowly alongside the platform, windows with arms sticking out like shoots from a plant and people leaping out of the doors or down from the roof before it was at a standstill. Smoke billowed past, the vendors started shouting, *'Chai … Garam chai … Narangi … '*

Roderick and I stood back to let the rush move past. As the smoke and the steam and the crowds thinned, we saw two little girls, waiting, quite still, foal-like in royal-blue cotton dresses, cardigans and black shoes. They each carried a cardboard suitcase in one hand and the straps of cloth bags draped diagonally across their chests. Their shiny black hair was cut in bobs level with their ear lobes, with very straight, chopped fringes. But it was easy to tell which was which.

Meena, the Indian girl, was skinny and long-legged, with big, mischievous eyes. Tashi was the smaller by far, unmistakably Tibetan with her strong cheekbones, rosy cheeks and gently slanting eyes. They stood holding hands as we approached, looking rather serious but quite self-possessed. Considering how long they had been on that train, they both looked fresh as daisies.

'Meena? Tashi?' Roderick said in his kindly way.

Grins broke across their faces.

'Hello, Uncle! Hello, Auntie!' they choursed.

So all Roderick and I could do was to enter into the spirit of things and parrot back, 'Hello, Meena, hello, Tashi!'

Meena, a pretty, string bean of a child, was a giggler. Although she was taller, she was in fact the younger – only nine. Tashi was ten, approximately. Most details about her origins were approximate in those days. No family was available to say exactly when she was born, but it must have been sometime in 1955 or '56, already in a country under Chinese occupation since 1951. And she knew she came from Lhasa, where the Tibetans had risen up to fight the Chinese in March 1959, starting three years of turmoil, during which many had fled the country. The guess about her age turned out to be fairly accurate.

During those days leading up to Christmas, these little girls entertained me a good deal. I sat on the verandah and watched them playing in the garden for hours. Sometimes Ginny was with me, snoozing. At times, while she dozed, splayed in a chair, I would look at her and remember my own heavy-bellied days in Barisal, how it had felt to carry my own little one. She woke once and saw me looking at her and I saw her face change.

'Oh, Auntie.' She reached for my hand and we squeezed each other's with gentle comfort. But I did not seek to dwell on it.

Because in front of my eyes were these children. They went tearing barefoot about the garden with Nip, who adored them both. They made games with buckets of water, a ball or hoop, or the rag dolls Ginny had made for them. And with them they had brought a repertoire of rhymes and clap-hands games. We could often hear their voices chanting somewhere.

'Aren't they lovely?' Ginny said, one afternoon as we sat watching them both play in the shade of a *neem* tree. 'I suppose your childhood was like that?'

'Early on, yes.'

'Oh. Of course.' She looked stricken. 'Sorry, I'd forgotten.'

I glanced at her. 'How old were you when your mother fell ill?'

'Seven.' She frowned. 'That's when it started, at least.'

We sat in silence for a moment.

'This is going to be a fine place for your little one,' I said. We smiled at each other.

What really struck me about the two little girls was their self-possession. They had lost so much, Tashi especially. Her country, her parents who might or might not be alive (she told Ginny she had witnessed her aunt being shot by the Chinese) – even her older sister who had fled Tibet with her was far away in Dharmsala, where the Dalai Lama had settled with the Tibetan government in exile. We knew less about Meena – it seemed she was truly an orphan. Despite it all, they both seemed so solid in themselves, had so much life in them.

They liked us watching them and every so often they would both come rushing up to the verandah.

'Aunties, watch!' Some cartwheel or singing game, which always ended with them both in a heap of giggles.

Quite soon, we were to be called Auntie One (me – age was the senior state, apparently) and Auntie Two, Ginny.

Tashi and I took an especial liking to each other. I don't know what she saw in me. I took to her because of her open gaze, with no artifice or pretence, her Tibetan way of speaking English, her joy when Ginny let her paint, first 'Auntie Two's' nails and then her own with rose-pink varnish, the way her almost stern face would crease into giggles.

One day, Tashi came and stood by the arm of my chair. Neither girl had many clothes to choose from, so Ginny had run up a little dress for each of them with straps that buttoned over each shoulder. They were very pretty. Tashi's was mauve. Meena, in her orange one, was playing on the floor close to Ginny.

'What do they teach you at school then?' I asked Tashi. A dull question, but I am not gifted with children. It was Meena who answered.

'To be good Christians.' She put her hands together as if in prayer but with such an air of mischief that Ginny and I could only laugh.

'Songs and rhymes,' Tashi said. 'Like, "Me no –"'

'Wait!' Meena scrambled to her feet and stood next to Tashi. They put their bare feet together and stood formally in front of us. Demure and innocent, they recited:

'Me no worry, me no care,
Me go marry a millionaire.
If he die, me no cry,
Me go marry some other guy.'

This was so much not the pious ditty Ginny and I had been

expecting that we exploded into laughter. And I was certain then that Tashi and I were going to get along supremely well.

28

It was late afternoon, a few days before Christmas, when I visited the banks of the river near Nimati Ghat. The sun was quite low in the sky, the light gentle, the water grey and almost still. The distant banks opposite merged with the sky, both pale and faded, so that however much you screwed up your eyes it was hard to distinguish one from another.

Every so often a long fishing boat went past, its owner standing to paddle it along. I met a few children scurrying among the scruffy bushes along the bank. But otherwise it was peaceful, with a light breeze and the sunlight's glitter on the water. Our spot was not hard to recognize and I came to it after walking for twenty minutes or so. I found a sandy patch, put my flowers on the ground and sat down. It felt much the same as it had forty-five years ago, when Bill and I were here together, even though I knew that at full spate the river must wash over it every year. How the small grains of everything change, slowly, unrecognizably, and suddenly we are old.

The letter that reached me in September was from the garden superintendent, a Mr Bhaduri. He was writing with great regret, to tell me that … His heart, they thought. Bill had been laid to rest 'with very full and dignified ceremony' in the Anglican cemetery in Jorhat.

I would go to the cemetery, but it was not the grave that mattered.

Sitting on the warm ground, I sat running the sand through my fingers, looking out over the water, filled with long, slow sadness. We could have been here together, I thought. Why did you have to go, Bill?

I told him then, in my mind, perhaps with my lips moving, all that I would have said were he here. About our little girl.

'When Persi and I laid her on the water, in her little leaf basket …' The tears flowed, warm down my cheeks. 'I felt as if I was sending her to you, along the rivers flowing between us. That they would always be there, between you and me – and her.'

And I felt as if Bill did sit beside me, his arm tightening about me as I spoke, heard his deep, gentle voice. 'Oh, my dear, dear girl …' And I knew, although I was speaking only to the breeze, and despite everything the future would now not hold, that in my life I had loved and been loved. All else is as dust.

After a time, I got up, reaching for the few flowers I had carried here. I took the little bundle I had brought with me out of my bag: the letter Bill wrote me from Calcutta saying he had seen Hughie, wrapped in Louise's white shawl along with a little vest she had worn. His more recent letters I could not bear to part with. I went down the bank and once again set loose a little barque of my heart on to the water, scattering pink and white hibiscus blooms on it as it moved away. The delicate white wool was soon sodden, sinking rapidly as it was carried away by the stream, leaving the flowers floating on the surface. Kissing my fingers, their tips wet from my tears, I blew the breath of my love after them.

This was but one branch of the great, mountain-fed body of water that had carried our Louise, then Sister Sushila, washed with Persi's tears and now my little souvenirs of Bill and our daughter. I stood for a long time, looking after them all along this river which would flow into the mighty Ganga, sweeping with her through the delta to the sea: that place of reunited souls where then is now, and now is forever and always.

29

1965, Christmas Day

'Auntie One!' Tashi commanded, marching out on to the verandah to find me. She was barefoot, wearing the little mauve dress, freshly washed. 'Auntie Two says you got to come!'

'Does she now, Tashi One?'

She shook her head fiercely. 'But there is only *one* Tashi.'

'There certainly is.' I smiled at Meena who was waiting nearby, chewing her fingernails. 'And one Meena. Too many Aunties, though.'

I hauled myself up from the chair.

'Come on, Auntie One – hurry!'

They each took one of my hands, which made me chuckle with astonishment. It was like being adopted. Ginny appeared at the door.

'Ah – there you all are!'

Her hair was up but escaping all over the place and she had an apron over her dress. She was blooming.

'I want to get everything ready and then everyone will be here and it'll be lovely!'

She was in her element, building a family about her, brick by strange brick: me, Tashi and Meena, Jessie – and there was to be another planter called Jim who would otherwise have spent the day alone. This young woman drew all us waifs and strays into her embrace.

'Now, Meena, Tashi – the glue is dry on those crackers you made. You can go and *very carefully* put one by each plate on the table, all right? And don't get in Bholu's way.'

'Yes, Auntie Two!' We heard their scurrying feet and their giggles receding into the house.

'Right.' Ginny perched on one of the verandah chairs. 'Look, I need to ask you something, Auntie – I'm so sorry, but I never thought to ask before.'

'Oh?' Heavens, what was this?

'Well, it's just … The friend of yours – Mr Ashton, was it, who you caught up with at the last minute last time you came? I don't know if he's got company for Christmas? I mean, he and Jim might get along rather …'

'No,' I said. I kept my voice light. 'I'm afraid the old boy didn't make it from that end of the year to this.'

'Oh, dear!' Ginny looked dismayed. 'I *am* sorry! Well, what a good thing you caught up with each other when you did!'

'Yes.' I smiled up at her as she hurried on towards her next task. 'A very good thing.'

And so, my dear Persi, we had our Christmas lunch, dining off those eternal scraggy Indian hens and all of us at last almost filling that vast dining table with a great deal of good cheer.

Roderick headed the table with Jim, the stray planter, and I on either side of him. I have to say I did a pretty fine job with Jim who was rather a bore, but I got him talking about sport and so on. I had plenty of catching up to do with Jessie as well, who sat beside me. Jessie (Auntie Three for the time being) looks much as she ever did, though her hair has gone the same washed-out grey as her mother's. She looks very twinkly behind her specs these days. There was a certain amount of joking with her about living in the 'Motherland'.. How did I stand it, living there? she wanted to know. Aylesbury didn't come out of the discussion terribly well, as you can imagine.

We agreed that there would be plenty of time for us to catch up properly when I visit Mussoorie. Jessie took a great interest in Ginny, who is looking plump-faced and happy, while the little girls sat gazing around and looking at the crackers they had made with much longing. I gave Tashi a wink, which she managed to return with some aplomb.

Roderick had saved the two decent bottles of claret I had brought over with me (after all, one needs to be sure of a decent tipple with Christmas dinner) and we toasted the coming child and absent friends – especially you, Persi.

'I do wish Miss Persimmon was here,' Ginny said. 'Tell her she must come with you next year, if she feels up to it. She would be so welcome. I'd love her to stay with us again.'

So I said, 'Am I to come next year then?' And they all cried yes and Tashi then wanted to know the same – and Meena. I saw Roderick and Ginny give each other a bit of a look and they said, yes, of course they could come. And then, what does young Tashi do but pop up with, 'Can I stay for ever?' I have a feeling young Tashi is already on her way to being family long-term – and perhaps Meena as well!

And I have to tell you, dear, that sitting round that table with the heaps of roast potatoes and lop-sided home-made crackers that never did go 'bang' but caused much fun all the same (Ginny had bought tiny hand-made trinkets from the bazaar to put in them and the girls were thrilled with all of it) … and with all the future laid out in front of these two improbable 'adult' children we met a year ago and who have taken us into their hearts, well, I knew there was nothing I could say to Roderick that day; that was not the moment.

I did sit him down yesterday, Boxing Day. I told him, gently, about Hugh. I took that book about temples down from the shelf and Hugh was so astonished by his father having been David Carterton that I do believe it softened the blow, just a fraction. I owned up to my own shame that I had not contacted Hugh and do you know what the pup said? 'Well, he had rejected you – us – rather soundly, hadn't he?' I had expected tears from him but in fact, though sad, he was more stoic than me. I seem to have become rather lachrymose in my old age. As he said, he had had so little of Hugh that I suppose there was no one to miss, as such, just the idea of him.

Only the day before, Christmas Day, I had watched him sitting back with a glass of red, pink-cheeked and happy; and Ginny, with that loose, softened look of soon-to-be motherhood. I wondered: how would it make things better in any way, if I tell them the truth about Hugh? Tell Roderick that his poor, damaged father not only left him, but lived on, kept silent and never once got in touch – except inadvertently, by a twist of fate, through an interest in rural temples? That Hugh made those brick edifices his project and his love when he had a flesh and blood boy? So far as Roderick was concerned then, his father died as some sort of eccentric hero, helping refugees escape Burma. Some of which is also the truth.

But in the event, as I say, he was quite calm. 'I suppose my father was very damaged.'

I agreed. 'As was mine.'

The boy took it all in and then he said, 'Well, I suppose all we can do is to try and learn to forgive them.'

It seems he is an old soul after all, broad and strong enough to accept what really happened, and that there is the blank in his life left by Hugh that will never be filled in. But I see that he feels blessed by all the life he has now – as do I, also, dear Persi, mightily, in mine. As you have taught me so many times throughout our lives, nothing is ever complete, but much is blessing.

Glossary

chowkidar – watchman/caretaker
'Koi-hai?' – anyone there?
charpoy – strong bed woven on to a wooden frame
dirzi – tailor
chai – tea
garam – hot
tonga – simple horse-drawn carriage
wallah – man, worker
bari – house, home
chappals – sandals or flip flops
didi – sister, usually older
dhoti – men's garment of cloth, tied at the waist and knotted
pani – water
narangi – orange

Acknowledgements

My thanks go to all the former Assam and Darjeeling tea-planters and their families who talked to me about how it was to live and work in the gardens of north-eastern India: Angela Johnstone, Caroline Findlay, Nod Thomson, Dick Ellingham, Mary Cherry, Denys Wild, Stephen Brown, David Rushton and Ann Lamb.

To the writers of numerous books about Assam and the tea gardens; to Rumer Godden's *Bengal Journey*, and to the British Library Asia and African Studies Department.

To the writing team, Oxford Narrative Group, for all their expertise and support in helping workshop this story month by month by year: Helen Newdick, Helen Matthews, Claire Spriggs, Yvonne Lyons, Rachel Norman, Pat Whitehouse, Benedicta Norel and an especially big thank you to Rose Stevens for her careful reading of and feedback on the completed novel.

To my excellent copy-editor Penny Rendall, whose eye for inconsistencies was invaluable in a book covering this many years and places.

To cover artist Elettra Francesca Cudignotto, who has been a joy to work with.

To my daughter Rachel Murray, for sharing the journey to Assam with me. It's a precious memory.

To Ananda and Swati Lal in Kolkata, for their hospitality and the Calcutta Writers Workshop volume – beautifully bound as ever – of Asif Currimbhoy's play *Darjeeling Tea?*

To the Banyan Grove outside Jorhat.

Above all, to my husband Martin Lloyd for his love and endless enthusiasm.

Please keep in touch – it would be great to hear from you.

You can find my website at www.abioliver.co.uk

Facebook is at www.facebook.com/AbiOliver12345

Twitter: @AbiWriterOliver